THE PAVONIS INSURGENCE

a novel of T-Space™

Alastair Mayer

Mabash Books

The Pavonis Insurgence

This is a work of fiction. Names, characters, places, and incidents are either the product of the author's imagination or are used fictitiously, and any resemblance to real people or incidents is purely coincidental.

Copyright © 2020 by Alastair Mayer

All rights reserved. No part of this book may be reproduced, scanned or distributed in any printed, electronic, or other form without permission. E-book editions of this book are available wherever fine e-books are sold.

Cover © 2020 by Mabash Books
Image credits:
    planet [spaceship] © Iurii - Depositphotos.com
    Jungle © kamchatka - Depositphotos.com
Images used by permission.

T-Space is a trademark of Alastair Mayer

For announcements about other T-Space books and special offers, sign up for Alastair Mayer's newsletter at
    http://www.alastairmayer.net/

A Mabash Books original.

First printing, April 2020
Second printing, minor corrections, January 2021

Mabash Books, Centennial, Colorado

Hardcover Edition: ISBN-13: 978-1-948188-19-7
Trade Paperback Edition: ISBN-13: 978-1-948188-20-3

THE PAVONIS INSURGENCE

A Carson and Roberts adventure in T-Space, number 5.

Dramatis Personae

Dr. Hannibal Carson - Exoarcheologist at Drake University, and part-time agent for Homeworld Security

Jacqueline "Jackie" Roberts - Pilot, owner/operator of the starship *Sophie*, occasionally works for Quentin Ducayne

Terran Union (*Union de Terre*) Homeworld Security

Quentin Ducayne - Head of the Sawyers World office of the Department of Homeworld Security, and in charge of most of that Department's extra-Solar operations

Jordan Burnside - Agent of Quentin Ducayne, until recently agent-in-residence on planet Tanith at 82 Eridani

Rico - Former criminal, now an agent for Quentin Ducayne

Avril Boutelle - Part-time agent, a graduate student in xeno-anthropology

Henry Prentiss - Agent-in-residence on Verdigris (junior to Burnside)

Drake University (Sawyer City)

Dean Matthews - Dean of the Archeology Department, Carson's boss.

Dr. Ellie Greystone - Head of the Biology Department. (See the book *Kakuloa: A Rising Tide* for her backstory)

Velkaryans (aka Church of Divine Interstellar Providence)

Klaus Vaughan - Head of Operations on planet Verdigris, recently out of Tanith. Owns the starship *Carcharodon*.

Ernest Dietrich - Head of Operations on Sawyers World

John Reid - Senior operations agent. Has had several hostile encounters with Rico, on both Earth and Sawyers World.

flight Paths, by Ship

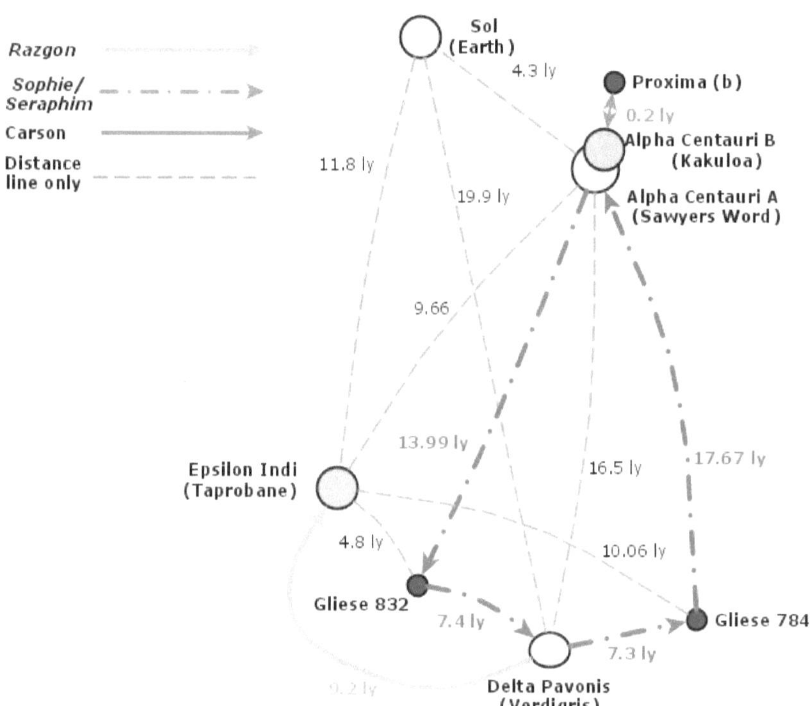

CONTENTS

THE PAVONIS INSURGENCE

a novel of T-Space ™

Alastair Mayer

Previously....

(Note to readers: The following synopses are to refresh the memory of those of you for whom it has been a while since you read the earlier books, and necessarily contain spoilers for those. If you haven't read the previous volumes, you will get more enjoyment out of The Pavonis Insurgence *if you start first with volume one,* The Chara Talisman, *and continue from there.)*

In *The Chara Talisman*, archeologist Hannibal Carson discovers a broken talisman in a stone tomb on the planet Verdigris, circling the star Delta Pavonis. Its slightly radioactive interior turns out to be a technetium betavoltaic battery –impossible technology for that stone-age culture. A similar, complete talisman had been found at a dig in another star system. Homeworld Security is interested, and Ducayne, head of their office on Sawyers World at Alpha Centauri (where Carson is based) follows up.

The markings on the talismans resemble a star map. Star-pilot Jackie Roberts, owner-operator of a small ship, determines that the intact talisman points to a star at the edge of T-Space, Beta Canum Venaticorum, also called Chara. Following that lead, Carson and Roberts discover a pyramid on the planet Chara III (aka St. Jacobs), which appears to contain a technology teaching museum, and, in a concealed chamber, a high-tech alien artifact.

After a run-in with the Velkaryans, a xenophobic quasi-religious faction who claim terraformed worlds were intended for humans, they return to Sawyers World. Ducayne informs them that more talismans have been located.

In *The Reticuli Deception*, Jackie Roberts correlates the star maps to a point-of-view somewhere near the Zeta Reticuli system, across T-Space from Chara. Carson and Roberts pursue that lead, where they find an abandoned planet whose cities have been devastated by war. They meet an alien, Ketzshanass, who warns them away from the system with a tale of attacks by the degkhidesh, a term translated as "enemies of the Kesh."

A Velkaryan ship, commanded by a man named Vaughan, has pursued Carson and Roberts to the Reticuli system. While there, his ship is damaged by a particle beam of unknown but presumed degkhidesh sentinel origin, but ultimately both he and Carson and Roberts escape.

Meanwhile, inspired by the possible connection between Zeta Reticuli and a legendary UFO incident on Earth in the 1960s, where an abductee later recalls, under hypnosis, a star map she was shown by the aliens, Ducayne sends Rico and another agent to Earth to acquire the original UFO report documents. The Velkaryans are also interested, and their man Reid apparently kills Rico in a shootout at the spaceport just as the other agent escapes with the files.

In *The Eridani Convergence*, another high-tech alien artifact is up for sale to Jordan Burnside, the agent-in-residence on the planet Tanith. The Velkaryans get wind of this, and Vaughan, who stopped at Tanith for repairs after leaving Zeta Reticuli, makes several attempts to get to it before Burnside does. However, he is recalled to Verdigris to resume supervision of Velkaryan starship manufacturing. Burnside acquires the artifact and hands it off to Carson and Roberts, and then, curious about Vaughan's sudden departure, follows him to Verdigris. This novel (*The Pavonis Insurgence*) picks up Burnside's story here.

On their way back to Alpha Centauri, Carson and Roberts stop briefly at the site of the crashed ship where the artifact was found. Other than the crash damage, they recognize other damage apparently caused by a particle beam similar to that used to attack Vaughan's ship at Zeta Reticuli.

In *The Centauri Surprise*, Carson, now back on Sawyers World, receives an anonymous package of undocumented artifacts, part of an illegal collection inherited by a donor who wants to be rid of them. One of the artifacts is yet another talisman, whose star map seems to point to Alpha Centauri. There is a mysterious, roughly pyramid-shaped hill which has been classified as a volcano remnant (see *Alpha Centauri: Sawyer's World*), but now Carson is convinced that it's a buried pyramid and wants to investigate.

Meanwhile, Reid (the Velkaryan who shot Rico on Earth) has returned to Sawyers World. It turns out that Rico was not killed, but recovered by the local police and put in a traumapod while they traced his identity. That traumapod was spirited away by Sawyers World security agents and eventually Rico recovers and is released. Reid, meanwhile, has raided Carson's excavation of the local pyramid, but is foiled as Carson turns the tables, and Rico shows up to assist. Reid is wounded in a brief shoot-out but manages to escape before the local authorities round up the other Velkaryans at the site. Carson gets the pyramid open, but it appears to have been not only deliberately buried, but deliberately filled in.

In light of recent events, Ducayne wants Carson to both visit pyramid sites on other planets, especially where there is Velkaryan activity, and, perhaps more urgently, re-contact the Kesh and ask them exactly what they're up to. There is evidence that they were responsible for trying to conceal the pyramid in the first place. He also wants Roberts, along with Rico and xenoanthropologist and part-time agent Avril Boutelle, to go to Verdigris, contact Burnside, and follow his direction from there.

This book picks up Burnside's tale as he arrives in the Delta Pavonis system at the end of *The Eridani Convergence*, then rejoins Carson and Roberts as of the end of *The Centauri Surprise*.

CARSON AND ROBERTS

Sawyer City, Sawyers World

Hannibal Carson woke from a pleasant dream, not immediately recognizing his surroundings. He was alone in a strange bed, but the sheets were warm, and the other pillow rumpled. There were doors—hatches—abutting the wall facing the foot of the bed in the small cabin. Then he awoke fully. This was the captain's cabin on a Sapphire. *Jackie's* cabin, on the *Sophie*. But where was she?

Just then the door on the aft bulkhead slid open and Jackie Roberts stepped out of the fresher, pulling a shirt down over herself.

"Come on, sleepy," she said, far more chipper than was normal for her before coffee. "Rise and shine. You have work, and I have a briefing with Ducayne later."

Carson looked at her and smiled. "And I thought you were a slave driver last night."

"You weren't complaining."

He got out of bed and stepped over to her. Between the bed and the desk, the cabin had not much floor space, and clothes littered what there was. "I'm still not," he said, hugging her.

She kissed him, but broke it off and gently pushed him away. "Neither am I, but now's not the time. Get dressed while I go fix coffee."

Carson sighed, but backed off. "Aye, Captain."

∞ ∞ ∞

Coffee and an omelette-like meal waited for him on the galley table when he came aft. Jackie was already most of the way through her mug of coffee and what looked like the remains of a cheese danish.

"Sit, eat," she said, gesturing at the food.

Carson sat. "About last night," he began, but Jackie put her hand up to stop him.

"I enjoyed it, and I don't regret it, and if you do, I don't want to know."

Carson shook his head, surprised that she would think that. "On the contrary, I—"

She cut him off again. "This isn't the best time to talk about it. We had something once, back before what happened at Raven's Rift—"

"That was—" he began again.

"—and for whatever reason, we both seem to have come away thinking that the breakup was the other's fault. Maybe that was all just a stupid misunderstanding, if last night was anything to go by. But we need to have a serious discussion before either of us assumes anything going forward, don't we?"

Carson thought he would rather grade papers than have the kind of serious discussion Jackie meant, but he knew she was right, and told her so. "Now?"

"No, that's just it. You have to be at work—"

"I don't have classes to teach until this afternoon."

"—and I have a meeting with Ducayne. He has a charter for me. I'll be off-planet for a while."

"Ah. So you want us to chill until you get back, is that it?"

"It's not a matter of what I want, not right now, but it's the smart thing to do. We can have that talk when I get back. Maybe over dinner?" She smiled at him. Dinner was how last night had started.

"Okay, but I can't promise Rick's Café again. Where's the charter to?"

"I probably shouldn't say, and I don't know all the details anyway. But you'll recall we were supposed to bring someone else back from Tanith, and didn't."

"Right, Jordan Burnside," Carson said, remembering. "Tevnar said he decided to stay at Verdigris, and parachuted in. Has Homeworld Security replaced the suit and retro-pack he borrowed?"

"They have. Ducayne is good about paying the bills. Speaking of, I'm going to have to kick you out. We both have work to do."

Carson swallowed the last of his coffee and stood. Jordan Burnside might be the reason Jackie had to rush off, but Carson didn't envy him. Using a reentry pack to land on a planet wasn't exactly fun—he'd done it himself once. Even less fun were the jungles of Verdigris. "I wonder how he's doing," Carson said.

"Who? You mean Burnside? I guess I'll find out when I get there. Now go. I'll call you."

PART I
VERDIGRIS, TWO MONTHS EARLIER

Chapter I: Burnside

Delta Pavonis system, above planet Verdigris, two months earlier
Jordan Burnside watched the airlock door slide shut as he drifted away from the *Razgon*. Neither he nor the ship had the velocity to maintain orbit, but neither were planning on staying. He was headed for Verdigris, the planet below, and the *Razgon* would be leaving the system.

As he drifted away to a safe distance, the ship's attitude jets flared briefly, putting more distance between them. They fired again to rotate the ship, pointing it at Epsilon Indi, nine light-years away.

He had never seen a ship go to warp from this particular vantage point. *This should be interesting.*

The ship held there, not doing anything. Captain Tevnar must be waiting to make sure Burnside's retrofire went without a hitch. That was considerate of her. He adjusted his own attitude so that the retrorocket on his de-orbit pack pointed forward, at the horizon. He could still see the *Razgon* from that angle. Good.

Burnside had a compact life-support pack strapped to his chest. On his back, a larger pack held a deployable heat shield. He activated it.

He felt a thump and then several vibrations as a polymer bag, shaped like a rounded, shallow cone, inflated out of the pack. The vibrations changed as the bag filled with a quick-setting ablative foam. Between the surrounding vacuum and his suit layers, he couldn't hear the hiss he imagined, but within moments he was half cocooned by the shield which would, so it said on the label, protect him from the heat of entry. He wondered wryly if there was a guarantee, not that he'd be able to collect on it if it failed. All right, he couldn't put it off any longer. Tevnar was waiting for him to depart, and it was time to make planetfall.

Simplicity counted for a lot in an emergency pack. The retro-rocket was a small chemical rocket motor, mounted at the apex of a triangular frame connecting it to his suit and the heat shield. Its nozzle pointed away from him, toward the horizon. Below, from what he could see, was the planet's swirly green skyweed layer, with the occasional white streak of high-altitude clouds. His nav system said that beneath the skyweed lay jungle, not ocean. *That better be right.* One final check that his emergency locator beacon was *OFF*—the last thing he needed was it broadcasting his position—and he triggered the retro.

It burst into life in front of him with a physical thump, its exhaust surprisingly faint although the nozzle glowed from the heat. He felt pulled toward it as it pushed back on the frame, decelerating him. The *Razgon*, meanwhile, continued in its own trajectory, pulling ahead of him rapidly as he slowed. Then, with a pale violet flicker, it winked out. It had gone to warp. He was on his own now, and as the retro burned out, he began falling toward Verdigris.

The retropack's attitude thrusters jetted briefly, turning him to place the heat shield forward. Things were about to get interesting . . . and hot.

∞ ∞ ∞

Before long, he felt the first gentle pressure as the thin upper atmosphere began to slow him, and the dark sky above him hinted at an orange glow as the faint traces of air ionized with the energy of his passage. As the glow grew more intense, he felt heat radiating back at him, almost as if it, and not the increasing gee forces, were pressing him back against the foam shield.

After a minute, smoke began to fill the trail he left. Then, with a jolt, a chunk of flaming insulation spalled off the shield, disappearing into his wake. The ride got rougher, shuddering and bumping, and he wondered just how long this particular entry pack had been in storage. *Maybe I should have had Tevnar land me af-*

ter all. But the whole point of this was stealth. A meteor could be shrugged off; a landing ship couldn't.

In the thickening atmosphere, the attitude jets were useless, and the retro blew off with another thump, dragging his drogue ballute out with it. It bobbled in his wake, and he hoped it wouldn't burn up or melt before it had done its job. But the fiery orange glow was already fading to blue.

The ride settled down. Was that the worst of it? Then there came a flurry of green as he fell through a skyweed layer. *I must be getting low. When does the heat shield jettison?* His main parachute couldn't deploy until the shield was gone.

And then it went, with an impact so sudden Burnside thought he must have hit the ground, until he saw the slabs of charred foam blow past him. *It jettisons at four thousand meters*, he remembered.

With a *THUMP* the ballute pulled a bigger drogue chute from its pack and released, taking the frame with it, and he felt another tug as the bigger drogue deployed, stabilizing and slowing him further. Finally, as he descended through a thousand meters, it extracted his main chute.

Burnside scanned the ground, or rather, the tops of the trees, beneath him. He couldn't see any clearing that he could reach as he descended. He was going into the trees. At least his spacesuit would protect him from small branches.

As he neared the treetops, he hooked his left foot behind his right ankle and squeezed his legs together. He did *not* want to hit astride a branch. He stretched his arms up, crossed in front of his helmet visor, alongside the parachute risers. With any luck, the canopy would catch in the trees before he hit the ground, yet leave him close enough to it so he could lower himself down. He tried to remember how tall the trees typically grew in the Verdigran jungle, but that factoid escaped him.

With a rush the upper branches brushed by him, and as best he could, he twisted his body to slip between the thicker branches below. Space opened up around him as the branches thinned, then he felt a strong upward tug as his parachute caught in the tree, the lines stretching slightly as he came to a stop some height above the ground.

Great. Now what?

∞ ∞ ∞

The jungle floor was about seven meters below. Too far to just drop, but his parachute harness held a rope he could slide himself down on, once he unstrapped. He looked up at the parachute tangled in the branches above him. It was still mostly open, and it was draped over much of the foliage. It would be obvious from the air. That wasn't good.

If it had been one of Covert Services' gadgets, it wouldn't have been a problem. The chute would have been a drab, camouflaged color to start with, and it would disintegrate in a few hours after exposure to the elements. But this one was part of the standard bail-out pack that Jackie Roberts had given him from the *Sophie* prior to this impromptu visit. This canopy was brightly colored, designed to be highly visible in case its user needed rescue. He had disabled the emergency beacon, but that canopy was a giveaway. He'd have to get it down somehow.

Experimentally, he pulled down hard on one riser, then on the other. The left one seemed to sag more than the right. Okay, that might work.

Burnside took the descent rope and uncoiled it, then looped one end through the buckle on the right riser. If this worked better than he hoped, he wanted to have some control over how fast he fell. Gripping both ends of the loop of rope in his left hand, he reached up and unfastened the right riser buckle. The strap jerked upward as his weight, now entirely on the left side of the parachute, pulled it over the tree branches and he started falling. The ropes slid through his left hand. He grabbed them tightly with both hands, and managed to slow, then stop, his downward movement. He was two meters closer to the ground.

He carefully eased his grip on the ropes, sliding slowly downward as, above him, the right riser of the 'chute rose, the parachute canopy starting to follow the lines and left riser, still attached to his harness, downward. It was working!

And then it wasn't. Burnside's downward motion stopped two meters above the ground. Looking up, he saw that the lines had become hopelessly tangled in various tree branches, but at least now most of the parachute was below the top leaves. He jerked on the remaining riser a few times, but made no further progress.

He pulled the descent rope loop free of the right riser buckle and then threaded it through the left, letting the ends drop to the ground. After undoing the rest of his harness, he slid down the rope to the ground.

Burnside unfastened and removed his helmet, taking a deep breath. The jungle air was warm and humid, smelling of damp soil and vegetation. His suit had been designed to keep him cool in space, not on a planet with atmosphere, and he had been working hard getting out of the tree. Despite the jungle's heat, taking off the helmet was a refreshing change.

He pondered what to do about the parachute canopy as he doffed the rest of his suit. There wasn't much he could do, but he pulled his descent line free. That might come in handy.

As far as he could tell from this angle, more than half of his canopy was now hidden from above by leaves. He'd come through a thick layer of skyweed on the way down, and anybody flying above that would see nothing. Hopefully, no one would be flying below it. Skyweed didn't stay aloft indefinitely. The tiny plants—aerophytoplankton—would get washed out by rain, and older plants got too heavy for their buoyancy sacs and winds to keep them afloat. With any luck enough of the weed would settle out over the chute to hide it from view before anyone spotted it.

Either way, he intended to put a considerable distance between himself and his landing area as quickly as he could. He just had to figure out the direction to Verdigris City, where he could contact the local *Union de Terre* security office. Fortunately, Verdigris had a navigation satellite system that wasn't bothered by skyweed, and he had downloaded what maps Tevnar had available to his omni. Less fortunately, large sections of those maps were marked with a single word: *jungle*.

Chapter 2: Vaughan

New Toronto, Verdigris

New Toronto was rapidly becoming the largest city on the planet Verdigris. Already the regional capital and biggest city on the continent, it was both an agricultural and major manufacturing center. The city lay on the shore of a large freshwater lake, some twelve-hundred kilometers from the site where Paul Fabron had first landed in the *Jules Verne* decades earlier.

Fabron, heir to a billionaire's fortune, had bought the ship—originally built for the 2069 Alpha Centauri expedition but never used because of mechanical issues—and refitted it with the latest solid-state fusion units and the newly available commercial warp modules.

It was a bastard design, lacking the warp-induced artificial gravity of newer ships. Furthermore, as had its sister ships of the first Centauri expedition, it relied on its chemical engines for lift-off from a planetary surface. Still, it was the *Jules Verne*, and Fabron had a certain Gallic pride in it. He was determined to find a new terraformed planet.

The yellow star Delta Pavonis was known to have an Earth-sized planet in its habitable zone, but while early observations had detected oxygen in its atmosphere—almost a sure sign of life—its overall color was wrong. Terraformed planets should look mostly blue and white, not green. It was low on the list of places to visit with the new V-class ships. That made it a prime candidate for the eccentric young Frenchman.

Even with the upgraded power and warp systems, Delta Pavonis was beyond the *Jules Verne*'s range of ten light-years. Paul Fabron was determined, though, and laid out a course that took him and his crew first to refuel at Alpha Centauri, then at Epsilon Indi—this was before the Terran Union, or *UDT,* had imposed restrictions on visiting Taprobane—and finally from there to Delta Pavonis.

The third planet appeared mostly green from space because of its vast clouds of aerophytoplankton, better known as sky-weed. After several orbits of radar imaging, the *Verne* found a thinner patch of weed over what their radar told them was a suitable landing site. They made their descent and landing, acquiring a film of scorched brown and green slime in the process. Being a rather irreverent fellow, Fabron named the planet Verdigris.

In a similar vein, he named its mottled-looking large moon after a particular creamy, semi-soft, blue cheese made in his home region of Jura, France: *Bleu de Gex*, now simply referred to as Gex.

His landing site, near the mouth of a large river, would later become the town of Louisbourg. The river itself, a major watershed for much of the continent, originated at a large lake. Given the lake's similarity to a Great Lake of North America back on Earth, he had named it *Lac Quebec*.

Some years later, another wave of settlers deemed the shore of that lake an ideal spot for their colony. It provided easy access to much of the interior of the continent and easy water transport to Louisbourg and thence to the other continent. However, they were no Francophiles. They couldn't change the name of the lake, but since it was about the size of Earth's Lake Ontario, they defiantly named their settlement New Toronto.

Now, several of New Toronto's major industries were owned by Velkaryan interests, and that organization played a dominant role in regional politics. Klaus Vaughan didn't care about the history of New Toronto, he cared that his Velkaryan superiors had ordered him here to resolve slowdowns in the Velkaryan-owned industries, with a particular focus on the production of armed starships.

∞ ∞ ∞

Velkaryan HQ, New Toronto

When he'd departed Verdigris, nearly a year ago now, Vaughan had left behind a smoothly operating assembly facility that was producing a complete, flight-worthy ship every ten days, with that rate projected to double within a few months. Now . . . well, fuselages were still rolling off the assembly line, but many critical subsystems were incomplete or missing entirely. His two highest priorities were to determine what had led to this shamble and fix it, and to inventory the existing ships to find out just how deeply the rot went and how long it would take to repair them. They were essential to Operation Jade Ribbon.

While the Velkaryan political party was strong in the New Toronto government, it didn't have absolute control. Vaughan wondered if other industries in the region were suffering a similar decay. If so, he might turn that to Velkaryan advantage. He had been turning things around in Harp City on Tanith before being recalled here, that nonsense with the fake alien artifact aside.

It was time to catch up on local events.

∞ ∞ ∞

New Toronto had been founded thirty-five years earlier, largely as a transportation hub for two industries: agriculture and mining. The jungle surrounding the area was thin and young. A few hundred years ago, the area had been more arid and savannah-like. There had been nothing unique about the forest, which extended to cover much of the continent. Much of the thin forest here, several thousand square kilometers, had been cleared and plowed under to make way for farms. The crops and, more recently, processed food supplied much of what was consumed in the other towns on the planet. A modest ship-building industry— sea-going ships, not starships—arose to fill the need for long-distance bulk transport.

That industry, in turn, had declined in recent years. There was still a demand, but it had leveled off after an initial rush. Associated businesses—the small manufacturers who made various fittings, plumbing and electronic parts for the ships—had turned to other products or gone out of business. The Velkaryans had taken advantage of this to buy up some of these, or engage them in long-term contracts at advantageous rates, and built up their own industries: small arms, farm machinery, starship subsystems, and more. All of which left the Velkaryans with money and significant political influence.

∞ ∞ ∞

Velkaryan HQ, New Toronto, Verdigris

Vaughan's inspection of the operation at New Toronto had left him in a sour mood. While significant progress had been made—the number of starship hulls on the landing field had been impressive, even if they had been left in the open—but other areas were severely lacking. Those starship hulls were mostly just that, empty hulls. Oh, they had life support and basic flight control systems installed, but only half of them had their fusion generators, and less than half of those were warp-capable. *What's the point of a starship that can't warp?*

Fusor and warp module fabrication was lagging sadly behind.

He had asked his assistant chief of production, Bill Cardigan, about that. "Why aren't we getting more warp modules? Are we embargoed?"

"Not officially," Cardigan had said. "Most of the available production on Earth goes to the shipyards at Kakuloa. There is a limit on what we can get from Tau Ceti. It's not just the constraints on what we can smuggle, but also because they're still getting the bugs out of their production lines. Maybe it's Skead's higher gravity."

If that were the case, Vaughan had wondered, why didn't they just move it to their moon? There were probably details he wasn't aware of. Warp module production was something of a black art as far as he was concerned.

On the plus side, the ships all had weapons hardpoints: laser turrets and missile launchers. Vaughan wasn't sure how space combat would play out. The lasers might work, but if an enemy ship saw a missile incoming, surely it could just make a millisecond warp jump and be hundreds of miles away. The trick was to program the missile to come in directly toward the enemy's bow; then, if it warped, it would warp straight into the missile. On the other hand, once an adversary figured out that tactic, a bow-mounted anti-missile laser was an obvious countermeasure. Did his own ships have those? It was a detail he'd have to check.

The latest communication from Earth had mentioned upcoming Space Force war games, possibly to be held in the Alpha

Centauri system. As far as Vaughan knew, most Space Force activities involved running down the occasional smuggler or per-
forming training exercises in unpopulated areas. He didn't really
see the point.

He shrugged. Space combat tactics weren't his specialty, nor
were they supposed to be. It was hypothetical anyway. Except for
a few space pirates—who usually ran rather than engaging in
combat—space warfare was mostly theoretical. His job was to
make sure the vehicles were available when the Velkaryan leader-
ship needed them. At least the munitions factories were running
on schedule.

Aside from the missiles, New Toronto had a sizable and
more-or-less legitimate small arms industry. Even the settled
planets were settled in name only. The most populated planets—
Sawyers World, Kakuloa, Verdigris itself, and a few others—had
each only a fraction of one percent of the human population of
Earth, with vast swathes of their planetary landmasses barely ex-
plored, much less settled. Sure, there was aerial and satellite im-
agery, and remote sensing scans, but nothing really matched a biologist's or geologist's feet on the ground.

Or intelligent natives having already discovered and exploited
useful minerals, or plants, or agricultural land.

Vaughan pushed that train of thought aside and reviewed his
inspection notes. Even without the warp drives, if they had fusion reactors for power, the ships could at least be flight tested.
How difficult was it to move the fusion plant from one ship to
another? Would it make sense to flight test what he could, then
transfer power units to the other ships to test them? Anything
that could be tested on ground power, such as instrumentation
and life support, should have already been checked out. *Should*
have. He'd better verify that.

He called his aide, a local man named Soleck. "I want you to
pull a random selection of the build sheets and logs for the ships
in the field. Then we're going to do a manual inspection to verify
those."

"Yes, sir. How many ships, or what percentage?"

"Pull the data for a quarter of them."

"That's a lot of inspections," Soleck said.

"We'll do a random sample of that sample. If we find problems, we'll do more." Vaughan thought for a moment. Bill Cardigan was competent, but he just wasn't up to managing something of this scale. No vehicle came off the production line in perfect condition. "Pull the quality check reports for those ships too, if that's separate from the build logs. Let's see what they found and fixed."

"Okay, will do. Anything else?"

"Not for now."

There should be roll-up reports on what sort of problems they ran into most often at the different manufacturing stages. That should be standard in any manufacturing, to identify bottlenecks and problem areas. He'd want to see those, too, but first, he wanted to discuss things with Cardigan.

∞ ∞ ∞

New Toronto

"So, what are the fundamental limitations of production here?" Vaughan asked Cardigan and his assembled production team leads.

"I think that's pretty obvious. We don't have enough fusion or warp modules. Fuselage assembly is well covered, likewise the life support systems, control systems, avionics—"

Vaughan cut him off. "Yes, I get that. You've done a reasonable job so far, but it's at the limits. What if we wanted to double production?"

"Double?" Cardigan's face paled. "We'd need to double the assembly facilities. We don't have enough staff. I'm not sure we could get the raw materials fast enough. And that still leaves us without critical engine systems. And, how would we pay for all that?"

"That's a good question, but one that can be addressed after we figure out if we *can* double production, and how," Vaughan said. "I want to see your production flow projections. I want to see where the bottlenecks are and where we're wasting effort overproducing."

"Overproducing?" one of the leads asked.

"If the life support team is producing two full systems for every hull that's manufactured, that's wasted effort. But you know this."

Cardigan nodded. That was basic production engineering. You needed some overcapacity to take up slack in a pinch, but otherwise, you were filling your warehouse with oversupply or paying your workers to sit idle part of the time.

"What do you suggest? It's not as if we can have a recycler technician assembling warp modules in his spare time."

"No? Perhaps not, but there may be skills that carry over. That's an extreme example. Have someone look into optimizing the workforce. That may include getting rid of workers we don't need."

"I think it's really more of a supply problem. As I said, we're short on components for critical engine systems, and so on. Homeworld Security monitors those. If we import more it will raise flags."

And there was the problem. They could import warp engine components, but if they weren't exporting a corresponding number of manufactured ships, flags would be raised. Homeworld Security's concerns included the possibility of random individuals warping off to parts unknown and disturbing some high-tech alien race that either didn't want to be disturbed, or might otherwise have hostile intent. Officially that wasn't a concern, because *officially* the likelihood of high-tech aliens was remote, but in fact both the Velkaryans and Homeworld Security knew full-well that there was at least one, and probably more than one, technological alien species out there. They also both knew that the other likely knew it too. No, the *official* concern was that one of those ships might bring back some alien plague that would devastate Earth, either humans directly or a critical food crop. The Quarantine Directorate played a strong, if discreet, role within Homeworld Security. And, Vaughan knew, a lot of other clandestine activities were rolled under the Quarantine Directorate's umbrella.

Either way, Homeworld Security tried to keep a rather close track of how many warp-capable ships were out there and who owned them, and if significant numbers of same went unaccounted for, they would wonder why. That someone was assembling a space fleet would be an obvious answer, and would in itself make them nervous.

That was why many of the critical components were already being smuggled in. None of those were installed in ships destined to be sold on the market, of course. It wouldn't do for some database comparison routine to notice that the serial numbers didn't correspond to anything which had officially been sold to a company on Verdigris.

Chapter 3: Arrival at Verdigris

Verdigris, in the jungle

The going here was proving to be tougher than Burnside had expected; the jungle in this part of Verdigris was thick. He remembered Carson saying something about hacking through the jungle on the expedition where he had found that first, broken, talisman, and Roberts had mentioned clearing a landing area with an improvised daisy-cutter bomb, but he had thought they were exaggerating. Burnside's experience in other forests and jungles had taught him that the upper tree canopy cut down on light to plants on the ground, so the undergrowth was relatively thin. Here on Verdigris, though, the undergrowth was as thick as it might be at the edge of a river or clearing elsewhere. Probably the local vegetation had adapted to light frequently dimmed by skyweed. *Good for it, bad for me.* Again, he regretted not taking up Captain Tevnar's offer to set him down near a trail.

∞ ∞ ∞

"What will you do now?" Tevnar had asked when, orbiting the planet, a break in the skyweed had let them spot the newly-manufactured ships lined up at the New Toronto spaceport. "Are you sure you don't want to come back to Taprobane with me? Roberts and Carson will be expecting you anyway."

"No, I need to check out what's going on down there," Burnside had said. "Vaughan was recalled here for a reason, one good enough to make him give up on the alien artifact you found."

"Perhaps the fake threw him off, and he decided he was being misled from the start."

"Maybe," Burnside said, "but he seemed in a hurry to get here either way. If the Velkaryans are planning something with those ships, I need to find out what."

"You think they're not just going to sell them?"

"With no marketing campaign ahead of time? That's unlikely. Anyway, there have been signs of funny business on this planet for a while. I need to get down there. Boots on the ground." He was certain Ducayne already had boots on the ground—all UDT-administered planets had some kind of Homeworld Defense department, and at least one intelligence officer—but a planet was a big place, and things could be missed. He would coordinate with the local office when he landed, but Tevnar had no need to know all that.

"Well then, clearly we can't land at New Toronto. Shall I head for Verdigris City, or to Louisbourg?"

"Neither," he said. "That would attract attention. Vaughan's people will be monitoring arrivals, especially anything coming from Tanith. They wouldn't ignore a timoan-owned ship. I'd rather go in covertly, then head into the jungle and try to contact the snake-eyes," Burnside said. "Some of them will have had contact with their counterparts in the cities. I want to learn what I can before heading to New Toronto."

"Snake-eyes? Why would you talk to the eyes of a snake?"

Burnside chuckled. "It's a nickname. It refers to the slit-pupils of the native Verdigran eyes, like a snake's. Each clan or tribe has their own term for themselves, much like some of your species when we first met, and most of them regarded *snake-eyes* as an honorific. They consider snakes to be silent and skillful hunters."

Tevnar shook her head. Most timoans were not fond of snakes. "There are natives? Don't you have the same hands-off policy with them that you do with us?"

"No," he said, "the native civilization on Verdigris collapsed thousands of years ago, and the circumstances of first contact were very different. Initially, we thought they'd all died out, but there are still Verdigrans living in the jungles, even a few that live on the fringes of the deserts." Burnside said.

"The current Verdigrans are believed to be a different sub-species from the original structure-builders," he explained, "something like the Neanderthals and Cro-Magnons on Earth, if that means anything to you. The existing Verdigrans are fairly primitive and reclusive; we didn't even realize they existed until settlement had started. They have small villages, but no stonework. Have you not visited Verdigris before?"

"Just once, but it was a brief stop at the Verdigris City spaceport. I never saw any natives, just heard a bit about what native life to beware of if I did wander off."

"Ah, generally, the natives here don't come near the spaceports, although there are some in the towns."

"Oh?" Tevnar said.

"They avoid anything to do with archeologists. The tribes, even widely separated ones, have superstitions about the stone ruins here. Won't go near them, although the reasons and stories are all different. Most of them involve punishment from the gods or something," he said. "You'd have to ask Carson. But they know the ruins are Verdigran-built because they were here before humans landed, and because of the carvings on a lot of them. A lot of the decorations are representational and look more like the snake-eyes than humans."

"Speaking of, I imagine you don't exactly look like a Verdigran native any more than you do a timoan. How do you expect to blend in? Do you even speak their language?"

"I don't expect to blend in. As for the language, I have a good ear, and a handy database of all known Verdigris dialects." He waved his left wrist, displaying his omniphone. "Of course, if the Velkaryans start doing a round-up, I'll be caught if they start checking out native villages. But a lot of the tribes are good at disappearing into the jungle. The story is that explorers often come across campsites that were recently abandoned but with no sign nearby of any natives. They could probably be found with an intensive search with IR and leaf-penetrating radar, but as far as I know, nobody has bothered. Some areas have been surveyed to get some kind of census, and as best possible keep human areas away from snake-eyes, but there's a lot of unexplored territory out there, if you don't count orbital scans."

"But what do you hope to gain? A few stone-age natives aren't going to make any difference to the Velkaryan's fleet building. You might keep some of them out of the camps, but are the Velkaryans even going to bother the ones in the jungle?"

"They may be stone-age, but they're intelligent. Mostly I want information, but if it comes down to it, they can learn to use modern tools and weapons—well, those that don't require reading or computer skills—as well as anyone. Those raised with computers can learn to use them, too, as you well know."

"That is true. But are you going to arm the natives?"

"That's not my plan," he said, shaking his head. It wasn't, at least not as a first resort. "If it does come to that, I'll figure out something."

"Would you assemble a snake-eye army together to fight the Velkaryans? Even if they fight as fiercely as timoans, surely they would be slaughtered!"

Burnside hid his amusement at Tevnar's comparison. He knew that timoans could indeed be fierce fighters, not unlike Viking berserkers by some stories, but the thought of iron-age timoans going up against modern weapons . . . of course, that wasn't what Tevnar had meant.

"No, not that," he said. "Just to disrupt their production systems a little. It's called asymmetric warfare. This probably won't mean much to you, but the various resistance groups in our World War II, for example, disrupted Nazi communications, transportation, factories, and so on, without necessarily shooting up Nazi soldiers. Although they did take out high-ranking officers when a good opportunity presented itself."

"The concept is familiar, if not the details. My planet has a history of clan warfare itself; we just hadn't developed the technology for anything bigger before humans showed up. But you seem to know a lot about it."

"Part training, part personal interest. Much of the training was so that I could recognize it if I saw it, not so much to implement it. But that too."

Tevnar slowly shook her head. "This whole thing is going in a dark direction. I hope Taprobane can stay out of it."

"I hope we can *all* stay out of it, but the Velkaryans seem to want to make the first move. Maybe I can do something here to frustrate their plans, give time for wiser heads to prevail."

"You seem set on this," she said. "I still think you should go back and report in first."

Ordinarily, Burnside would agree, but time might be of the essence. "I don't see another way," he said. "I can do more good here. You can take my reports back to Carson, who will get them to my boss. If I leave with you, getting someone back here will only get harder. Do you see any other options?"

She didn't. She shook her head. "No, but neither of us has all the information."

"Nor does my boss. Even if he does know about their ship-building—which he might have figured out from other data—he won't know how far they've gotten or what they're doing to the local inhabitants," Burnside said grimly. "And if he does know, he can't prove it. If we can get him evidence that someone could bring to the UDT council, it might persuade them to do something."

"You staying here won't change that one way or the other."

"It might, and I can give him an ace in the hole if things turn nasty."

She scoffed at that. "Just how is he going to contact you?"

That was something Burnside had given some thought to. His omniphone could contact a ship in orbit, if the ship knew to listen, but it could also be overheard, and what if he lost it? He could use the local UDT intelligence office, of course, but that would mean staying in constant communication with them, and it would hamper what he intended to do. He would find a way; he just needed to know if there was anyone to contact. "I'll contact him. If he needs to get my attention, I'll be looking for a sign at regular intervals. The details will be in my report. He'll know what to do."

"All right, if you insist on going AWOL and taking an extended vacation here, I can't stop you." She gave him the timoan equivalent of a grin. "Not short of kidnapping you and keeping you on the ship until we're at Taprobane."

"You could, but you won't. You know I need to do this."

She sighed. "I do. All right, figure out where do you want me to set you down. If I can land near a lake, I can refuel."

"I'd rather you didn't take the ship down, too much risk of it being detected. Do you have to refuel?"

"Yes, to make it to Taprobane, but this system's gas giant, Zeus, has an ice moon where I can refuel. Why don't you come along until I'm done with that? It will give you time to plan your next moves and give me any information you want to pass on to your boss. Don't forget that Captain Roberts will be waiting for me on Taprobane."

"Yes, that's a good idea."

"Are you planning to use the bail-out pack, then?"

"I'm looking forward to it," Burnside had said.

Tevnar made a gesture that Burnside took to mean something like "okay, it's your funeral" and went forward to set course for her refueling stop.

Burnside strapped himself into a seat at the galley table and brought up maps of Verdigris on a monitor. He had some planning to do.

∞ ∞ ∞

The gas giant, Zeus, had several icy moons. The one Tevnar picked to land on was much like Saturn's moon Enceladus, about 500 kilometers in diameter and covered with a thick, icy crust. They had found life on Enceladus, primitive microorganisms, in the ocean under the ice. Burnside idly wondered if this moon had the like.

Like Enceladus, periodic geysers through cracks in the crust spewed water high above the surface, where much of it immediately froze and settled out as clean, white snow. As far as Tevnar was concerned, that made it ideal for refueling the *Razgon*; there would be a minimum of impurities to filter out.

The fueling operation itself was straight-forward; exploration ships were designed for just such a contingency. A robotic arm extended two hoses out, one narrower, carrying high-pressure steam, and the other wider, which would carry back water and water vapor that the steam had melted from the ice. The only tricky part was making sure that operation didn't undermine the ice that the *Razgon* had parked on.

"All right," Tevnar said after she came back in from making sure the equipment was functioning properly. "So, you have been busy. Have you worked out your plan?"

"Yes, I think so." Burnside swung the display around so she could see it. "I think if you drop me somewhere around here—he pointed to a spot about two hundred kilometers south-west of Verdigris City—I can make my way to the city in four or five days."

"So far? You know that is jungle. It won't be like hiking on open plain. Can you cross it that quickly?"

"I think so, but a few more days won't matter."

"I thought you wanted to go to New Toronto?"

"I can catch commercial transportation for that. I'll want to set up a cover first and get an idea of what I'll be going into."

"You humans. Never straightforward."

"And you creating a fake copy of the artifact you found was?" Burnside said, amused.

"It seemed the path least likely to lead to complications."

"Well, and so does what I plan. I might even get there before you get back to Taprobane."

"And even if you're not, it will take another two or three weeks at least before the information gets back to your boss and he sends somebody out to pick you up, if that's the plan."

"Well, yes, a pick-up would be nice eventually, although I can work something else out if I have to."

"Do you have a pick-up plan?" Tevnar asked, eying him dubiously. "They're not just going to land in New Toronto and call your omniphone."

He cringed at the thought. "I would hope not. It should be okay for them to land at Louisbourg or Verdigris City. If I'm at one of those I'll check with the spaceport. I'll try to get a message out as to which. But if I am in or near New Toronto . . . ." He looked back at the chart. "No, see this lake here?" He pointed to small lake about two hundred kilometers north-east of the city. It was connected by a narrow river or creek to the much larger Lac Quebec, where New Toronto sat on the southwest shore.

"Yes. That's just as long a hike, unless you were going to swim across the lake?" Tevnar made a face at that. Timoans were not fond of water.

"I should be able to find a boat. There's a lot of water traffic in that area. I can cross Lac Quebec and then up that small river to the rendezvous lake. I don't think it has a name, but it's thin and curved like a buckhorn. Call it that.

"What is a buckhorn?" Tevnar wondered aloud.

"It's the horn or antler of a—" Burnside groped for a Taprobani equivalent "—a *pragarth*. Did I say that right?"

The timoan seemed amused. "A good try. So how will you know when to be there?"

"I'll give you details of my plans to pass on to Roberts and Carson. I'll be watching for some kind of signal at regular times. If I get such a signal, I'll try to be at the rendezvous four days later."

"Verdigris days?"

"Yes."

"And if you miss the signal, or your meet-up?"

"I've put contingency instructions in the packet for Roberts. But otherwise, I'll figure something out. Maybe I'll steal one of Vaughan's starships. I figure he owes us."

"Can you fly a starship? Especially one you've never seen the inside of?"

Burnside shrugged. "How hard could it be?"

Tevnar gasped, but before she could say anything, Burnside hastily added, "I'm joking. I'm not as experienced as you or Roberts, but I do have pilot training."

Tevnar just muttered something. To Burnside it sounded like "*Boys!*"

She rose from the table. "I told you I wouldn't try to stop you, but I think you are crazy. Anyway, the refueling should be done. I need to see to it."

∞ ∞ ∞

In hindsight, Burnside mused, maybe he should have taken his chances on the *Razgon* being spotted and let her land him. A Taprobane-registered ship even at the Verdigris City spaceport would have invited too much attention, but somewhere nearby could have worked. Odds were the locals would have just assumed it was artifact smugglers, and he wouldn't have had to hack through so much damned jungle.

Chapter 4: Verdigris City

Verdigris City

Burnside didn't want to be seen entering the UDT offices, which was safest to assume were under observation. Although he had managed to clean himself up a bit upon entering the city, he would probably still attract attention he didn't want. He did need to talk to the resident intelligence officer, though. A quick search of the online directory wasn't helpful, but Burnside hadn't imagined it would be.

He called the UDT consulate.

"Terran Union Administration, how may I help you?"

Burnside smiled to himself. The English name for the *Union De Terre* was less often used; its initials were unfortunate. "Yes, can you connect me to the Quarantine Directorate office, please." That office name hadn't been used in decades, but it got the receptionist's attention.

"Yes, sir. May I ask what this is about, to better direct your call?"

"Just tell them I'm a recent arrival and need to check on a few things."

"One moment."

A moment later, another voice came on the line. "This is the Office of Plant and Wildlife Control. Did I understand that you had a question about quarantine?"

"Indirectly. More a concern about local wildlife. I'd rather not come into the office. Could we meet somewhere?"

"I'd have to get back to you on that. Can you give me a number?"

Burnside recited a number. It was an identity string, not his omniphone number. He waited a moment while whoever he was talking to validated it.

"Got it, sir. As it happens, something just opened up. Can you make it to the Hungry Snake in a half-hour?"

Burnside checked the location on his omni. It was an eatery a few blocks from the UDT, or TU, office.

"Yes, I can do that. Who should I expect?"

"Henry Prentiss. Tall, thin, blond hair, grey eyes. And you?"

"Just average. I'll find him." Burnside clicked off.

Most of that rigamarole had probably been unnecessary, the line had been encrypted and theoretically uncrackable. But it never hurt to play it safe. Burnside checked the map display again. At a brisk walk, he could make it to the Hungry Snake in plenty of time. He preferred to watch the door for new arrivals when arranging a meet. Probably Henry Prentiss, or whoever he really was, did too; the Hungry Snake was an even shorter walk from the UDT building.

∞ ∞ ∞

The Hungry Snake

The eatery—it didn't really deserve the term restaurant—was an older establishment, with a dozen tables and a handful of booths along one wall. It was moderately lit, and three of the tables were occupied. There was a bar along the back wall, with a couple of patrons. A mirror behind the bar would theoretically let a patron watch the front door, if he could see between the bottles and glasses on the shelves in front of it.

Burnside scanned the clientele as he entered the place. He didn't see anyone who might qualify as tall, thin, and blond, although with them all sitting down, the first was a guess.

He walked over to a booth and sat facing the doorway. A man wearing a shabby apron stepped out from behind the bar and came over.

"What can I get you? Or do you need a menu?"

"Just a beer for now. I'm expecting someone."

"What kind?"

Burnside didn't really know what brands were available here, but he'd scanned the bottles and taps behind the bar as he entered and noted one. "Do you have Emerald on tap?" He knew that they did.

"Sure do. You want a glass or a pitcher?"

"Just a glass, thanks."

The man came back a few moments later with a frothy glass of brew. Burnside was relieved to see that it was amber, not green. After two days trekking through the jungle, he was sick of green. "Cheers."

A couple rose from their table and left, and as the door swung shut behind them, it opened again. A tall man, wearing a hat, entered. He paused in the doorway, removing the hat and looking around. Blond hair. That was probably his man.

"Henry!" Burnside called and waved. "Over here."

The man paused, staring intently at Burnside for a moment, then scanned the room before walking over to the booth.

"JB?" he asked quietly, before sitting. The data linked to the code Burnside had given would have told him that much. Initials and minimal data, not enough to pose a serious risk if it leaked.

Burnside nodded. "Henry Prentiss? Did we speak earlier?"

"We did. You mentioned being a recent arrival. What's going on?"

The bartender was back. Business must be slow. "Something for you?" he asked Prentiss.

"Same as my friend," he said, then looked at Burnside. "Are you hungry?"

Burnside was famished. He'd arrived in the city early this morning and had eaten his last ration bar shortly before that. "I could eat," he said.

"Two of your burger platters," Prentiss told the bartender/waiter. Make mine medium-rare."

"And yours?" the bartender asked, turning to Burnside.

"The same, thanks."

As the bartender walked away, Prentiss said, "That ought to keep him busy for a while. They don't use an autochef for the burger platter. So, care to explain yourself?"

"I'm Jordan Burnside, recently out of Tanith. I followed a Velkaryan agent out here. He had dropped everything and left in a hurry."

"So why are you here and not in New Toronto?"

"Interesting question. What's going on in New Toronto that would cause you to think a Velkaryan would go there instead of here?"

"I wish we knew. I haven't heard from our agent there in weeks. We just don't have the manpower to investigate."

"Have you reported it?"

"Of course. I was hoping you might be the reply, but apparently, you're not."

"How safe is it to talk here?" Burnside had turned on the built-in jammer in his omni as soon as Prentiss had entered the restaurant, but that didn't mean they were impervious to bugging, or to plain old-fashioned eavesdropping.

"We'd be better back at the office, but we keep an eye on this place. So how did you get in? There hasn't been a starship landing here recently. Did you come in via Louisbourg?"

Burnside grinned. "I came in through the jungle. Reentry pack."

Prentiss's eyes widened at that. "You jumped? Do I take it then that you're more an active field agent than an analyst?"

"You could say that," Burnside said. "But don't," he added with a grin.

"Ha. So, do you have a place to stay?"

"No, I was hoping you could help with that, at least for a couple of days."

Prentiss nodded. "We have a safe house. It doesn't see much use, and it's not very fancy."

"I'm sure whatever it is beats sleeping on the ground in the jungle."

"All right. I'll take you back there after we eat. It's secure; we can brief each other there."

Chapter 5: Safehouse

UDT Safehouse, Verdigris City

The safe house was a small apartment in an older area of Verdigris City, within walking distance of both the Hungry Snake and of the UDT offices, near the edge of what would be considered downtown.

"We keep a retainer on this place through a couple of cutout companies. The usual arrangement," Prentiss said as he showed Burnside in.

"I'm familiar," Burnside replied. He had maintained just such during his post on Tanith. "Does it come with the usual accoutrements?" Meaning, in addition to spare clothing and supplies for a short stay, did it have the usual collection of tools that might be useful to an agent.

"It does. Clothes in the closet here," he said, opening the cupboard's sliding door. "Now, set the room thermostat to forty-two—"

"Isn't it hot enough in here already?"

Prentiss stepped over to the thermostat and adjusted it himself. "Not an issue," he said. "Now ask the autochef for 'tea, Earl Grey, hot.'"

Burnside smiled and stepped over to the autochef, pressed its request button, and did as Prentiss had instructed. The autochef didn't seem to do anything, but there was a muffled sound from the closet. Intrigued, Burnside strode over to it. Prentiss was there already, pushing the hanging clothing aside.

Part of the back of the closet had slid away, revealing a hidden compartment. It contained an assortment of electronic devices, tools, and hand weapons.

"Very cute," Burnside said, "but what if I need to get in there in a hurry?"

"We'll take care of that now," Prentiss said. There was a keypad built into the side of the hidden compartment. He tapped out a sequence. "Okay, place your hand there." He pointed to the closet wall beside the opening.

"Left or right?"

"Whichever you're most likely to use."

Burnside placed his right hand flat against the indicated area of the wall. It felt just like a normal, painted wall; smooth, dry, and only slightly cool to the touch.

Prentiss tapped another sequence, and the pad beeped. "Okay, you can take your hand away."

Burnside did so, and Prentiss tapped another key on the pad. The panel slide down, hiding the compartment. The crack that outlined the panel then faded, and the back wall was now seamless.

"Smart materials?" Burnside asked.

"Yes. Nothing too fancy, it works best on a smooth, plain background. Okay, give it a try. Just slap the wall where I showed you."

Burnside stepped forward again and slapped the wall. The panel slid open almost instantly. "Very nice." His place on Tanith had nothing similar, just concealed mechanical latches.

"It's probably overkill," Prentiss said, "but my predecessor had a hankering for toys."

"And a fondness for old science fiction references, I gather."

"Oh? What makes you say that?"

"The code— Never mind. We should get down to business," Burnside said, and closed the panel again.

"Agreed. So, why are you pursing a Velkaryan agent here from 82 Eridani? What's he up to?"

"The man's name is Klaus Vaughan. I believe he was stationed here some time back."

"Yes, I know the name. Fairly high up in the Velkaryan organization. He departed on his ship, the *Carcharodon*, about, oh, five months back. Not sure where he was going, but now that you mention it, a report did come through a while back that he was on Tanith. Your report?"

"Most likely. He landed there about three months ago, with slight damage to his ship. Even after repairs, he stayed on to organize the local party. With some success, I would add. There's a minority of timoan settlers on the planet, and he was stirring up resentment against them for various imagined incidents."

Prentiss grunted acknowledgment. "Yeah, they do that here too. Not against timoans, but against the native Verdigrans, the snake-eyes. What brings him back here?"

"That's what I was curious about. It seemed to be urgent. He and his crew were in the middle of another operation that they seemingly abandoned to head here. My guess is that he got orders from Velkaryan headquarters. Is there some local operation of theirs that needs help?" Burnside was pretty sure that it somehow related to the starships he'd seen, but he wanted to hear Prentiss's opinion without influencing it first.

"I suppose there are a couple of possibilities," the other man said. "The local Velkaryan political party does try to keep things stirred up, but there are no elections scheduled for a while."

Verdigris was, like many of the other terraformed planets with human settlements, officially UDT territory under the nominal direction of an appointed planetary governor. However, these territories, particularly the older, more-settled ones, had their own local elected governments, with the UDT appointee more of a symbolic governor-general, acting on the advice of the local government. He or she could overrule the locals if they violated the UDT charter, and had a small contingent of UDT Space Force to back that up, but it was largely symbolic. The Velkaryans, however, objected even to that symbolism, and were constantly pushing for more autonomy—in no small part because their own anti-alien agenda was contrary to the UDT charter, although they downplayed that in places where it wouldn't go over as well.

"Anything else?" Burnside asked.

"Did you know they have a number of manufacturing businesses in New Toronto? Not all officially, but controlled by Velkaryan supporters, at least."

"Somewhat aware, yes. What kind of manufacturing?"

"A little of everything, in particular light machinery including firearms, and the ammunition to go with it. They've also been getting into aircraft and spacecraft manufacturing, with a company called Hansa Astrospace. However, from the reports I've seen, Hansa's sales are underwhelming. I'm not surprised, it takes a while to build up a reputation there. Earth-based companies like Mitsubishi and SpaceX still dominate, and the shipyards in the Alpha Centauri system have a strong lead for second place."

"And first place for the weapons, with companies like Maclaren Armaments," Burnside mused. The frontier nature of all the terraformed worlds generally meant that almost everyone went armed when away from settled areas, and a good many did so within cities. A sidearm was an expected piece of protective gear, like good boots. There was a large market, and weapons from Earth were overpriced and—except for impossible-to-obtain military weapons—unreliable, their numerous built-in safety systems tending to fail on the side of *safe for whatever you might want to shoot*, rather than *safe for the shooter*. People who might be uncomfortable with proper defensive tools weren't the sort to come out to space in the first place.

"Exactly, although Maclaren weapons come at a price premium, so the local industry does pretty well there."

"Exports too, or is the price markup just shipping?"

"No. Maclaren charges more at the loading dock. Their build quality is somewhat better, but not enough to justify the price, in my opinion anyway. Plus, we're closer to some of the outlying settlements than Alpha Cee is, so there's an advantage there, too."

"Huh." Burnside's recent home, Tanith at 82 Eridani, was almost equidistant from both Alpha Centauri and Delta Pavonis, so he hadn't really considered how that might play for the settlements at stars like Zeta Tucanae or Beta Hydri, which, if he remembered right, were considerably closer to Verdigris.

"Okay. What about the ships? I ask because, as we approached the planet, we spotted a large number of ships on the field at New Toronto. If they're not selling them, why build so many?"

"That would depend why they're not selling. It could be that they've built a backlog because they couldn't get warp drives or power units for them—those are strictly import items. Who wants a starship that can't warp? But when they get the supply chain unplugged, they'll start moving."

"That seems like a strange way to run a business."

"Maybe they had a contract, but their supplier fell through."

"No local source, then?"

"Not for warp drives, that's restricted technology. There's some local manufacture of fusion power units, but it's older tech, deuterium based, not the newer stuff."

"Deuterium? That *is* old tech." Modern fusion units, using elements of warp technology to carefully control the reaction chains, could run on almost pure ordinary hydrogen, not the heavier deuterium. Burnside didn't know the details, all he knew was that it was easier to get deuterium to fuse, making the technology simpler.

"It's fine for most uses," Prentiss said. "It just limits your range in a starship. But deuterium fusors are something we can manufacture on Verdigris."

"Well, that's a plus. Still, the ships aren't much use without warp drives, unless you're just going from here to the moon."

"That's probably why they have so many ships sitting on the field. Although you would think they'd put a hold on construction until they nailed down a source of warp modules."

"Is there no way those could be manufactured locally?" Burnside pressed. "Even illegally?"

"Unlikely, but I'm no expert on warp module technology. My understanding is that some parts of the module are no more complex than a deuterium solid-state fusor, so there's that, but other parts require exotic materials and fabrication techniques."

"Have they sold any starships?"

"I think so. We do get occasional imports of warp modules. We get reports because those are on the restricted list. But they can't be importing enough for all the ship hulls you say they have."

Since creating a warp field in atmosphere, or on a planet's surface, could create a huge explosion, the devices—especially when not installed in a ship, with its layers of safety protocols—were understandably considered dangerous. In theory those same protocols prevented activation of an uninstalled warp module, but any device could be hacked with enough time and determination, and perhaps access to leaked specifications. A starship manufacturer, of course, would have access to those specs, but why build a fleet of starships if you just wanted to use the warp modules as bombs?

"Okay, then. I think I want to pay a visit to the Hansa Astrospace Corporation. I've decided I'm in the market for a starship. Possibly several. Can you arrange that, and a suitable cover?"

Prentiss looked momentarily nonplussed. "Not the sort of thing we usually do, but potentially, yes. There are a couple of big biopharmaceutical companies based here in town. If not a starship *per se*, how about modifying one as an aircraft for harvesting skyweed? They have something similar already, big and lumbering. Maybe you could be looking into that?"

"Whatever gets me into the plant. I want to ask a few questions and take a closer look at the operation."

"I should warn you, our last man in New Toronto seems to have gone missing," Prentiss said.

"Missing? Yes, you mentioned that before. When?"

"His last report was several weeks ago. We've tried contacting him, with no response. I've mentioned it in my reports."

"Was he undercover? I assume you've checked with the local authorities?"

"Yes, and yes, so our checks had to be discrete. Many of his personal items had been removed from his apartment, but not all. Officially there was no sign of foul play, so as far as they're concerned, he just decided to move on."

"You don't think so?"

"He wasn't the sort, and he would have notified us. His rent was paid up and we've extended that, hoping to get someone in there to take a closer look. I don't think he just left."

Burnside understood the implication. If his cover was blown, or if he were merely suspected, he too might be disappeared. "A chance I'll have to take. We need more information about what's going on. Just make that cover story solid, all right?"

"Of course."

∞ ∞ ∞

A few days later

"It's set up," Prentiss told Burnside. "You're John Fisher, a senior purchasing representative for Otani Biochemicals based here in Verdigris City. You're booked on a commercial air flight to New Toronto, meeting with Antonio Serbinski, the Sales Director for Hansa Astrospace."

"He's expecting me?" Burnside asked.

"Yes. You contacted him three days ago via email. There's a transcript of all the communication between you two in the dossier."

"Very good. What else?"

"The background is all in the file, you'll have time to read it on the flight. Essentially, Otani is looking for up to three ships now, one to replace an aging, small transport, S-class, and two new ones as cargo carriers. Business is at the point where Otani thinks it will be cheaper to operate their own, although you'd be interested in a lease-back arrangement if Hansa is willing, or if they can recommend a third party who is. There's a Velkaryan-owned firm, Constellation Capital, who does that sort of thing, so expect their name to come up. Otani's not making a commitment at this point, but if business growth goes as planned, there may be additional starship purchases down the road.

"Again, read the files. Otani actually did look into this recently, although they hadn't come to any decision, and they were thinking more of acquiring previously-owned Sapphires than anything new. Still, there's enough there to pass a cursory background check. They probably already did that when *you* first contacted them."

"Excellent work," Burnside said. "I appreciate the effort you've put in." Burnside had spent the time familiarizing himself with places and events in and around Verdigris City, and with the business operations of the larger companies. He wanted to be comfortable if any of that came up in conversation while undercover.

"Aren't you worried that Vaughan will recognize you?"

"I'm not planning to meet with him, and anyway, we never met each other in person."

"If he had you under surveillance, he will have seen photographs of you. After all, you know what he looks like."

Burnside had already considered that, but didn't see any other option. "I guess that's a chance I'll have to take."

"One request," Prentiss added.

"Yes?"

"I've included information about our missing man, Peter Franks. Details of his apartment, and so on. It's completely secondary to your main mission, of course, but if you can find out anything about what happened to him, we'd appreciate it."

"Of course. Do you want me to take any action on what I find?"

"That's up to you. If it turns out someone else was responsible for his disappearance, we'd certainly like to discourage that sort of thing in future." Prentiss seemed to enjoy understatement. "But not if it jeopardizes your operation."

Burnside understood him perfectly and agreed. "I'll see what I can do," he said grimly.

Chapter 6: Hansa Astrospace

New Toronto, Hansa Astrospace Co.

"John Fisher to see Antonio Serbinski," Burnside announced himself at the reception desk of the Hansa Astrospace building. The building itself was unimpressive by Earth or even Alpha Centauri system standards, a relatively plain four-story concrete office building that abutted a larger steel-framed assembly building.

"Certainly, Mr. Fisher. I'll have someone escort you."

A few minutes later, Burnside was being introduced to Hansa's head of sales.

To Burnside, Antonio Serbinski seemed like a typical sales rep, well dressed and with an enthusiasm that came across as just a bit forced.

"Mr. Fisher! Welcome to Hansa Astrospace. Call me Tony," he said, shaking Burnside's hand. "I trust you had a pleasant trip? I understand you came in from Verdigris City?"

"Thank you, Tony. Call me John," Burnside said. "That's right, I'm based in Otani's head office, but I like to get out when I can."

"I understand perfectly. Perhaps later we can show you around a bit. So tell me, how can we help Otani Biopharmaceuticals?"

Burnside recapped the cover story, about how Otani was looking to upgrade its aging fleet of ships. Serbinski already had most of that background as part of the meeting setup, but the conversation would be an opportunity for each side to ask questions and discuss details that weren't mentioned earlier -- and for both men to get a feel for the other's bargaining position.

For Burnside, it was also an opportunity to get an idea of just where the Velkaryan-owned Hansa stood in its production capability. The delivery time on a customized ship, for example, gave him an idea of just how quickly they were being manufactured.

"Now, in terms of serviceability," Burnside said, "are the powerplants locally manufactured, or might we have to wait for off-world parts if something needs repairs?"

"That's a great question, John, and the answer comes down to which you would prefer. We can go with either PNF powerplants produced right here in New Toronto, or with something from Maclaren Industries on Sawyers World or Mitsubishi on Earth. The latter would both cost a bit more, but Hansa would commit to retaining an inventory of spares on-planet. Not that any model fusor needs much in the way of maintenance, of course."

"Of course. What are the advantages and disadvantages?"

"I can give you an overview, but if you want technical detail, let me get a sales engineer up here."

"Oh, no need for that, I wouldn't understand all the details. Let's set up a meeting later between your sales engineer and our chief of flight operations. Right now, I was just curious."

"Okay, sure. Well, the PNF modules are more economical to purchase, and every bit as reliable as Maclaren or Mitsubishi. You're avoiding the brand-name markup and shipping costs. The only drawback, and for your purposes it's not really an issue, is that they run on deuterium only. Of course, that also means they're more reliable."

"So, the imports can run on unenriched hydrogen?" Burnside knew they could, but "Fisher" might not.

"That's correct, and that's part of what accounts for their higher cost. Of course, whether you opt for the PNF modules or imports, that's just for the power production. Thruster reaction mass can be plain hydrogen or water. You really only need the imports' flexibility if you're refueling in the wild, so to speak, but it sounds like you don't need that. If you do, my engineering team can talk about what would be involved with adding a deuterium extraction unit."

"No, I don't think we'd need that," Burnside said. "But now I am curious, what is the lead-time on the imported fusor units? Would that be a hold up in our expected delivery?"

"Oh, no, not really. It would take about a month for order and delivery, that's just the basic turnaround time for ordering anything from Alpha Centauri. Add a couple of weeks if you want something from Earth. But we'd just fit that into the build schedule."

"Is there anything else that would have to be ordered from off-planet? What about avionics, for example, or warp modules?"

"Yes, the local manufacturing base for that isn't where we'd like it be just yet. However, word is that there have been recent investments in new facilities."

Have there now, Burnside thought. *Interesting.*

"But," Serbinski continued, "since we have standing orders for what we expect to need, that's just part of our standard supply line. It wouldn't affect the delivery time unless you wanted to commission a large fleet order, a dozen or more ships. We'd have to ramp things up a bit for that."

"Well," Burnside said, smiling, "we are hoping to expand, but not quite that fast."

The conversation continued in that vein for a few minutes longer, each of them making notes on their respective datapads, with Serbinski providing "Fisher" with digital copies of the configuration and service manuals for the proposed models. Finally, Serbinski offered what Burnside had really wanted all along: a tour of the plant.

∞ ∞ ∞

New Toronto

Burnside exited the autocab several blocks from his destination, a nondescript apartment building, and walked the rest of the way.

The tour of the Astrospace plant had been interesting, but not as informative as Burnside had hoped. Unsurprisingly, much of the facility was off-limits to outsiders, and probably even to plant workers without the proper clearance. He had noticed several doors with security scanners.

More useful was what he had seen of partially assembled ships; that was more enlightening than perhaps Serbinski had realized. Burnside had noticed the extra structural members at key points on the airframes, as well as other details like power conduit routing and cooling tubes. It was unlikely that it was all for additional warp modules; nobody built ships with seven engines. No, those were hardpoints for weaponry of some kind: missile racks, rail guns, or lasers, maybe all three.

He had begged off of Serbinski's invitation to dinner, saying he was still lagged by the trip from Verdigris City, far enough away to have an eight-hour time difference. Instead, they'd meet for lunch in the executive dining room the next day.

There was little traffic on the streets at this late afternoon hour, before most businesses ended shift or closed for the day, but Burnside kept an eye out for anyone who might be following him or watching the apartment. It seemed clear, and he entered the four-story building as though he lived there.

He took the stairs to the third floor, then down the hall to number four. This was the apartment registered to Prentiss's missing agent, UDT had kept up the payments. Burnside let himself in.

It was small, little bigger than the safehouse he'd been staying at in Verdigris City. It looked lived-in, in that there were the expected accoutrements around; a large vidscreen, clothing in the bedroom, food and dishes in the kitchen area. There were no dirty dishes, though, and no perishable food in the refrigerator. Similarly, there was no dirty laundry anywhere, the bed was made, and routine toiletries like toothbrush and comb were absent from the bathroom. He could see why the police had concluded that the man's absence was planned. But to Burnside's eye, there was still something off about it.

He examined the apartment more carefully, beginning with the kitchen. It was a standard small kitchenette, with an autochef, a sink, a refrigerator, and several cupboards for storing food or dishes. No stove or oven, the autochef would suffice for most people living in a place like this, and no dishwasher either. He checked the cupboards. Plates, bowls, cups and glasses in one, canned and boxed food in another. Cutlery in a drawer under the counter, with some cleaning supplies in a lower cabinet. What was he missing?

Missing! There was no trash can or open trash bag anywhere that he could see, nor was there any waste disposal slot. Whoever had last taken out the trash had not put out a new bag. He checked the dish cupboard again. Aside from a couple of odd glasses and mugs, it seemed to be a four-place set of ceramic plates, bowls and cups. Except that there were only three plates. Well, it was possible one had been broken.

Burnside took a plate from the cupboard and dropped it on the floor. It hit with a clunk, bounced slightly, and wobbled to a stop. He picked it up and rapped it smartly, but not too hard, on the edge of the counter. It thunked, but otherwise ignored the impact. Okay, rule out accidentally breaking a plate. There had been no sign of disposable plates, either. He checked the cutlery drawer, counting the knives, forks and spoons. There were four of each, except for a missing fork. *Interesting.*

Burnside envisioned the scene. Peter Franks comes home, orders something simple from the autochef, and gets a plate and fork to eat it with. Maybe a glass too, for something to drink. He's eating when an assailant either breaks in or lulls him into opening the door, but either way is overcome, leaving the remains of his dinner on the table.

If the assailant wanted to make it look like Franks had gone on vacation, he would stage the scene. Aside from getting rid of the body, he wouldn't leave a half-eaten dinner on the table, he might just throw it, dishes and all, in the trash. Why take the time to actually wash them? What other clean-up shortcuts might he take? Burnside went back to the bedroom.

Sure enough, not only was there no dirty clothing left in the open, he couldn't find any sign of a laundry basket or hamper. If Franks had just used a hamper bag, the cleaner would have taken it, and perhaps a few other clothes to make it seem like Franks had packed, and thrown them in the trash too. Not a completely professional job, but good enough to fool cops who don't have a dead body to investigate.

He went back to the living/dining area and began searching around the edges of the counters, table legs, and the like. Eventually, he found a few traces of reddish-brown substance in a difficult-to-clean crack. He didn't think it was dried ketchup. *Either the cops didn't bother spraying the floor with luminol, or they did a half-assed job of it*, he thought. Probably the former, although depending on how the scene had been cleaned, a luminol test could be swamped with false positives.

Burnside had seen enough. It wasn't enough to prove the agent had been murdered, but that seemed the likeliest scenario. He'd give Prentiss the details and let him take it from there.

∞ ∞ ∞

As Burnside left the building to walk the few blocks to where he planned to pick up an autocab, he didn't notice the small camera affixed to the streetlight across the street. There was no particular reason he would, since it was designed to look just like the standard photosensor that would turn the streetlight on and off. But someone was monitoring that camera.

"Boss? Mignon here. That guy Fisher, he just left Peter Franks' apartment building. And you were right, he does look an awful lot like that guy Smith from back on Tanith."

∞ ∞ ∞

New Toronto, lunch meeting

Serbinski put down his omni. "I'm sorry about the delay, John. My boss wanted to meet you, and he got held up. He says to go ahead and order and he'll be here shortly."

"That's quite all right," Burnside said. He glanced over the menu, not particularly caring what was on it. He had a vague, uneasy feeling, but had no good excuse to leave. Besides, Serbinski had promised to get him a look at some of the factory they had skipped yesterday, before the meeting with a couple of engineers to discuss detail design modifications. It was worth sticking around for. He looked up at Serbinski. "I really can't decide. Is there a special?"

"Yes, there is. Roast polcken"—a domesticated native bird, something like chicken—"with a roast vegetable mix. I was planning on having it."

"I'll have that too, then."

Serbinski signaled the waiter, a slim man who nevertheless had an edgy, tough look about him. "Two of the special, please."

"Yes, sir," the waiter said and returned to the kitchen.

"I think you'll find—" Serbinski began, then broke off as two men entered the dining room. "Ah, here he is now," he said, rising from his chair. Burnside rose also, trying to catch a glimpse of the second man, who was partially hidden behind the larger man in front of him.

The two came over to the table, and the larger man pulled the chair back for the other. Burnside felt a knot in his stomach as he recognized the other man, and hoped the recognition wasn't mutual. The other man was Klaus Vaughan.

"Mr. Vaughan," Serbinski said, "may I present John Fisher of Otani Biochemicals. John, this is my boss, Mr. Vaughan."

"Pleased to meet you, sir," Burnside said, extending his hand.

"Yes," said Vaughan, gripping Burnsides hand. "I don't think we have met face to face. But John, wasn't your last name *Smith* back on Tanith?"

Burnside felt his gut clench. "I'm sorry?" he said, hoping he could bluff it out.

"My mistake," the Velkaryan said. His eyes bored into Burnside's, and his grip, still holding Burnside's hand in an extended shake, squeezed. "For a moment I thought you looked like somebody else. Do you have a twin, or a clone? I'm sure he looks just like you."

"Hah, poor fellow," Burnside said, making a joke of it as he squeezed back, then released his grip. "Not someone who owed you money, I hope?"

"Not exactly," Vaughan said, seating himself. "But I do hope *you* will soon enough, if we can do business. Or rather, your employer."

Serbinski glanced nervously at his boss as he and Burnside sat down. The big man, who had not been introduced, remained standing just behind and to the side of Vaughan's seat. "We're still talking about what we can do for Otani," Serbinski said, "we're not ready to discuss financing yet."

"Relax, Tony, I'm just playing along with the joke. Besides, we all know what this is about. I'm sure Mr. Smith, I'm sorry, Mr. Fisher here doesn't expect us to just give him something for nothing."

"No, of course not," Burnside said, "and please, call me John. It might help prevent confusion."

"We certainly wouldn't want any confusion," Vaughan said. "So perhaps I should just call you Jordan. Burnside, isn't it?"

Shit. Burnside tensed his legs beneath him, ready to launch himself from the chair. One hand was already on the edge of the table, ready to push it away or flip it over. He wondered how far he'd get if he had to run for it. "Who?"

"You can drop the act," Vaughan said, in a tone that left no doubt the verbal sparring was over. "You were followed last night. Why would a purchasing exec have an interest in the apartment of a known UDT undercover agent, I wonder?"

"Was it? I was just—"

"I said drop it! Mignon, take him."

As the big man started to step around the table, Burnside jumped up, twisting the table and pushing it into Mignon's path. Mignon stumbled once, then pushed it aside. Burnside had already turned and was sprinting for the exit.

And then the waiter stepped in front of him, pistol in hand. Burnside kept going, advancing into the waiter and past the extended gun hand, grabbing the wrist as he did. His momentum carried the waiter backward, staggering, but it had slowed Burnside down. A heavy arm came up under his, breaking his grip on the waiter's wrist, while another arm came around his neck. Mignon had him.

He tried turning to put his captor between himself and the waiter's gun, but the man holding him was too heavy and skilled to allow that.

"Enough!" Vaughan shouted. "If he keeps struggling, shoot him in the leg or something. Don't kill him yet."

The *yet* was something, anyway, and it would be easier to try another escape with both legs functioning. Burnside relaxed, still with Mignon's arm around his throat. He slowly raised his hands. "Okay," he gasped.

"You're becoming something of an annoyance to me, Mister Burnside," Vaughan said icily. First you interfere with my negotiations to buy an artifact on Tanith, and now you show up here. Just what are you doing on Verdigris?"

Burnside remained silent. Vaughan turned to the waiter, who still held his pistol. "Shoot his foot."

"Wait," Burnside said. If he was going to escape, somehow, it would be easier with both feet working. "I was following you, actually. You left in such a hurry I wondered what you were up to. You didn't even come back when you discovered you had a phony artifact. Please tell me you looked in the crate before you got all the way here."

Vaughan's jaw clenched. Burnside wondered if he would tell his men to shoot him anyway. Then Vaughan said, "And how do you know what was in the crate?"

"Because I got the real one. I laughed myself silly when I heard they'd been switched."

Vaughan's eyes narrowed, his jaw clenching again. "And where is it now?"

Burnside could guess, but he didn't actually know. "I have no idea. I don't know anything about alien artifacts, so I passed it off to an archeologist."

"Carson!" Vaughan said it like it was a curse.

"*Gesundheit*," Burnside said.

Vaughan's left hand lashed out, slapped Burnside hard across the face, rattling teeth.

"Enough of this," Vaughan said, standing to leave. "I have better things to occupy my time. Mignon, Richards, take him out and get rid of him. Make sure he can't bother us again."

Burnside felt an impact on the back of his head, and things went dark.

∞ ∞ ∞

New Toronto

The two Velkaryan thugs dragged Burnside down to a car parked by a rear entrance to the factory. It rode high, on large wheels, like a vehicle often driven on rough roads, yet not a truck. Burnside had recovered consciousness, but he was still groggy, and his head hurt. He pretended to still be out, waiting for an opportunity. Unfortunately, Mignon had a gun trained on him, perhaps wary of just such a move.

He assumed that wherever they were planning to take him, he wouldn't be coming back, but even if he could wrestle free of the two, there wasn't anywhere near enough to get to cover before Mignon shot him. He clung to the hope that a better opportunity would present itself. In the worst case, he intended to take at least one of the thugs with him.

"Why don't we just shoot him now?" the waiter, Richards, asked as they bundled Burnside into the vehicle.

"Are you going to clean the blood off the seats?" Mignon asked in return. "We'll take him to the jungle. The scavengers will take care of the body."

With Burnside lying across the back seat, Richards took the driver's seat while Mignon rode shotgun, turning to keep his pistol pointed at Burnside.

The car pulled out and headed up the road. As it hit a bump, the jostle shook Burnside's head and he let out an involuntary groan. There was no point trying to pretend he was unconscious, so he raised his head to look around.

"Just relax, you," Mignon said, gesturing slightly with his gun. "I shot you once, I'll do it again, and this time it won't be a tracking dart."

"A tra . . ." Burnside said, but he remembered. It had been back on Tanith, just before his first rendezvous with Jackie Roberts. He'd gotten rid of the dart, but had to have the *Sophie*'s traumapod stitch him up. "So that was you, was it?" Burnside added it to the list of things owed for. Not that would change any of Burnside's plans, assuming he came up with any.

Mignon just smiled, if that's what that half snarl was.

"Could you at least take your finger off the trigger? I'd hate for your gun to go off if we hit another bump."

"Don't worry, I've got a steady hand," Mignon said, "and fast reflexes." But he did move his finger off the trigger, resting it against the trigger guard.

Burnside figured that might gain him a tenth of a second. He'd take whatever he could get. If they were taking him to the jungle, he had a few minutes. Lying on the seat like this limited his range of motion. The seat back would interfere with him trying to kick Mignon, and the thug was watching his arms, with the gun pointed roughly at his chest. Richards, the waiter, was focused on driving, if Burnside could deal with Mignon's gun, he'd have a few moments before Waiter could draw his. He wondered what level of autonomy the vehicle had. Any vehicle had some, although Waiter obviously hadn't engaged it. Maybe "the jungle" wasn't a specific enough destination for the car to understand.

By now they'd left the built-up area of New Toronto. The road was getting rougher, they were probably in surrounding farmland. The trees wouldn't be much further. Mignon was still turned toward the back, watching him. *What the hell*, Burnside thought, *we're in a car, it's worth a try.*

"Look out!" he yelled, looking out the front window in horror.

Reflexively, Mignon turned to see, and Burnside grabbed for his gun hand, pushing it forward as he twisted to get out of the line of fire.

BANG!

Chapter 7: Fayettesville

Fayettesville, Verdigris, five days later

Fayettesville was a small town on the Lawrence River, about a third of the way between New Toronto and Louisbourg. It had taken Jordan Burnside three days of slogging through jungle, and another two on the water, to arrive here. He had made much better time on his makeshift raft, thanks to the current, and vowed to arrange for some kind of boat the next time he had to make an overland trek. Not that he'd had any advance warning before this one.

The town had a landing field. Burnside doubted the place had off-planet traffic very often, but maybe he could catch a flight to somewhere that did.

"What's the usual outbound schedule?" Burnside asked the dispatch clerk at the field's small office. "Heading to Sawyer's World."

"From here? Once in a blue moon," the man said, chuckling. Verdigris' moon was, in fact, bluish, but rarely visible as other than a glow through the skyweed. "But let me check the Louisbourg schedule. Would that be a message, package or passenger?"

"A small package." Burnside needed to get the information he'd collected to Ducayne, and a message wouldn't cover it all.

The dispatcher consulted his terminal. "Next scheduled departure is Thursday, and there's an air flight to Louisbourg tomorrow. You might get lucky; you never know when a freelance courier will be coming or going."

Thursday was three days hence. Add another fifteen days in warp, and a couple of days for in-system maneuvers. His package would get to Ducayne in three weeks.

"Of course," the agent added while looking at his screen, "if you're only sending email, the *Alacran* hasn't left the system yet. You've got a couple of hours before it goes to warp."

"That will work. I still want to send the package, but I can let them know it's on the way. Give me a few minutes."

"*C'est sûr*," the agent said agreeably.

∞ ∞ ∞

Burnside stepped back to a corner of the dispatch office and withdrew his omni. It was a simple, generic omniphone that he'd bought when he arrived in Fayetteville—fortunately the two thugs had had cash on them. He didn't trust the omniphones he had taken from them. But that meant it didn't have the sophisticated crypto package installed on his personal omniphone, just simple commercial cipher apps. The Velkaryans could probably crack those, but then so could Ducayne's office. Since he couldn't send them the key, that was to his advantage. Besides, he wasn't going to be telling Ducayne anything the Velkaryan's didn't already know, even if they did intercept the message.

He composed a simple message, out of habit substituting keywords and names.

"Arrived Greenland. Visited Fort York. Confirmed building aeroplanes and engines. Package to follow. Will continue research. Request lift home as arranged. Notify me when arrive."

He encoded the message and sent it, then went back to the clerk.

"Okay, I still want this package to go out," he said, handing it over. "And there'll be a final data upload before the *Alacran* goes to warp?"

"Yes, that's standard procedure." The clerk took the package and set it on the pad of a boxy apparatus that weighed it and scanned its dimensions. "Any biologicals, flammables, explosives, or radioactive materials in there?" he asked.

"No," Burnside said. "Mostly just papers."

"What about archeological artifacts?"

"None of those, either." Burnside was mildly amused, thinking back on what Tevnar had given Carson and Roberts to take back to Alpha Centauri. He also suspected that his package had been sniffed, x-rayed, checked for radiation, and scanned with terahertz waves while it was being weighed and measured.

"Okay." The clerk tapped away at a keyboard, then looked back at Burnside and told him what it would cost.

Burnside shrugged, tapped an account number into his omni, and authorized the charge. It would be billed via a dummy account back to the UDT office in Verdigris City.

That taken care of, Burnside left the dispatch office to consider his next step.

He needed to make his way back to New Toronto, to "continue research" as he had put it. It would be dangerous, Vaughan would have men looking for him, but the trip back ought to be easier than how he'd gotten here.

∞ ∞ ∞

Five days earlier, a car outside New Toronto
From the back seat, Burnside had yelled and reacted as though the car were about to crash. Reflexively, Mignon had turned to look, and Burnside grabbed the gun hand as he twisted away from the muzzle.

BANG!
The noise of the gunshot had been deafening in the car. Burnside had smashed his free hand hard into the side of Mignon's face. He doubled his grip on Mignon's gun hand and smashed it against the side of the driver's seat.

That's when he saw the blood flowing from Richards' right arm, as he clutched at it with his left. Mignon's stray shot must have hit him.

Mignon was struggling to get either arm free. Burnside had hold of his right, the gun hand. His left was hampered because he'd been twisted around in the seat, but the man was strong.

Burnside pulled the gun arm back, keeping the muzzle pointed away as Mignon fired again. The noise and flash were blinding, but Burnside hung on. He levered his feet against the seat-back in front and pushed, pulling Mignon's arm back further. Then he leaned forward and sank his teeth into Mignon's wrist, hard. Mignon yelled and relaxed his grip enough for Burnside to pull the gun free.

He was bringing it to bear on Mignon as the car veered off the road and slammed into a ditch. The gun went off again. Mignon's head was covered in blood, but Burnside wasn't sure if from the bullet or from the impact with the windshield. Either way, Mignon was no longer moving.

Burnside turned to check on the driver, who wasn't moving either. The steering-wheel airbag had deployed, and there was blood on it. Leaning forward to look closer, Burnside saw that the waiter had coughed up a lot of blood. He moved the wounded arm. The bullet had gone right through and into the man's chest. He was gone.

"Well," Burnside muttered, "so much for the autopilot."

He climbed out of the vehicle, both relieved to still be alive and a little disappointed that neither of the thugs had survived to be questioned. If Mignon had been on Tanith, he might have known quite a bit about Vaughan's operation.

Looking around where they'd crashed, it was clear that they were close to the jungle proper. The land here had been cleared, but was not yet an established farm. Thick trees loomed a kilometer further up the road. He wondered if the car was drivable, assuming he could get it out of the ditch, so he scrambled around it to check it over.

No such luck. With a front wheel bent out of alignment, and the two rear wheels in the air with the vehicle high-centered over the edge of the ditch, it wasn't going anywhere by itself. He checked the bodies, relieving them of weapons, IDs, cash, and omniphones. That could all come in handy, although the omnis could likely be tracked. He'd ditch those shortly.

Satisfied that he'd salvaged everything worth carrying from the wreck, he set off up the road toward the forest.

∞ ∞ ∞

There was no way for him to get back to Verdigris City, that was on another continent, but he needed to get a message out to Ducayne, either via Prentiss or directly. Louisbourg was twelve hundred kilometers away, but downstream at the mouth of the New Lawrence River. He would need to make his way back to Lake Quebec, or a river that led to it, and find a boat that he could either stow away on or steal. There were a few scattered small towns along the shore; it should be possible.

But he would have to do all that while avoiding any patrols looking for him. Vaughan would certainly have men looking for him, once Mignon and the other failed to return, and he might also invoke the local police. The latter would depend on whether Vaughan could come up with a convincing story, or if the cops were already in the Velkaryan's pocket.

Either way, Burnside had some more hacking through the jungle ahead of him. Well, not hacking, he had no machete. This was not going to be fun.

Chapter 8: Burnside's Encounter

Verdigris, Northeast of New Toronto, three days earlier

Burnside had been making his way northeast for a full day now. The going was slow; the jungle here was thick. At least he had an omni to navigate with.

He had, he hoped, disabled the transmitter function of Mignon's omniphone. He had kept it both for its navigation function, and for the fact it had a translation app for several of the local snake-eye dialects. It was also a simpler model, easier to modify than the waiter's had been. He had smashed that one, after using it to confirm—as best he could—that Mignon's was no longer able to transmit. Still, he kept it switched off except when checking his location.

Following the track the omni showed him was a different matter. It had maps of the planet, but the most detail was around the towns and settlements; the maps didn't show game trails or much of any other detail in the forested areas. He'd come across several streams that would have been navigable if he'd had some kind of boat, but he didn't. He didn't even have a machete, so he was constantly having to detour around thick patches of vegetation. He was barely making twenty-five kilometers a day.

He was also being followed. He wasn't sure by who or how many, but for the past several hours there'd been signs of someone, or several someones, tracking him. Sometimes they were behind, sometimes paralleling his course. Not often, but at intervals there would be sounds of rustling in the bush, or an occasional startled animal cry. Whoever it was—he hoped it was natives rather than some large predator—was very good at not letting themselves be seen.

By now, Burnside had become accustomed to the usual appearance of this jungle, so it became easier for him to spot the unusual. Broken branches, an absence of certain small-animal signs that had been prevalent until some kilometers back, scuff marks in the groundcover that suggested footprints. Burnside was sure he was getting closer to a native village. He just wondered what sort of reception he'd get, if any.

∞ ∞ ∞

He found out soon enough. As he rounded a curve on the narrow trail he was following, the trail opened up into a clearing. As he stepped into it, he heard a sudden rustling in the brush around the periphery, and a half-dozen vaguely humanoid creatures, each about a meter-and-a-half tall, stepped out. Their jaws seemed oversized for their otherwise more-or-less human-like skulls, although their noses were flat, more like an ape's, with thin vertical nostrils. Their eyes were large and wide-set. In the brighter light of the clearing, their pupils had contracted to vertical ellipses, like the snakes they were nicknamed for, or like a cat's, except there were no felines on this planet. Their skin seemed gray, but it was daubed in shades of green like so many Special Forces members wearing jungle camo. These natives were hardly wearing anything. They wore breech clouts, some wore beaded armbands or necklaces, and Burnside could see three with arrow-filled quivers slung over their shoulders. These carried short bows, with arrows at the knock and drawn. The others had spears. All were pointed at him.

Burnside slowly raised his hands, palms open and facing forward, to level with his shoulders, half outstretched. He became acutely aware of the small game animal hanging from his belt. He had killed it earlier, intending to make a meal of it. He wondered how the natives felt about poachers. "Hello," he said calmly, "do any of you understand me?"

The only response was that a few of the Verdigrans looked at each other before looking back at him. He tried something else. *"Bonjour. Est-ce que tu me comprends?"*

This drew more puzzled looks, if he was interpreting their expression correctly, from the armed group surrounding him. There was one more thing to try. He slowly moved his left hand—with the omni wrapped around the wrist—closer to his mouth. "Omni," he addressed it, "translator on; Verdigran dialect near New Toronto. 'Hello. I mean no harm. I am a traveller.'"

There was a brief pause, and the omni emitted a string of syllables that Burnside barely caught. The natives surrounding him, however, reacted, gesturing with their weapons and several talking at once.

His omni announced *"Unable to parse input. Too many speakers."*

Burnside sighed. *That was helpful*, he thought sarcastically.

One of the locals—Burnside noted that he was taller and wore more beads—said something in a raised voice. The others stopped talking, and his omni helpfully translated: *"Be quiet!"*.

The leader pointed to one of the others and said something his omni described as *"Untranslatable, possibly a proper noun."*

The other Verdigran took a step back and walked around behind the others to the leader. It would have been quicker for him to walk across the clearing, but that would have put him in the line of fire from the rest of his group, Burnside noted. The leader seemed to whisper something to the other snake-eye.

The other then turned to Burnside and said, "I shpeak. Who you?"

Well, so one of them spoke some English. Burnside slowly patted his chest and said, "My name is Burnside. I would like to talk."

The other turned to the leader and held a brief whispered conversation, then turned back to Burnside. "You shpeak, Burnshide. Why here?" He sounded as if he was speaking through a mouthful of marbles.

Burnside remembered something he had heard about many species of Verdigran mammals, something unique about their teeth. What was the word? Multituberculates, that was it. An ancient mammalian line that had survived the end-Cretaceous extinctions only to die out on Earth some thirty million years ago. They had particularly large and specialized teeth toward the rear of their mouths. *I guess that explains the speech.* He gestured to the ground. "May I sit?" He could stand there all day if he had to, but, since he was taller than all of them, he hoped this would help put them at ease. Maybe they'd lower their weapons.

The other gestured at him, a downward motion. Burnside lowered himself to sit cross-legged on the ground. "Shpeak."

It took a while, but between his omni and the Verdigran speaker, and Burnside picking up a few words of the dialect himself, he managed to get across the idea that he had heard stories that the humans in the big village to the north were doing bad things, and he wanted to find out the truth.

This snake-eye tribe, as it turned out, stayed well clear of human towns and villages. They had heard stories from other tribes, but they didn't necessarily believe them all. It wasn't unknown for other tribes to make up warning tales to keep each other out of their respective hunting and grazing areas, but there had been traders, and the traders' stories were more likely to be believed. If true, the stories were grim.

Snake-eyes had been rounded up in jungle areas near New Toronto and put to work clearing the forest to make way for agriculture, and even been put to work on the fields. Burnside at first found this hard to believe, surely machines and automation would be more efficient at this than, well, slavery. Digging through the database on his omni, apparently slavery was not unknown to Verdigran tribes, some of whom occasionally engaged in raids on other tribes, so there might be some inter-tribal thing going on there. Perhaps it was easier to train a snake-eye from one of the more hostile tribes to drive slaves than to drive a bulldozer. Burnside's disgust with the Velkaryans grew.

"This is very bad," he said to the group's leader by way of the translator. "These men are breaking many of our laws. I would see them punished."

The leader barked a laugh. "How? You are one, they are many."

"I must report it to my people. We are many-many. But I must see more for myself. My people will want me to see with my eyes, not rely on stories told by traders."

"This is wise."

"Also, there may be things I can do." Burnside wasn't sure he could, or even should, explain the concept of sabotage. Any such actions would have to be targeted; not everyone living in or around New Toronto was a Velkaryan, and many of them would be ignorant of what was going on. At least, Burnside hoped that was the case, but he'd seen what Velkaryan disinformation against the timoan settlers could do on Tanith.

The day drew to a close, and Burnside contributed some of his rations, and the game animal he had caught earlier, to the communal meal. He wasn't exactly welcomed, but he was at least tolerated. As best he could gather, this village had decided to treat him as a trader. Not part of the group, but someone who could be tolerated briefly for their potential benefits.

That night, Burnside slept on the ground near the fire pit, reasonably convinced that if they had meant him harm, they would have inflicted it already. When he awoke just after dawn, the Verdigrans had vanished, and most signs of the village with them.

Ghosts, indeed.

∞ ∞ ∞

As he ate breakfast around the remains of the campfire the Verdigrans had left for him, Burnside realized he was still being watched.

"Hello?" he called out. "Would you care to join me?"

A rustling from the nearby trees, and then two Verdigrans trotted out to sit by him. "Burnshide, we would shpeak."

It was his translator, Tuktoyahu, of the day before, and another male, whose name Burnside hadn't learned.

"Then speak, please."

"Last night, you shpoke of things you could do, against the bad men."

"I did, yes. What of it?"

"Are these things we could do? Can you teach us?"

Well now, Burnside thought, that puts things in a different light. If they're asking. . . .

"I can show some things. But they can be dangerous. You could be hurt or killed. Or the bad men could take retribution against your tribe."

"Re-tri-bu-sshun?"

"Punishment."

The two Verdigrans looked at each other and made the sounds Burnside recognized as a laugh.

"What is funny?"

"Everything is dangerous. Animals in the forest, shnakes in the tree, bad men in the big village. Bad men already punish other tribes. We have tell you thish before."

Burnside nodded. "This is true. You did."

"Then teach us. We would know. Maybe not do, but know."

He couldn't fault their logic. "All right."

∞ ∞ ∞

The natives invited Burnside to travel with them, and over the next two days he learned at least as much from them as they from him.

His general training and experience on other planets had already made him skilled in walking stealthily through a forest, but the snake-eyes made him seem like a blundering oaf. They glided through the vegetation almost like a fish through water, rarely leaving a broken branch or leaf behind. They also pointed out to him many subtleties of the native vegetation, and how to spot various insects and animals in the bush.

In turn, he hoped to further ingratiate himself by teaching them some tricks to improve their hunting or trapping skills, but the fact was that they were far better at it than he could ever hope to be. For every improvement he tried to show them, they were already aware of it or something similar, and could demonstrate why it wasn't really better. He had more success when he explained how the commerce of the humans was an expansion of the traders they were already familiar with.

They were amused by his attempts to explain agriculture. It turned out that they were quite familiar with the concept of planting crops, tending them, and later harvesting them. They just thought it was a waste of time and energy. With the jungle providing plentiful resources for their hunting and gathering lifestyle, why tie themselves to one spot and work every day keeping weeds and pests out of the fields? Burnside had to admit that they had a point. He had read once that humans in a hunter-gatherer society had more free time than most of those in an agricultural one, resources permitting. He wondered how well that difference might explain why this particular subspecies of intelligent Verdigran had survived while the supposedly more advanced stone structure builders elsewhere on the planet had died out. Who was really more intelligent?

He also taught them, at least the few who were interested, about the various technological devices he carried with him. Some of the natives, especially Tuktoyahu, his translator, already had some familiarity through previous dealings either directly with humans or with other Verdigrans who had had such dealings. They grasped the concept of firearms quickly. Projectile weapons are a simple concept, and the Verdigris jungle was home to an insect very like Earth's bombardier beetle, so they got the concept of explosive propulsion too. What they thought ludicrous, though, was the idea of using a weapon with disposable ammunition.

"You can't use bullet again? I can use arrow again, or fix if broken, or make new. How you make new bullet?"

"Well, there is a special place where bullets are made—"

"A magic place? Puts the beetle magic in the bullet?"

"No, not magic. Just a place where different traders bring things. The metal for the bullet. The powders and juices that make the fire. Other things. Then skilled men use special tools to assemble these into bullets, then trade bullets for more things."

Tuktoyahu made a gesture that signified negation or disbelief. "Lot of work and trouble. Arrows more simple."

"Does everyone in your tribe know how to make arrows?"

"Yes, but not small children."

So much for that approach, thought Burnside, but he pressed on. "Are all arrows the same?"

"No. Some fly straighter, or farther. I make pretty good arrows. Mikatoaha makes best arrows."

"Is Mik—" Burnside stumbled over the name "—Mikatoaha your best hunter?"

Tuktoyahu laughed. "No. He makes good arrows, but can't shoot them."

"So could your best hunter trade food to Mikatoaha for best arrows?"

"Why? All share food. All share arrows."

"What if someone from another tribe made even better arrows?"

That got Tuktoyahu thinking. The tribes had trade between each other, so the concept wasn't foreign, but he was clearly trying to apply the concept back to the discussion of bullets.

"We could trade. But would have to be very special arrows."

"And if those special arrows broke or got lost? You couldn't make more special arrows."

"Would have to trade again, if arrows so good. Are bullets like very special arrows?"

"Very, very special."

"Huh. And gun is like special bow for special arrows?"

"Exactly."

"Still seems like lot of trouble. Maybe gun can shoot straighter and farther than bow, but in forest, can't see any farther past trees anyway."

Burnside looked around. The tribe had been temporarily camped in a small clearing, and sightlines through the vegetation beyond that weren't even five meters, at best. The snake-eye had a point.

∞ ∞ ∞

"I need to get to a town, so I can send a message," Burnside tried to explain to Tuktoyahu.

"We were in village. What messhage?"

"No, I mean a human village, big. Special message to make report to my people, like I told you before."

According to the map on his omni, the town of Fayetteville was probably the closest, but it was still many days hike through the jungle.

"No human village near. We stay clear. Powpakki tribe closer."

"Powpakki tribe? Can they guide me?"

"Maybe, if you find them. Better to go to human village by boat."

"I don't have a boat."

"Make one."

Sure, I'll just set my fabber and print one right out, Burnside thought. "I don't have tools. I have never made a boat before. Have you?"

Tuktoyahu made a sound that Burnside assumed was a snort of derision. "Many times. Good way to travel."

"Could you teach me? How long would it take?"

It turned out there were two kinds of boats the natives used, both canoes. One was made from thin sheets of bark wrapped over a frame, like a birchbark canoe. That was light and more suitable to smaller rivers, but there were no suitable "birch" trees nearby. The simpler boat was a dugout, made by hollowing out a large split log, and usually equipped with an outrigger if they were venturing out on Lake Quebec.

The lake itself was less than an hour's hike away, they had been paralleling the shore since the day before. When Burnside understood what Tuktoyahu was suggesting, he managed to get across the idea of making the outrigger bigger, and not spending the time to hollow out a large log. Instead, with Tuktoyahu's help, he lashed several branches across two logs, making a crude catamaran. The current and prevailing winds were in his favor, although he lacked anything to rig a sail with. That was probably just as well; anything Burnside knew about sailing he'd learned from watching entertainment vids, hardly a reliable source.

"Burnshide, you shay you never make boat before," Tuktoyahu said to him after he had taken the catamaran out briefly. "It look like fine boat."

"Beginner's luck," Burnside said, ignoring Tuktoyahu's puzzlement at the expression. "I just hope it holds long enough to get me to town."

The Verdigran had inspected the craft, tugging on the lashings and pounding on the logs. "It ish good," he pronounced. "Fare well, Burnshide."

∞ ∞ ∞

Sure enough, the catamaran had held up, and he had guided it ashore in Fayetteville the second day after that. After using the cash he'd taken off the bodies of Vaughan's two goons to buy a replacement omniphone, he had managed to contact Prentiss to arrange for access to more funds.

"What are your plans?" Prentiss had asked.

"I have information I want to get to get directly to my boss, so I'll get that out on the next ship. Then I'm going to head back to New Toronto, via more modern transport. I want to keep an eye on what the Velkaryans are up to there, and I owe Vaughan."

"Do you need me to set up another alias?"

"No, I'm going off-grid for this. But I will send you reports when I can."

"Thank you. Did you have a chance to—"

"Check on your man? Yes. Bad news I'm afraid. There were signs that his apartment had been searched, and not by the police. It had also been cleaned up, but they missed some bloodstains. I don't think your man is coming back."

"I was afraid of that. Well, take care of yourself. And give them one from me, too."

"Oh," Burnside said grimly, "I'll give them several."

PART II
CARSON AND ROBERTS

Chapter 9: Leaving Centauri

UDT Headquarters, Sawyer City

"So, when do we leave?" Rico asked Ducayne. Rico, Jackie Roberts, and Avril Boutelle were all in Ducayne's office, being briefed on their planned mission to Verdigris.

"I had hoped tomorrow," Ducayne said, "but your arm is in a sling." Rico had been shot when Velkaryans tried to take over Carson's dig site at Pete's Peak.

"I told you, it's fine. The traumapod fixed the cracked bone and sewed me up. I can leave tomorrow."

"The *Sophie* has a traumapod," Jackie said. "It's two weeks to the Delta Pavonis system. He can sleep in the traumapod; it will accelerate the healing. He'll have the sling off in a few days." She looked over at Rico. "That is, if he's willing to be in a traumapod again with me around."

He grinned back at her. "The *Sophie*'s traumapod is almost a second home." He had spent most of the trip back from Chara, several weeks, in it a while back.

Ducayne looked from one to the other. "All right, that will work."

"That still doesn't answer the question of the *Sophie* landing at New Toronto," Jackie said. "They wouldn't let me last time. The Velkaryans in charge there must know the ship."

Ducayne nodded. "That's true, and if Velkaryan presence there has expanded, they may not let you land anywhere. If there's a flag in their Space Traffic Control database, they'll be watching you from the moment your transponder squawks when you enter the system."

"That shouldn't matter if I want to land at Verdigris City or Louisbourg. I'm just a charter pilot and courier." Jackie looked at Rico and Avril, then back to Ducayne. "It might complicate whatever you want to do, though."

"It might." He looked at Rico and smiled slightly. "You said you knew how to handle that. How?"

"Another test? Let me think a moment." Rico's omni was on his wrist. He tapped and swiped it as if looking for something. He nodded to himself, then looked up at Roberts. "You and Ducayne had some work done on the *Sophie*, right?"

Ducayne's smile widened. Apparently, Rico had figured out whatever Ducayne had wanted him to.

Jackie's eyes narrowed. "Yes. Repaired a warp module, installed a range extender and some radio gear. Why?"

"How do you feel about changing the name of your ship for a while?"

"That won't help. The real identification is an encrypted string hard-coded into the ship's systems. You can't change that." She saw Rico's and Ducayne's smug we-know-something-you-don't expressions, and her eyes widened. "Wait, *can* you? I thought that was impossible."

Rico grinned. "Sure it is. Unless the ship has certain additional hardware modules installed."

Of course, Jackie thought. She should have known. "Can it be changed back afterward?"

"It wouldn't be very useful otherwise," Ducayne said. "Well, unless you were in the business of stealing ships, which we're not. And those who are usually just strip them down and rebuild them, or head off into the unknown where nobody cares."

Avril Boutelle looked surprised at this. "Wait, you mean space pirates actually exist?"

The others looked at her as though she were a naïve schoolchild.

"They don't call themselves that," said Ducayne, "and probably don't think of themselves that way, but yes, they exist."

"Oh," Boutelle said, at a loss for other words.

"As long as whatever we do doesn't jeopardize my courier license," Jackie said. "Aside from helping me make a living when I'm not running errands for Ducayne, it's a damned good cover when I am."

"She has a point," Boutelle said.

"She does," agreed Ducayne.

"Also, you can't change the identity before we leave," Jackie continued. "Traffic Control will have no record of the new ship landing. Even if you hack their records, somebody might wonder why they'd never heard of that ship before."

"We'll have to take that into account." Ducayne agreed. "We can fake a departure record after the fact, it's unlikely anyone would go back and check." He rubbed his chin, thinking. "Jackie, what happens when you've got a charter to some uninhabited star system? Suppose someone wanted to check out the asteroids in a red dwarf system or something. Does that ever happen?"

Jackie nodded. "Not often, but it does. I still let the courier office know where I'm headed and file a flight plan, but the odds are near zero that they'll have something to deliver there, and there won't be anyone at that end to close the flight plan anyway. I just close it at the next inhabited system I reach."

"Good. Figure out something near Delta Pavonis where nobody is doing research and file for that. Once you're out-system, Rico knows how to change your ship's ident."

"What about me?" Avril asked.

"You're Jackie's cover. A xenoanthropologist visiting Verdigris is nothing unusual, even if, *especially* if, you've been there before. It'll just be a routine university expedition, except that the ship won't be courier licensed so there's less of a data trail to worry about."

"Okay, that works."

"Right, then. Meet back here tomorrow for a final briefing before you depart. Meanwhile, get yourselves ready. Oh, and Roberts, let me know whatever new temporary name you decide for your ship, so I can make sure the records match."

"Got it."

∞ ∞ ∞

Sawyer City

Hannibal Carson sat at the desk in his apartment, going over the reports that Ducayne had given him. The analysis Avril Boutelle had done was surprisingly thorough. It showed potential pyramid locations throughout T-Space, even unto Pete's Peak here on Sawyers World that he had only confirmed was a pyramid a short time ago.

Officially, that pyramid was still the remnant of a volcano. It didn't help that it had been filled with dried mud that would take a major excavation to clear. Carson would much rather be working on that, but that was on hold until the Sawyers World government figured out just how, or whether, to release the news. At least that mud fill had frustrated the attempt the Velkaryan, Reid, had made to loot the pyramid before Carson and reinforcements could turn the tables.

The other report on his desk was Homeland Security's analysis of Velkaryan activity, not just on Sawyers World but throughout the planets of T-Space. There was nothing, however, in the document making any actual reference to Velkaryans. That data was masquerading as obscure statistics on economic data, just on the off chance a copy of the document fell into the wrong hands. Carson didn't think it likely, but his apartment had been broken into once before, by thugs working for an illicit artifacts dealer.

His omni chimed, and he looked at in annoyance. Then he saw the caller ID and smiled. He answered. "Jackie, I'm glad you called. If you'll settle for less than Rick's Café, we can do dinner again."

"Are you sure dinner is what you're after?" Jackie said, amusement in her voice. "Although I certainly have no complaints about last night. That was lovely."

"Then—" he began, but she cut him off.

"I'm sorry, Hannibal, but I can't. Ducayne wants me to head out by tomorrow night, so I need to preflight and provision my ship."

"Oh. Well, you did warn me. How long are you gone for?"

"At least five weeks. Possibly more, depending on how much time we spend on-planet or in-system, but I hope not much more."

"Five weeks? But—" He shut up when he noticed the hint of a whine in his own voice.

"Come on, Carson. You've been without my company longer than that. You'll survive. I thought you said you had classes to teach and papers to grade?"

"I do. That doesn't mean I have to enjoy it. I'd rather be coming along."

"Aren't you always complaining that space travel is boring?"

"Well, it *was*, but. . . ." But last night in the *Sophie,* Jackie had reminded him of something they could do to pass the time, and it had been anything but boring.

"Look, Carson, last night was fun, and I'm not averse to doing it again, but—notwithstanding what we did on the *Arabella*, or maybe because of it—I have a policy about passengers. . . ."

"Oh. Sure, I understand." It was logical, but that didn't mean he was happy about it.

As if sensing his disappointment, she added, "Although, it is the captain's prerogative to change policies. You'll just have to wait until our next expedition together to find out."

He glanced over at the documents he'd been reviewing. "About that, we might have some extended trips coming up."

"Oh?"

"It will keep until you get back," he said. Ducayne had proposed two missions to him, one to return to Zeta Reticuli and recontact the Kesh, the other to visit all the known worlds with both pyramids and Velkaryan activity. "I'm still working out the details, and as you said, I have classes to teach in the meantime."

"All right, be mysterious. I guess I deserved that. Now I do need to get the *Sophie* prepped. Try to stay out of trouble, Carson."

"Me? Of course, Jackie. Fly safe."

"Always," she said, and clicked off.

Carson gazed at the omni for a while, thinking about the previous night, and of the times Jackie had flown anything but safe. Although, he smiled to himself, those times he knew of were because he had not stayed out of trouble.

Chapter 10: Velkaryans

Sawyer City, Church of Divine Stellar Providence

Ernest Deitrich, head of the local Velkaryan contingent, entered the medical bay tucked away in the church headquarters offices. His agent, Reid, had been brought in the week before, in a traumapod. He was still in it. "What's his status?" Deitrich demanded of the medical technician.

"I've seen worse," the tech said, "but that's not saying much. The separation at the shoulder could have been cleaner, there were still bone fragments from the humerus, as well as a few metal shards, probably bullet fragments. But the socket's clean, it shouldn't be too hard to fit a replacement."

"A robotic arm? What about regrowing a new one?"

"That will take longer, and requires a full autodoc, not just a traumapod. That would actually be easier if there'd been anything left of the upper arm, but it's doable. He's well enough along now that we could transfer him. It will take about two months to regrow, maybe less if we can use a cellular fabricator to rebuild the basic matrix for the cells to grow on. If we—"

"Fine," Deitrich cut him off. "I don't need all the details. A biological arm can wait. When can he be up and around?"

"Tomorrow, if necessary. The arm and blood loss were the main issues. We don't have a spare arm, though."

The story, as Deitrich had heard it, was that Reid had escaped from the Space Guard team that intervened at the pyramid dig site, after having been shot in the shoulder. On his way back to the transport hidden in the jungle, he'd been attacked by a Finley's leopard, probably attracted by the smell of blood. What saved Reid, ironically, was that very gunshot wound. The leopard had gone for the injured arm first, and torn it off as Reid struggled. While the animal was distracted, Reid managed to get away, the pseudo-cat settling for the arm.

He'd stumbled up to the transport, and the waiting pilot had managed to get him into the vehicle's traumapod. That Reid hadn't lost more blood with a dismembered arm was, again, related to the gunshot wound. Someone had applied a bandage to the original wound; it had served to slow the bleeding.

Reid had been barely coherent, and Deitrich wanted him awake to get the full story. All he knew was that the rest of Reid's team had been taken by the Space Guard, who had shown up in force as Reid was about to get the pyramid open. That information had trickled out from inside informants, but the whole thing was being kept very quiet. There was no news about the incident on the net, and no mention of the pyramid. As far as the Sawyers World public was concerned, the lone peak in the middle of a wildlife preserve was still just an old volcanic remnant.

"Very well," Deitrich told the med-tech. "Give him another day while you locate a suitable arm. Then I need to debrief him."

"A day? It might take me more than that to—"

"We could always give him yours."

The med-tech paled. A transplant wouldn't be that easy, but that wasn't Deitrich's point. "A day. Yes, sir."

Chapter II: Departure

Sawyer City

Jackie Roberts' ship, *Sophie*, accelerated down the spaceport runway, the lights beside it flashing by against the dark night, and Jackie eased in the lift fans to shorten the take-off. At this time of night, there were noise restrictions in the vicinity of the port, and the fans were quieter than thrusters. They also improved *Sophie's* climb. It most places this wouldn't matter. The ship was perfectly capable of rotating to vertical and reaching space entirely on its aft thrusters, but again, the Sawyer City noise restrictions at this time of night ruled that out.

As it cleared the field, the ship retracted its landing gear and climbed rapidly away from the city and the spaceport. Jackie called it in.

"Sawyer Control, this is the *Sophie* calling clear of the zone. Requesting climb out."

"*Affirmative*, Sophie. *You're clear to climb. Maintain heading and report clearing the atmosphere.*" There was no clear boundary to the atmosphere, of course. There was the Karman line, the altitude where the air became so thin that an aircraft had to be going at orbital velocity anyway to fly aerodynamically. The minimum "safe" altitude to go to warp was usually taken as twice that, although it depended on the level of radiation to which a pilot was willing to subject her ship and its passengers. That was the altitude where Jackie would report clear, 180 kilometers.

"Roger that, Control. Climb on current heading, will report clear."

Jackie lifted the nose as she increased the throttle, then hit the switch to cut the fans and close the lift gates. The *Sophie* leaped toward space.

One of the indicators on the monitor panel glowed yellow. Jackie glanced at it and muttered, but took no other action.

"What's that light?" Avril Boutelle asked from the copilot's seat.

"The fan gates didn't lock closed. Nothing to worry about now, I'll cycle them again in orbit."

"If you say so."

∞ ∞ ∞

Two minutes later Jackie called clear of the atmosphere, and shortly after that had established a high orbit. She reported her status to Space Traffic Control.

"*Roger that*, Sophie. *You're clear in that orbit. Your flight plan shows your destination as Gliese 832, correct?*"

"Affirmative, Control." That was on the other side of the planet at the moment. Their orbit would bring them into position in about forty minutes.

"*Cleared for departure at your discretion then. Have a good trip.*"

"Roger that. Thank you, Control. *Sophie* out."

She turned back to the panel. "Okay, let's see about that fan gate." She tapped the screen on the yellow indicator, and it opened to a window showing a schematic of the *Sophie* and its three lift fans. The aft two were green, but the forward one was highlighted yellow. She muttered something under her breath.

"Problem?" Boutelle asked.

"It's the forward ventral fan gate. It's a set of louvers. When the fan is not in use, they fold flat to streamline the surface. They're supposed to lock into place so they don't vibrate. Lately they've been getting a bit flaky. *Sophie*'s an old ship." As she was speaking, she had tapped the screen again to open a short menu beside the recalcitrant fan on the schematic. She tapped the item marked OPEN.

"I never really thought about how many moving parts a ship like this has," Boutelle said.

"Too many," Jackie said. "But it gives her personality." The display now showed the fan covers open, but red.

"Red is bad?"

"It could be, but now it's just warning that we're in space and they're open. That's an odd condition. Nothing to worry about at the moment." She tapped the CLOSE button.

"What do you mean, *at the moment?*" On the screen, the graphic changed to yellow and showed the flaps closing.

"We wouldn't want to enter atmosphere with that one open, it's on the heat shield side. If there's a real problem, it will be flashing red." The graphic now showed the cover closed, but still yellow. "Damn it," Roberts said.

"That doesn't sound good."

"It's not locking." She hit the OPEN button again, waiting until the fan gate showed fully open, and then hit CLOSE. It cycled closed but again, remained yellow.

"I take it that it should show green?"

"Yes, there's a latching mechanism that engages to lock them against buffeting during reentry or atmospheric flight. Except it's not engaging. I guess we'll have to fix it."

"Fix it? You're going to go outside?"

"Not if I don't have to. There's a drone for that."

"You have a drone for fixing the fan covers?"

Jackie chuckled. "No, it's a general-purpose external inspection-and-repair drone. A robot with a couple of cameras and arms that can fly around the outside of the ship. Maybe if it gives the shutters a whack it will lock them into place."

"Seriously? You're just going to hit it?"

"That or give it a mighty heave. Sometimes that's all it takes. Relax, it's a time-honored tradition in spaceflight, going back to Skylab if not earlier."

"Okay. It's your ship." Boutelle sounded less than enthusiastic.

Rico had come forward and been listening to the conversation. "Relax," he said. "I've seen some of what this ship can do. She's a tough bird."

∞ ∞ ∞

The inspection-and-repair drone was kept in a storage compartment midships, near the port-side hatch. Roberts retrieved it and maneuvered it to the airlock. It was a boxy device less than a meter long, and half that in either sideways dimension, with four mechanical appendages, as well as cameras, illumination and navigation lights, and small control-thruster quads on each surface.

After verifying that its batteries had a full charge and its thruster tanks were pressurized, she positioned it by the overhead docking hatch and returned to the *Sophie*'s cockpit, securing the inner lock door behind her. She began the depressurization sequence on the lock while running a communications check with the drone.

"What's the range on that thing?" Rico asked.

"Do you mean the communications? About a kilometer. As far as physical range, in space there's nothing to slow it down. There's enough delta-vee in the thrusters to get into trouble, but it's programmed never to go further than it can return from, and to stay in comm range," Jackie explained. "Why?"

"I just like to know what things are capable of. You never know when you might want to put them to some unusual purpose."

Jackie could imagine some of the *unusual purposes* that Rico might put a drone to, especially with longer communication range or with the come-home disabled.

"Well, it's not exactly stealthy, so that probably eliminates some of your unusual purposes."

Rico nodded, slowly. "Yeah. Pity."

Jackie grinned to herself. She put several of the drone's camera images up on the main console, and activated the hatch built into the overhead of the airlock. This was the circular hatch typically used for ship-to-ship or ship-to-station docking, not the side door normally used planet-side. She had already slaved the drone to the panel's control joysticks, and she maneuvered the drone out through the hatch, then rotated it so its long axis was parallel to Sophie's hull.

She flew the drone around to the forward ventral fan. The hub of the fan housed a lift thruster; in use, airflow from the fan would cool and quiet the thruster exhaust. Around that were the fan cover shutters, which, sure enough, were slightly ajar. A camera sweep didn't reveal any obvious obstruction, but she hadn't really expected one. Cycling the covers would usually clear something like that.

"Guess I'm going to have to give them a thump," she told
her audience. The other two had gathered around the console to
watch.

"Don't you need something to hold on to, or are you going
to use the thrusters?" Boutelle asked.

"Neither." Roberts touched a control, and the "hands" on
three of the drone's arms spread wide and flat. She touched another control, then moved all three arms so the hands lay flat on
the hull, bracketing the fan louvers. The arms flexed slightly,
pulling the drone closer to the ship.

"Magnets?" Rico asked.

"No, the hull isn't magnetic. It uses electrostatics, the same
principle as the hold-down pads on the galley table and on some
of the deck and wall surfaces. Just like the feet of an insect or a
wall-climbing lizard, it's a microstuctured surface. It can be
switched on and off, just like the hold-down pads."

"Logical. Can't be very strong, though."

"It doesn't need to be. It's strong enough for this though." So
saying, she directed the remaining, fourth arm to thump around
the frame of the gates. "That should do it."

She switched off the drone's gecko-pads and backed it off,
then cycled the fan gate control again. She watched as the louvers
moved all the way open, and then closed. The display lit up with
a green CLOSED to confirm that.

"And we're done. That was easy."

"Almost boring," Rico said.

"Boring is good," Jackie said. "In space, there are too many
ways for *exciting* to suddenly become *terrifying* and then *fatal.*"

"*I* thought it was interesting," Boutelle said as Jackie commanded the drone back to the docking hatch.

"Yeah," Jackie allowed, "interesting is okay." She said it with
a smile, but the fact was she was concerned. Not about the fan
gate, which was an annoyance that, in the worst case, could be
worked around, but it was a symptom of her ship's age in general.

Ducayne had paid for some maintenance and repairs of damage incurred on missions for Homeworld Security, but mostly for
enhancements useful only to such missions. The range extender

could be a plus, but the paperwork and licensing to be able to purchase antimatter was hardly worth the trouble even if she could afford it, and the gravity wave sensor had no practical use in commercial operations. She wouldn't normally need to detect ships going in or out of warp.

Routine maintenance was her problem, and *Sophie* would only need more of it as time went on. Carson had mentioned something about wanting to take some extended trips. It would be a good idea to give *Sophie* an overhaul before that. She wondered if the university would be paying for the trips, or Ducayne, and if they would front payment for the work.

The joys of being a starship owner/operator, she sighed to herself. But she couldn't imagine herself doing anything else. It sure beat being the first officer on a passenger liner.

Chapter 12: A Slight Detour

Deep space, aboard the Sophie, *a day later*

Jackie Roberts checked the instruments and then announced to the others, "Okay, secure for zero-gee. I'm going to bring us out of warp."

"Is there a problem?" Avril Boutelle asked while making sure any loose items were stowed.

"Nothing urgent, but we're going to come into Delta Pavonis with nearly five light-years less fuel than we should, with this diversion to Gliese 832," Jackie said.

"What? Are we going to run out?" asked Rico.

"No, there's enough, not even counting reserves. It's just that someone might notice when I refuel."

"Is that all?" he asked. "Does anyone pay attention to that?"

"No," Jackie admitted, "not unless it's a specialized fuel, highly pure or deuterated or whatever. But Sapphires aren't fussy. They'll take plain water, even dirty water, although that's not good for the filters."

"Then why do you want to drop out of warp?" Boutelle asked, although her tone suggested she had an idea why.

"Partly it's my perfectionist streak," Jackie said. "But also, I need to do a systems check on the emergency-reserve system anyway."

"Need to or want to?" Boutelle said. "I think you just want to try the antimatter engine."

Jackie grinned. "You got me."

"Wait," Rico said. "Antimatter engine?"

"Did you sleep through that part of the briefing?" Boutelle asked him.

"It's not really an antimatter engine," Jackie explained. "It's just an alternate power source for the warp pods. It's an emergency range extender. It adds a few parsecs."

"But, *antimatter?*" Rico said. Jackie couldn't tell from his tone or expression whether the idea worried him, or whether he thought the antimatter might be a cool new toy to play with. She suspected the latter.

"Thanks to Ducayne. Same thing that powers message torpedoes. There's not *much* antimatter, about two kilograms."

"*Two kilogra*— Geez, and I thought *I* liked dangerous toys." Rico shook his head, but he was grinning.

"Relax, Rico. We're not going to be blowing anything up. It has multiple fail-safes; the containment system will last thousands of years." She paused for effect. "Or so I've been told."

"So, you want to do five light-years on antimatter?" Boutelle said. "What's involved?"

"Not much. I enter a few commands to reroute power from the fusion module, enter the authorization code for the antimatter system, and everything else behaves normally."

"Oh, okay."

"Either that," she added, "or we blow up in a twenty-megaton explosion. We'll never know what hit us."

"*What?*" Boutelle exclaimed.

"Joking! It is *really hard* to make an antimatter containment system explode."

Rico looked doubtful—probably thinking of a few ways he could brute-force it—but he said, "Oh, well, that's all right then."

"I'm glad you approve," Jackie said with a smirk. "Is everything secured?"

Boutelle strapped herself into the co-pilot's seat. Rico, after a quick glance back at the rest of the ship, grabbed one of the yellow handrails affixed to the bulkheads. "Roger that, all secure."

"Cutting warp in three, two, one, now." Jackie hit the control and gravity went away.

∞ ∞ ∞

In spite of her earlier claim that *not much* was involved in switching from the fusion engine to the antimatter system, Jackie Roberts first carried out an intense sequence of diagnostics on both systems. Shutting the fusion system down and bringing it back online again was routine, a normal part of operations. There was sufficient battery capacity to maintain life support and electronics for days. The full power of the fusion module was only needed at takeoff—to power the plasma jets—and while in warp.

The antimatter power system was something else. It had a monitoring system running at all times, but that was for its "static" stand-by mode. Shifting it to full power output meant actually manipulating the stored antimatter, directing it to the reaction chamber to generate the power needed to drive the warp module. If something were to go wrong, that was the most likely time, what with the transients involved in switchover.

The diagnostic routines simulated this to the extent possible, but failures happened when real-life didn't match the simulation.

Finally satisfied, Jackie hit the EXECUTE control to reconfigure the power system. There was no obvious effect.

"That's it?" Boutelle asked. "Nothing happened."

"No, nothing is supposed to happen yet. I just told the computers to draw warp power from the antimatter instead of the fusor. It won't actually do that until I engage the warp drive, although below-decks there was some heavy-duty power line switching. Right now it's just drawing a minimal amount to power the ship."

"Oh."

Jackie raised her voice, although the other two were still in the cockpit area. "Is everything secure for warp? Gravity's about to come back."

Rico and Boutelle acknowledged that. There hadn't been time to unstow anything.

"Okay, engaging warp in five, four—"

"Or blowing up," Rico said.

"—Two, one . . ." Jackie reached for the control. "Warp."

Outside, the stars went out, while inside gravity came back.

"Looks like it worked," Jackie said. "Standby." She cut the warp drive, and again they were in freefall.

"Something wrong?" Rico asked?

"No, I just wanted to check that everything matches what it should." She scanned the panel. Everything looked nominal. "Okay. Next stop, halfway to Gliese 832."

"Only halfway?"

"Position check, then we go the rest of the way."

"Ah."

"And away we go." Jackie engaged the warp drive again, and gravity was back. She unbuckled and stood up from her control chair. "I'm heading back to the galley. I don't know about you folks, but I'm hungry."

∞ ∞ ∞

Somewhere in deep space, aboard Sophie

Jackie Roberts and Avril Boutelle were at breakfast in the ship's galley. Jackie had finished eating and was working on a second cup of coffee, watching idly as Avril toyed with a bowl of oatmeal.

"Feel free to tell me I have no need to know," Jackie said, "but how did you end up working for Ducayne? I wouldn't have taken you for a spook."

Avril looked up from her oatmeal and grinned. "Well, of course not. Else I wouldn't be a very good one, would I?"

"Fair point."

"Anyway, there's not much to tell. As an undergrad I'd already shown some talent for alien cultures and Verdigris history, so I was approached to do some analysis work. One thing led to another, and before long, I was doing some assignments on the side along with my academic field trips. After a while, I asked for more challenging assignments and got trained in fieldcraft. But most of it is just keeping my eyes and ears open and reporting what's going on. A lot is indistinguishable from journalism, except that we keep a lower profile and don't publish. What about you?"

"Me? I'm just a pilot-for-hire. Well, and a ship-for-hire. Ducayne wanted Carson to follow up on something he'd found, and my ship was available."

"But you already knew Carson, didn't you?"

"You could say that. And I wonder if Ducayne knew that. But we hadn't seen each other for a couple of years."

"Oh. I thought . . . never mind."

"It's complicated," Jackie said, guessing Avril's thoughts. *Even more complicated since two nights before departure*, she reflected.

"What about Rico?" Avril asked, breaking Jackie's reverie.

"Somebody mention my name?" Rico said, arriving in the galley from his bunk just then.

"I first met Rico on that mission with Carson," Jackie said. "It was . . . interesting."

Rico laughed. "You could say that." He turned to Avril. "I was working for somebody else. I guess you could say we were on opposite sides. But later Roberts here saved my life, dragged me out of a wrecked ship and put me in her traumapod." He nodded toward it, across the corridor from the galley.

"He exaggerates. I couldn't drag Rico anywhere. That was mostly Carson. I just got the stretcher out of the ship."

"If you say so," Rico said. "I was kind of out of it."

"Anyway," Jackie said, "he returned the favor later. Helped us get away from a hostile ship and ended up back in the traumapod in the process."

Rico shook his head. "I have spent entirely too much of the last year or so in traumapods. It's a habit I'm trying to quit."

Avril had been looking from Jackie to Rico and back again as they talked. "You know," she said, "I've never had to use one, let alone be in one, and it's been a while since I trained. Maybe you should check me out on the *Sophie*'s traumapod, Captain."

"The whole idea is that they're about as easy to operate as an autochef," Jackie said, "but sure."

"Just don't ask me to play patient," Rico said, shaking his head with a wry grin.

Chapter 13: Reid

Sawyers City, Velkaryan HQ, a few days later

"So? Have you located Rico yet?" Reid demanded. He had been out of the traumapod for a day. He clenched his mechanical right hand. He wanted payback.

The other man, Aston, was one of the local Velkaryans, part of Deitrich's team. "As far as we can tell, Rico's no longer on-planet. If he is, he's lying low. Maybe wherever he was hiding for the last few months,"

"No," Reid said. "Our sources say that he was in a traumapod for much of that." They had learned that much. "Apparently Space Guard was investigating him for his connections to Hopkins, for artifact smuggling."

"Since when does Sawyers World care about artifact smugglers?" Aston said. "It's not like there's anything worthwhile here."

"I suppose some people might be interested in old arrowheads, but no," Reid said, shaking his head. "The reasons the Guard might be interested have to do with treaty obligations, and the fact that anyone involved in artifact smuggling might be involved in other kinds of smuggling.

"Anyway," Reid continued, "that's irrelevant. The Guard doesn't have him now. Best guess is that he's working for Homeworld Security, so he's either holed up at their base, or he's off-planet. Have you checked passenger lists and flight plans?"

"Of course," Aston said, sounding almost offended. "There was no Rico or anyone matching his description, but not every small ship operator files a flight plan. There was one thing, though."

"What?"

"The starship *Sophie*, belonging to a Captain Roberts, departed a few days ago. That's a ship of interest, right?"

"It is. Where was it headed?"

"It wasn't to one of her usual destinations. This time it was a red dwarf star, Gliese 832. The funny thing is, her last trip was also to a red dwarf, to Proxima. Suppose there's a connection?"

Reid thought about it. Roberts and her ship, *Sophie*, were nominally a space charter and courier operation, and most of her flights reflected that. But there'd just been a couple of incidents where she had been in the same place with Velkaryan operations gone wrong, and she'd shown up along with Rico at Pete's Peak. It was possible that Ducayne was just using her as an available ship, but why the interest in Gliese 832? If there was some kind of ongoing research on red dwarf planets, it was conceivable that someone at Proxima had wanted to send a package to a colleague at GL 832, if there was anything going on there. Was there? That was worth looking into.

"Maybe it's just a courier run," Reid said. "Did the flight plan say anything about passengers?" It wouldn't list specific cargo, charter captains, and especially couriers, considered that private.

"No names, just 'two pax'. I suppose Rico could have been one of them."

"Why would he want to go to GL 832, or why would Ducayne send him? Two passengers? I assume Carson is the other one?"

"No, Carson's still on-planet, still teaching."

"Hmm. So why there?" Reid tapped his omniphone. "Give me information about Gliese 832," he told it.

It responded almost immediately. *"Gliese 832 is a red dwarf star located 13.99 light-years from Alpha Centauri. It has a gas giant orbiting at 3.4 AUs, a super-Earth orbiting—"*

"Skip planetary data," Reid interrupted. "Historical information?"

"Historically Gliese 832 was used as a refueling stop as an alternative to Taprobane Station in the Epsilon Indi system—"

"Stop," Reid said, disgusted. There would never have been a need for an alternative if the meddling UDT hadn't put Taprobane off-limits because of the natives. These days, ships had about twice the range they used to, so a lot of those old refueling stops were obsolete. They had been abandoned or repurposed. Wait, refueling stop to where? Reid tapped his omni again. "On what routes was Gliese 832 used for refueling?"

"The Tau Ceti to Delta Pavonis run, the Tau Ceti to Zeta Tucanae run, the Alpha Centauri to Delta Pavonis run, the—"

"Stop." Reid looked at Aston. "They could be headed to Delta Pavonis."

Aston looked skeptical. "Why not just go directly? It's only five parsecs. The *Sophie*'s a Sapphire; it must have at least a six-parsec range."

"Do we have any operations at 832?" Reid knew that they occasionally made use of such abandoned facilities as temporary bases, and there might be something going on there he hadn't been informed of.

"You'd have to ask Deitrich. I don't know of any."

Reid dismissed the thought. If there was such an operation and Homeworld Security suspected it, they'd be unlikely to send Roberts and her Sapphire directly there. He would mention it to Deitrich, however, just in case. As to why they would go to Gliese 832 at all, perhaps it was a diversion. "Maybe they're going to 832 just to keep us guessing."

"Why bother? It's not like we could tell Verdigris that they're on their way."

Reid nodded. "You have a point." Except that he didn't. Reid knew that ordinarily there was no way to get a message to Delta Pavonis from here before a ship that had left a couple of days earlier would arrive. Even the higher speed of a message torpedo would be hard-pressed to overtake a ship with enough of a head start. But Reid also knew of the FTL communication system between Earth and Verdigris. Not the details, of course, but that it existed; more than most Velkaryans knew. It was a closely guarded secret. Reid thought it through. A message by regular ship would take four days to get from here to Earth, and then a few hours from there to the Delta Pavonis system. It would take a ship close to fifteen days to travel from here to Delta Pavonis directly.

He would talk it over with Deitrich. It could well be just a routine charter on the *Sophie*'s part, or Deitrich might know of some operation involving GL 832 that Reid didn't. They didn't use the FTL comm system without good reason. If the *Sophie*'s crew had reason to believe that anyone on Verdigris had been expecting them, they would wonder about that, and might deduce something about the communication method. Better if they suspected nothing, or that it was just heightened alertness after Carson's and Roberts' previous visits to Verdigris. He'd leave that decision to Deitrich. There was still plenty of time to get a message to Verdigris to let them know that the *Sophie* and a couple of Ducayne's agents might be paying them a visit. More information would help.

"All right," Reid said. "I'll take care of it. Maybe I'll have someone pay Carson a visit."

Chapter 14: Carson Makes Plans

Sawyer City, Carson's apartment

Carson put aside his datapad and got up to get something to eat. Reviewing his students' end-of-term assignments was a slog, and he needed to change gears. His apartment's kitchenette wasn't much bigger than the galley on a Sapphire-class starship, but at least his fridge held fresh food. He swung its door open. *At least, it would if I had bought any recently,* he thought, and closed it again. He tapped the omniphone on his wrist. "Remind me to pick up groceries on the way home tomorrow," he said, deciding not to order them for delivery. It was nice to get out somewhere other than home or campus once in a while.

He hadn't heard anything from Ducayne in a couple of weeks, and of course there was no way to hear anything from Jackie. Messages didn't travel any faster than the starships that carried them, unless there was actually something to Ducayne's theory that the Velkaryans might indeed have a pair of working alien FTL transceivers. He idly wondered if there was any connection to the alien artifacts that had been recovered from the pyramid on Chara III, or the one pulled from the wrecked alien ship at Kapteyn's Star. Ducayne was keeping him in the dark about those. Not that Carson could blame him. Reverse engineering millennia-old alien high tech was pretty far outside Carson's expertise, although he wasn't sure into whose area of expertise it would fall. Maybe cross out "millennia-old" and "alien" and it would fall into the domain of industrial espionage and normal technological spying. Ducayne probably had plenty of experts in that. *What does he tell them about where those gadgets came from?* Carson wondered.

Carson ordered up a snack from his autochef—that, at least, was kept stocked, thanks to an automatic reorder when it ran low —and took it back to the living area. He settled back in his chair and picked up the datapad again. Speaking of aliens, Ducayne had left him with two puzzles. The bigger one, at least in terms of as-trographic area if not in implications, was that of following up on Avril Boutelle's report on all known extraterrestrial pyramids, or pyramid-like structures, and how their presence on a planet might correlate with Velkaryan activity. And to find first any Spacefarer-built pyramids the Velkaryans hadn't.

The other puzzle likely had more significant long-term im-pact: to figure out just what exactly the Kesh were up to. Carson had met exactly one of the vaguely saurian aliens, at Zeta Reticuli, and Ketzshanass, as the alien had called himself, specifically said that their species wasn't ready to make formal first contact with humans. More specifically, that humans weren't ready.

Yet there was pretty good evidence—still classified—that the Kesh had been watching humans for some time. Just over fifty years ago Elizabeth Sawyer, in charge of the first landing team on this planet, had spotted one near their landing site before it acti-vated some kind of active camouflage system and disappeared. Then there were the remains of a Kesh scout-ship found in the waters off Belize a few months back—remains that could be as much as two-thousand years old. And someone had deliberately buried the Spacefarer pyramid on this planet. The evidence sug-gested it was the Kesh, but why? Not only buried it, but filled it in. Carson still remembered his feelings of shock and disbelief when he'd finally got the entrance open, only to find the passages beyond clogged floor to ceiling with dried mud. Yes, he definitely wanted to ask the Kesh what they were playing at.

He opened an astronomical database program on his pad. It wasn't as fancy as anything Jackie would have on hers, let alone what the *Sophie*'s navigation computer would have, but it might do. Carson wanted to figure out where the Kesh homeworld might be.

He, along with Jackie and his timoan colleague Marten, had found cities, ruined cities, on the third planet of Zeta 1 Reticuli. Ketzshanass had explicitly refused to say anything about the Kesh homeworld, but Carson had the impression that Zirth, as he had unofficially dubbed Zeta 1 Reticuli III, was not it. What they'd seen from orbit had all been modern cities, with no signs of older buildings within them. They had also been spaced out in a manner that suggested easy long-distance transportation. Neither was a feature he would expect of a planet where civilization had arisen, rather than been transplanted to. But then, he mused, the Kesh may have had interstellar travel for at least two thousand years.

They had not continued on to Zeta 2 Reticuli, even though it was a mere tenth of a light-year distant, closer than Proxima was to Sawyers World. Vaughan's ship *Carcharodon*, which had followed them to the system, had been attacked by some kind of automated defense system, and the *Sophie* had almost been similarly attacked. Ketzshanass said that the Kesh had been attacked by a species he referred to as the degkhidesh, or enemy of the Kesh, sometime after going through a civil war of their own, and strongly suggested they stay away from both systems. The alien ship—presumed Kesh—they'd found crashed on a planet orbiting Kapteyn's Star had shown similar weapon damage.

But if not Zeta Reticuli, then where? Almost certainly nowhere closer, they would have been noticed. Zeta 2 was a possibility, but what about further out?

Ketzshanass had implied that his years and Earth years were about the same length. That strongly implied a G-type star as their sun. That fit with the terraformed planets humans had so far discovered. Not that they were all G-types, some were the smaller K-type, and perhaps a factor of two in year difference wouldn't have made much difference in the context of his discussion with Ketz. That was about the difference between Kakuloa and Sawyers World years, neatly bracketing Earth's standard year.

So, what G- or K-type stars were at some reasonable distance beyond Zeta Reticuli?

It seemed a simple question, but the program on his datapad wasn't equipped to answer it. At least, Carson couldn't figure out a way to ask it that. He could set the origin at Zeta Reticuli and it would happily show him what the sky looked like from there. He could even pinpoint individual stars and it would identify them and tell him the distance. He picked out a few stars that looked right.

HD-28255? That was a double star, types G4 and G6. There was nothing wrong with double stars, so long as they had stable orbits in at least one of their habitable zones. Carson lived in a double-star system himself, triple if one counted Proxima Centauri, and Zeta 1 and 2 Reticuli were another such. Although, the HD-28255 system was over fifty-two light-years from Zeta Reticuli. That didn't rule it out, but it would be easier to check out closer stars first. Statistically, there were thirty to forty G-type stars in a volume fifty light-years in diameter, at least if T-Space was anything to go by. Jackie would know. He started to reach for his omni, then stopped himself. She was off-planet. *Damn.* He wished she were here, and not just for her navigation skills. With a sigh, he turned back to the star charts.

What about that one, HD-36435? A singleton star, about twenty-seven light-years from Zeta Reticuli, or sixty from here. That was a long trip. But he was planning to take a sabbatical, he had plenty of time. Would Jackie be willing to commit to a twelve-week round trip, plus whatever time that detours to refuel would take? Well, she had been born on a starship, on a four-year mission. Maybe. Could *he* stand it? Perhaps. Anyway, odds were that wasn't the right star either.

It would make sense to check out the Reticuli system again and see what they could find out. He and Marten had had a chance to explore just one building in the ruined city they had visited, and that one had been cleaned out. But there should be something on the planet, or perhaps in the Zeta 2 system, that gave a clue as to where the Kesh were really from. *If*, that is, they could manage to get in, search until they found something, and get out, all before either a Kesh ship showed up or the automated defense systems noticed them.

He tossed the datapad back down. He wasn't going to solve it tonight.

Chapter 15: Gliese 832

Gliese 832

The *Sophie* arrived in the Gliese 832 system a week later.

A red dwarf star, it held little of interest to beings evolved under a yellower sun. There was a cold gas-giant orbiting at 3.4 AUs, and a large Venus-like super-Earth in an eccentric orbit, grazing the inner edge of the system's habitable zone. That eccentricity was enough to keep the planet from being tidally locked into keeping the same side toward its sun, so it rotated three times for every two orbits of its sun, like Mercury.

The gas giant had a few moons, and the system had a scattering of smaller, Pluto-like bodies and asteroids. On one partially ice-covered moon of the gas giant, there was an abandoned refueling station, left over from an era where Delta Pavonis was beyond the fifteen-light-year reach of many ships.

The usual route from Alpha Centauri would have been to Taprobane in the Epsilon Indi system and then on to Verdigris, at just under ten light-years per hop. When the UDT had restricted landings on Taprobane in light of the local timoan civilization, refueling stations had been established elsewhere in the Epsilon Indi system as well as at Gliese 832. They, along with other stations dating to an era of shorter-range ships, had largely fallen into disuse. Some were still used as scientific outposts if there was anything else interesting in the system, and popular entertainment often portrayed them as used for pirate or smuggler bases.

Jackie had never put any credence in such stories. The logistics didn't make sense, and it didn't seem logical to base an illegal operation somewhere so obvious. The Space Force made occasional visits to such outposts just to discourage that.

"What do you think, Rico?" she asked him. "Did you ever know anyone to use those old refueling stations as a base?"

"Not that I'd ever heard. As an out-of-the-way refueling stop, maybe, but even at that, most illicit operations use ships that are capable of refueling in the wild. There's no reason to hang out at a base that may be in disrepair and without supplies."

"That's what I figured. Anyway, we have no reason to land. Nobody is answering my hails, so I think we'll just turn around and leave. We've established our cover. *Sophie* did a run to Gliese 832, and she is now leaving."

"Actually," Rico said, "how much of a hurry are we in to get to Verdigris, and how much time did we pick up using the antimatter?"

"You want to check out the base," Jackie guessed. "Why?"

"Just because there's nobody there now doesn't mean there wasn't someone there recently. Maybe they left something interesting behind. Seems a shame to waste the trip."

She eyed him speculatively. She got the feeling there was something he wasn't telling her. Was this a side-quest Ducayne had given him? She turned to Boutelle. "Avril? What do you think?"

Boutelle shrugged. "If it's really abandoned, it might be interesting. Just so long as we don't run into pirates. Would we need to suit up?"

Jackie turned back to her console and tapped out a query. "Telemetry shows that the base is still pressurized and at nominal temperatures, although perhaps on the cool side. It also indicates the docking tunnels are still operative. We shouldn't need full suits, but I'm going to suggest we wear shipsuits anyway."

Shipsuits were coverall-type garments, comfortable enough for everyday shipboard wear, but designed to tighten to a pressure suit in case of sudden exposure to vacuum. A flexible hood-helmet was built into the collar, along with a fifteen-minute oxygen reserve. Aboard ship, that should be plenty of time to get to a safe area or find and attach a longer-duration air pack. They were no substitute for a proper space suit, although Jackie had been known to use hers for short trips outside, as during refueling operations on an ice moon. Of course, in those cases, she coupled it with a proper helmet and protective boots and gloves, but it was still easier to work in than a full EVA suit.

"We're landing, then?" Rico asked.

"Affirmative. Everyone strap in."

Chapter 16: Dean Matthews

Drake University, Sawyer City

The formal meeting of the university's Board of Regents had broken up, and Dean of Archeology Eric Matthews had joined the others in a nearby hall for a reception, including drinks and snacks.

He turned away from the buffet table, drink in one hand, a small plate of sandwiches in the other, and surveyed the hall. The problem with these affairs, he thought, is that you either need a third arm in order to actually eat the sandwiches, or you needed a table to put your plate on. While there were a few, fully occupied, stand-up tables, the other tables—still not an adequate number for all the guests—were all sit-down, limiting one's ability to mingle.

"That's always a problem, isn't it?" a tall, swarthy man nearby said.

"I'm sorry?"

"You looked like you were trying to figure out what to do with your food. I make sure I eat before coming to these things, that way I only have to hold my glass." He raised the one he was holding. "Cheers."

"Oh, uh, cheers," Matthews said, raising his glass in turn.

"I'm Rajesh Dejois, by the way; one of the board members."

A Dejois and *a board member.* Matthews wondered if he was related to the first settlers, one of Jennifer Singh and Roger Dejois' descendants. *Probably, with that first name.* "I'm Dean Eric

Matthews, Archeology," he said, introducing himself. "I'd offer to shake hands but. . . ." He held out his arms, plate in one hand, glass in the other, and shrugged.

"Hah, no worries. I'm not big on formality. Archeology, eh? Were you the one involved with that find in the Anderson Preserve?"

"Find?" Matthews was at a momentary loss. He wasn't aware of any find. Hannibal Carson had been temporarily attached to an ecological survey, since it was near an area where ancient stone tools had been found, but Matthews didn't recall him saying much about it. Typical, Carson was getting shoddy with his paperwork. But Dejois was still looking at him, expecting more. "I'm sorry," Matthews added, "but I'm not sure what find you're referring to."

"Ah, so not you then, or you're keeping mum. I'd heard a rumor that the survey team had found evidence of some ancient structure. No details, apparently it's all being kept very hush-hush. Of course, you wouldn't want the souvenir hunters and smugglers to get in there before you can do a proper excavation, right? I understand you wanting to keep mum about it. Still, a nice bit of publicity for the university when it can be revealed, eh?"

"Um, quite." Structure? What was this man going on about? Matthews decided he needed to have a long talk with Hannibal Carson. "Of course, these things need to be evaluated carefully before any announcement is made. Tomb raiders aside, sometimes a natural phenomenon can be mistaken for something artificial, and then there'd be red faces all around."

"Right. Wouldn't want that," Dejois said. "But look, I'm keeping you from your sandwiches. I'll go off and bother someone else. It was good chatting with you, Matthews."

"Oh, not at all, no bother. A pleasure to meet you," Matthews said, but by the end of that, Dejois was already wandering off to talk to Doctor Greystone of the biology department.

Chapter 17: Base 832

Refueling station, Gliese 832

Jackie tried to contact the base again as she brought the Sophie in toward the landing area. There was no human response, but the landing lights did come on at her coded signal. That was something, at least.

"So it still has power," Rico said.

"That's not surprising. It's a refueling outpost, so it will have plenty of fuel for a fusion reactor. I imagine that on standby, it could last for years, maybe decades. The question is how much of the mechanical equipment works without maintenance."

She did a low pass over the base. As expected, all the landing pads were clear, although there was a ship—it looked like an old Staravelle model—in one of the long-term parking areas. From the windblown dust accumulated on it, it had been there a while.

The planet had a thin atmosphere, not enough to go out without a pressure suit of some kind, but enough to blow dust around. A bit like Mars, Jackie decided.

"It doesn't look like anyone's home," she said.

"What about that ship?"

"It's an old design, at least twenty years." But then, so was her *Sophie*. "And look at the dust on it. It's been here a while. Probably had some problem that couldn't be fixed easily, and was still awaiting parts when the base was abandoned. We can check the station logs, maybe even board it if you're interested."

"We can play that as it comes," Rico said.

Jackie grunted an acknowledgment as she turned her attention to landing. Between the thin air and relatively low gravity, she just brought the Sophie into a hover a hundred meters above one of the landing pads and lowered the ship vertically, orienting it to allow the docking tunnel to connect with the starboard hatch.

With the ship on the ground, Jackie ran through the post-landing checks and secured it from flight.

"Now what?" Boutelle asked.

Jackie gestured at one of the view screens. "See that tunnel? Keep an eye on it."

As Boutelle and Rico watched the viewscreen, Jackie linked her control console to the base's computers, that were designed for just such. A schematic of the docking tunnel—a distant cousin to old airport jetways—came up on her screen, along with a command menu and status indicators. They were all green; so far, so good.

She initiated the extension sequence, and the schematic showed the tunnel slowly extending its telescoping joints.

"It's moving!" Boutelle noted.

"Good." Jackie looked up at the viewscreen, just in time to see the tunnel shudder to a halt.

"It's not moving," Boutelle said.

Jackie looked back at the console. A status light was now yellow. A "Motor stall" warning dialog popped up, then changed to "Resequencing." Jackie hoped it was just a bit of dirt in the track.

One of the tunnel's sliding joints retracted a short way, then extended again, this time pushing beyond whatever had hung it up. The previous warning dialog was replaced by another: "Motor operation restored," and the indicator flickered and turned green again, then back to yellow, as the tunnel lurched to a halt once again. The "Motor stall" warning came back.

"Damn it." Jackie shut the power tunnel power off.

"What now?"

"Probably just more dirt. I'll give the motor a chance to cool off so it doesn't overheat, then try again."

"And if it doesn't work?"

"Then we either suit up, or give this little tourist excursion a pass."

"Oh."

Jackie waited another minute, then sent the command to start the tunnel retracting. It slid back smoothly. She stopped it half-way, then ran it forward again.

The tunnel extended again, rolling smoothly as it approached the spot where it had stalled before. There was a hesitation and the ramp slowed for a moment. The warning light flickered yellow and then went back to green as the ramp surged forward, having pushed past this second obstruction.

"It's moving again," Avril said, "getting closer!"

The tunnel kept coming, and Jackie poised her hand over the "Emergency Stop" in case it didn't when it touched *Sophie*'s hull. Then, with a slight bump, the tunnel extension came to a stop on its own.

Jackie ran through the sequence to fine tune the tunnel's docking adapter against the opposite adapter around *Sophie*'s hatch, and a series of clicks from starboard signaled that the latches engaged.

"Okay," Jackie said, exhaling the breath she'd been holding. "Let's give it a couple of minutes to purge any outside air"— she entered a command to start that—"then we can go take a look."

∞ ∞ ∞

Rico had observed the trouble with the tunnel with growing concern. "Should we suit up anyway?" he asked. "If that base has been empty for a while. . . ."

Roberts had been working the control panel while waiting for the docking tunnel's atmosphere to purge. "No need," she said. "The readouts confirm the telemetry we got earlier. They show that all the airlock seals are intact and the base's life support is still operating normally. It has plenty of power. The only issue is the parts exposed to ambient conditions, things like dust blowing into the seals, temperature changes, and such like. Some of the outer lock doors may be a bit reluctant, like the tunnel was, but everything inside is showing green. Mind you, I wouldn't go wandering in there in shorts and a tee-shirt, just in case, but shipsuits will be fine."

Rico looked over at the two women. "And here I was looking forward to you both in shorts and tee-shirts," he said, smiling to show he was joking. Often as not, that was normal shipboard wear anyway. "No, shipsuits work. But I'm going armed."

"Why?" Roberts asked. "The base is empty. No life-signs on the monitors, and that Staravelle has been there for what looks like years."

"Or that's what they want you to believe, and the monitors have been hacked not to show life-signs. Humor me, I just like going armed."

"I say we humor him," Avril said. "I wouldn't mind a sidearm myself."

"All right," Roberts said. "I know you're both trained." She touched a control on her panel. "The weapons locker is unlocked, bring one for me too."

Rico stepped aft to where he remembered the weapons locker was from his previous trip on the *Sophie*, back when they'd had to refuel at Lalande 21185 and encountered Hopkins and his gang. Opening it, he surveyed the contents. Unsurprisingly, there was nothing really heavy—no fully automatic weapons or explosives. What there was, though, was good quality. He withdrew three pistols, 10mm Maclarens, plus gun-belts and magazines for the pistols. He checked the pistols' operation but left them unloaded. With no immediate danger, that could wait until they were off the ship.

He came back forward and distributed the gear to Roberts and Boutelle. "Anything else we need? Will our omnis work in the base?"

"They should," Roberts said, "but we're not splitting up."

"Good," Avril said. "I'm getting a weird horror movie vibe about this whole thing."

"Seriously?" asked Rico. "You can stay in the ship if you'd rather." He looked at Roberts. "Is that okay, Captain?"

Boutelle answered before Roberts could. "No, I'll come with. I'm curious to see the base too. Let's just stick together."

"That's the plan," Roberts said. "Okay, are we all set?"

"Yes," Avril said.

"Whenever you're ready," said Rico.

"Okay," Roberts keyed open the inner airlock door. "It's a bit crowded for three, but we can squeeze in."

They did, and with the inner lock door closed, Rico watched as Roberts checked the sensors again confirming that the docking tunnel was attached and pressurized.

"Okay," she said, "slight pressure change between us and the tunnel, stand by."

She activated a valve and there was a slight hiss as the airlock pressure dropped to match that in the tunnel. Rico felt his ears pop slightly.

Taking a final look at the outside view—the tunnel was illuminated and empty—Jackie opened the outer lock door. A wave of cooler air drifted in, with a slightly unpleasant odor of dust and hydrocarbons.

"I thought you purged the tunnel air?" Rico said.

"I did. Probably just traces stuck to the tunnel walls. It's nothing toxic."

"I hope it clears up inside," Boutelle said. "Or I'm pulling my hood up and sealing my suit."

"It should," Roberts said.

They had already stepped out of the *Sophie's* airlock and into the tunnel. Rico took the opportunity to load his pistol while Roberts closed the outer lock door. Boutelle, noticing this, unholstered hers and loaded it too, then re-holstered it.

Rico had already started down the tunnel to the door to the base. Behind him, he heard Roberts check her own weapon.

"Is there another airlock behind this, or is it just a hatch to the inside?" Rico asked when they reached the inner door. It had a small window in it.

"There should be an airlock," she said, "in case someone needs to use this as an exit with no ship attached."

Rico looked it over, noting the small control panel beside it. "Yes, standard airlock controls." He peered through the window, but it was too dark to make anything out. He touched the small panel beside the door, and an indicator lit up green. "And we have pressure inside. Stand by."

He drew his pistol, flipped the safety off, then held it ready as he touched another control. The hatch opened, revealing a small chamber slightly larger than the *Sophie's* own airlock, with another green light on a panel on the far wall. It was empty. "Wait here. I'll go through first," he said.

"It's big enough for all of us," Boutelle said.

"And if someone *is* here, and waiting for us, that would be a perfect trap. Let me check that it's clear. If not, go back to the ship."

"What about you?"

"I'll figure something out. But it's probably clear." With that he stepped into the airlock and closed the door behind him.

Again, holding his gun at the ready, he pressed the OPEN button for the inner door. Nothing happened for a moment, and Rico tensed, then the door slid open. The corridor behind it was dark and empty. Rico relaxed.

He stepped back into the airlock to give Roberts, who was watching through the window, a thumbs up, then went back into the corridor to wait, closing the door behind him.

Roberts and Boutelle came through a few moments later, by which time Rico had found an on-switch for the lights.

He gestured down the corridor. "Shall we?"

∞ ∞ ∞

Their exploration confirmed Jackie's initial premise that the base was, indeed, abandoned. She noted that it was cool but not unpleasantly so, and the air was breathable if dry. The life support was tuned for human occupation, which the base hadn't had in some time. Jackie knew from years of shipboard experience that the presence of warm bodies would naturally tend to raise the base's temperature and humidity.

The lights, except for strips of emergency lighting, had been off, but now came on automatically whenever they entered a new room or corridor. Rico's on-switch must have activated the whole system. As the telemetry had said, everything seemed to be functioning nominally. The base had been abandoned because it was no longer needed, not because of any mechanical problems.

Avril Boutelle must have been thinking along the same lines. "Why didn't they just shut it down completely?" she asked.

"Probably just in case someone stopped by," Jackie said. "With a fusion power supply, it's easier just to keep it on standby than shut it down and have to reboot it from a cold start. The computers would shut it down cold if there were a problem or the fuel ran out, but that might not be for years."

"Or," Rico said, "this place does get used from time to time, so they leave it on standby."

"Are you still thinking about pirates or smugglers?" Jackie asked.

"Or squatters, perhaps? Could someone live here?" Boutelle wondered.

"Not likely," Jackie said. "The life support will maintain air and water, but they'd need food. And it seems like a lonely place to live, especially with no way to leave."

"Stuck here with that damaged Staravelle?" Boutelle wondered aloud.

"And no food, once it ran out," Rico said. "I don't think so. Come on, let's go find the main control room. Maybe the base logs will show us when someone was last here."

∞ ∞ ∞

Control Room, Gliese 832 Base

To Jackie, the base control room was unremarkable, looking much like any technical operations center. Display screens, now dark, covered one wall, and facing that were several desks, each with its own monitors, keyboards and control panels. Aside from the darkened displays, the place had an air of everyone having just left for lunch, with some desks and chairs neatly aligned, and others where the chairs were turned away and the odd paper or pen left haphazardly on the desk. Here and there was the occasional desktop toy or decoration, although no pictures. Any items with sentimental value would have been removed with the last of the departing crew.

"It doesn't look like it's been touched in years," Boutelle said. "It's almost creepy."

"Actually," Rico said, "two of these desks were used more recently." He pointed at them. "See, the dust layer isn't as thick as on the others."

Jackie looked at the desks, ducking down to view the table-tops at an angle. "You're right. Some of the others show signs of dust disturbance, but not as much as those two." She looked for some sign or other indication of their purpose, but saw nothing. None of the consoles had any such indication, meaning that they were all general-purpose consoles, or the signs had been removed. That only two of them had seen use suggested the latter.

"Let's power these up and see what they control." With that, she toggled the power switch to the monitor she was standing near. Rico did likewise at the desk near him.

"This one's the refueling facility," he said as he examined the display. "The deuterium tanks are full, and the processor is at idle. What have you got?"

Jackie recognized her display as very similar to one aboard the *Sophie*. "This is base life support," she said. "Air recycling is fully operational—we knew that—water and sewage are on standby, with heaters on to keep things from freezing. Plenty of water in the tanks."

"What is the significance of that, if any?" Boutelle asked.

"I'd say that someone has been here within the last year or so, and probably stayed for a while," Jackie said. "Let me see if I can find the traffic console. It should have comm gear."

She walked from desk to desk, looking closely at the dust on the surface and checking for a microphone or headset. She knew it was quite possible that any comm headset could be wireless, but there should be some provision for interference or dead batteries. *There.* She found what she was looking for, a small box beside one of the desk monitors, with a pair of jacks and control knobs, probably for volume. She checked the desk drawers and found a headset in one. It had a cable terminating in a plug that matched the jacks.

"Found it," she said, turning on the monitor. The dust on this desk had also been disturbed relatively recently.

The monitor screen was now on, but displayed a login prompt. "It wants a password," she announced, and Rico and Avril came over to see.

Jackie entered "comms/comms" at the prompt, not really expecting it to work, and it didn't. She picked up the keyboard to check the underside, but there was no helpful scrap of paper or anything else that might indicate the password. Rico began going through the drawers.

The upper right one was locked. Rico grunted, then pulled out a knife and slid it into the gap between drawer and desk, jimmying the mechanism. With a clunk, the drawer slid open, but to all their disgust, the drawer was empty.

"Why would anyone lock an empty drawer?" Boutelle asked.

"Habit. Whoever it was must have cleaned it out before they left."

"Well, dang," Jackie said. "I was hoping to access the comm logs. That should tell us when the last traffic was."

"I'm going to download all the base logs anyway," Rico said. "That will have the information."

"Wouldn't it be encrypted?" Jackie said.

"Maybe, but even so, it will be twenty-year-old encryption with what were UDT codes to start with," Rico said. "Ducayne can unravel it."

"So that was why you wanted to check out the base. What if someone has changed the codes in the meantime?"

Rico shrugged. "He may still be able to decode it."

"Even if not," Avril added, "the fact that the codes were changed tells us something."

"That someone has been using this base and doesn't want UDT to know about it," Jackie said.

"Exactly."

"All right. Rico, you said something about downloading the base logs. How do you propose to do that?"

"From the server room. Worst case I just pull out the drive modules, but it shouldn't come to that. Come on," he said, "it should be this way."

Jackie and Avril followed, Jackie wondering if this was something Rico had been recently trained to do, or if something like this had been part of his duties back when he worked for Hopkins. Given how easily Hopkins had followed the *Sophie* to Chara III, the latter wouldn't have surprised her.

∞ ∞ ∞

Aboard the Sophie, *departing Gliese 832*

True to his word, Rico had siphoned off the data from the base's computers without having to remove their storage modules. He *had* removed some back panels and physically connected cables between something in their interiors and the portable unit he'd carried in with him, muttering all the while.

Jackie thought she was used to old tech, given the age of her ship, but these computers seemed more primitive than even that. She caught Rico muttering something about stone knives and bearskins, but he seemed amused, not frustrated.

With Rico's mission accomplished—she was sure it was one —the trio secured the base much as they had found it, then made their way back to the *Sophie*.

Although they discussed it, there was really no point in speculating about just who had been using the abandoned base. There was some unencrypted data in with what Rico had taken, but it was mostly routine—and outdated—navigational data, copies of regulations or manuals, and similar not very useful information. Until the relevant logs were decrypted, they didn't have sufficient information to tell whether the previous visitors had been Velkaryans, pirates, or just sightseers.

Their own sightseeing satisfied, the *Sophie* departed, climbing away from the planet so it could make the warp jump to Delta Pavonis.

Chapter 18: Trouble with the Dean

Drake University, next day

Hannibal Carson had just dismissed the class when his omni beeped a message alert. He looked at the text.

"*Report to my office. Now. - Matthews.*"

Uh oh, Carson thought. *What paperwork have I forgotten this time?* He finished packing up his things and, after a brief stop at his own office, made his way to the Dean's. The door was open. He rapped on it as he entered, and Matthews looked up from his desk.

"You wanted to see me?" Carson said.

"Close the door and sit down, Dr. Carson."

Carson did so, with a feeling of trepidation at his boss's tone.

Matthews studiously ignored Carson for a moment, finishing up something on his desk computer, then he looked up. "You never told me what you found on your little expedition to the Anderson Wildlife Preserve. I'm glad to see you weren't eaten by any leopards."

"Uh, no. Thank you, sir." Carson paused, wondering what this was really about. "The fact is, we didn't find any arrowheads, spearpoints, or any other evidence that the area had been part of the range of the ancient Sawyerites. We did a few test digs, but we didn't find anything like that."

"So, you found something else?" Matthews said, leaning forward.

Did he know something? How? "I didn't say that."

"It's precisely what you didn't say that concerns me. I had an interesting but, frankly, embarrassing conversation at the reception after the board meeting last night."

Uh oh. "Conversation, sir? What about, if I may ask?"

"When one of the board members asked me 'were you the one involved in that find in the Anderson Preserve,' and I had no idea what in the world he was talking about, what do you suppose my reaction was? And he was talking about an archeological find, not anything related to biology or ecology." Matthews leaned forward, his voice lowering ominously, "So tell me, Carson, what *did* you find, and why did you see fit not to tell me?"

"I wanted to tell you," Carson said. It was true. After all of Matthews taunts about von Dänikenism and ancient astronauts, he would have loved to rub Matthews' face in it. Just not like this. "But the government wants it kept secret, at least until they decide how to release the news."

"Seriously? You want me to believe that there's a government coverup over some archeological find? The term 'structure' was used. What was it really, a few stones piled up into a hunting fence or something?"

Carson understood the reference, of course. Some paleolithic societies, on Earth and elsewhere, had constructed angled stone fences, also called kites from their shape, to funnel stampeded prey into a corral or a killing zone. Finding such on this planet would be interesting, the first evidence the natives had ever been so advanced, but hardly worth keeping a secret. "Not exactly," he said.

"Then what, exactly? What's this big secret? And I don't want to hear that you can't tell me."

"But—" *Screw it.* "All right. It was a pyramid. With evidence of advanced construction techniques."

Matthews' face turned deep red; his fists clenched. "I've had enough of your von Däniken nonsense, Carson. I'm this close to having your ass walked out of here. . . ."

As Matthews shouted, Carson calmly unfastened his omni, expanded the screen, and brought up an image of the entrance to the pyramid, its door partially open, and showing the elaborate carvings surrounding it. Carson and his guide, Dundee, were standing in front of it. Alex Finley had taken the picture. Wordlessly, he handed the omni to Matthews.

"What's this?"

"That was taken at the base of Pete's Peak. Look at the metadata for the time and location if you want. It's not a volcanic plug, it's a pyramid, covered over with a meter or so of soil and some vegetation."

Matthews examined the image. While he might have been a bit of a martinet when it came to administrative details, he had also been a pretty good field archeologist in his day. He zoomed and panned the image, the redness fading from his face. He looked at Carson.

"Has this area ever been cleared? Any sign of forest fire or the like? Drought?"

"No." Carson knew why he was asking but didn't say anything else.

"But this vegetation doesn't look more than a couple of hundred years old, yet well over fifty. That isn't possible. What kind of stone is this?" He pointed at the pyramid itself, where the carvings had been cleared of dirt.

"I'm not certain," Carson said. It had defied ready analysis. "The image color is pretty close to reality, a kind of grayish pink, like granite but very fine-grained. Maybe rose quartz, but not translucent. Hard."

"I don't recognize the style of the carvings, but I suppose there's no reason I would. But why haven't we seen any other signs of old Sawyerite civilization?"

Carson chose his next words carefully. "I'm not at liberty to go into details, sir, but I have seen similar carvings before. Just not on this planet."

Matthews glared at him. "If this—"

Carson held up his hand to cut off the tirade before it started. "Sir, do you remember about a year ago, when I had been jumped by tomb raiders on Verdigris?"

Matthews paused, thinking. "Do you mean that time you came in here with a story about being left with nothing but a radioactive talisman? One you couldn't show any providence for because the site had been contaminated?"

"Exactly."

"I don't see the connection."

Carson reached into his pocket and pulled out the talisman he'd retrieved from his office. He handed it to Matthews. "The one I found on Verdigris was like this one, but broken. Notice the shape?"

"Of course, a kind of squared circle. What about it?"

Carson picked up his omni and zoomed in part of the image, saying, "Technically, it's called a supercircle, a particular mathematical construct. But that's not what's important." He handed the omni back to Matthews, the image now focused on a detail in the carvings around the doorway. "Notice that recess?"

Matthews looked. "It's the same shape."

"Exactly. When this talisman is inserted into that recess, the door slides up. Or at least it would, if the interior passage hadn't been choked with mud. We got it open about a meter."

"You're saying this talisman is a *key* to that pyramid?"

"Not just that. This pattern?" Carson pointed out the irregular pattern of colored gems inlaid on one face of the flat stone, together with engraved lines connecting some of them. "That's a star map. The stone in the center represents Alpha Centauri."

"If this is some kind of elaborate joke, Carson—"

"It's not. Look, Doctor Matthews, it's hardly controversial that the planet we're on was terraformed some sixty-five million years ago, and likewise for many other planets in our neighborhood. Correct?"

"Correct," Matthews grudgingly conceded, "but—"

"And we know of some half-dozen planets with species currently or in the relatively recent past capable of making tools, yes?"

"I know where you're going with this, Carson. You wonder if it might not be possible that somewhere a civilization arose sooner than it did on Earth, just as we got a head start over the timoans or now-extinct Sawyerites, or the others. That's the argument you want to make, right?"

"Yes."

"All right," Matthews said, "for the sake of argument, let's ignore the jumpstart human civilization got by having access to hundreds of millions of years' worth of fossil fuels that recently terraformed planets just don't have. And yes, by comparison to

Earth's age, sixty-five million years is recent. Even ignoring that advantage, where are they? Why didn't we bump into them as soon as we arrived in the Alpha Centauri system for the first time? Better yet, why didn't they visit us even before that?

"And don't give me any of that von Däniken bullshit. You know as well as I do that humans were perfectly capable of, and did, build everything on Earth that he claimed ancient astronauts were responsible for."

"I won't. I completely agree with you on that." Carson was sorely tempted to spill the whole story, about the pyramids on St. Jacobs and Verdigris, the ruined Kesh city at Zeta Reticuli, the crashed alien ship at Kapteyn's star, and even Elizabeth Sawyer's encounter and the possible connection with some UFO sightings in the old Project Bluebook files. He was tempted, but he knew that Matthews would only take it as evidence that Carson had lost his marbles, and it would reveal information that Homeworld Security and, now, the Sawyers World government wanted kept secret.

"But," Carson went on, "consider the possibility that such spacefaring aliens, if they existed, would have their own agenda and might well have their own reasons for avoiding contact. Look at how we've limited contact with most of the natives on Taprobane, for example."

"Limited, yes, but not avoided completely. You've worked with a timoan on some digs yourself, haven't you?"

"All right, that's fair. But our discussion makes the government's point, doesn't it? If we as archeologists can't even agree on what this represents, then consider the effect that releasing evidence, however ambiguous, of possible spacefaring aliens would have on the general population. What do you think the Velkaryan Party, for example, would do with it?"

"Those lunatics?" Matthews settled back in his seat and shook his head. "Very well. I understand why you were asked not to publicize this. But you should have let me know. I can keep a secret as well as the next person, and I wouldn't have been caught unaware when someone asked me about it. That makes the department look bad."

"I'm sorry. Can I ask who mentioned it? You said a board member?"

"I don't know if I should say. He just mentioned that he'd heard a rumor."

"Never mind, then. I was just curious." Carson knew that most of the board members were either senior academics, retired politicians, or well-connected business leaders. That number certainly included several with family ties to the First Landers, by now they all must know about the pyramid. Pete Finley's grandson had been with him when they uncovered it, although anyone closely connected to him wouldn't have had to ask about a rumor.

"I'll let this incident slide, Carson, because you seem to have had an honest reason for not telling me. But I get the distinct impression that there's a lot more you're not telling me, and frankly I don't like that. I'll be keeping my eye on you, and if I find you doing anything not in the university's best interests, well. . . ."

Carson pocketed the talisman and retrieved his omni. "I understand, sir. I always keep the university's interests in mind." *Well, mostly.* "Will that be all? I have end-of-term grading to work on."

"Very well, Carson. Get back to it, then."

Carson made a hasty exit before Matthews thought to ask any more questions, like just where he got the talisman or how he knew it would open the pyramid.

As he walked back to his office, he knew he was going to have to discuss this with Ducayne. For one thing, he should be told that rumors of the recent find were already spreading. Carson also wondered what to do about Matthews. If the Dean could be read into the whole thing without blowing a gasket, he could be very helpful in covering for Carson. On the other hand, Carson was planning to take at least a year's sabbatical to go chase Ducayne's rabbits, so maybe he should just let it lie. Either way, he should talk to Ducayne.

Chapter 19: Secret Identities

Interstellar space, three days later

"I'm going to take us out of warp for a position check," Roberts announced. "Everyone secure for zero-gee."

"Okay, good," Rico said. "We want to change the registration before we get to the Delta Pavonis system anyway. Might as well do it now." He reached a seat and strapped himself in. Boutelle also buckled in.

Roberts gave them a quick look to check they were secure, then dropped *Sophie* out of warp. She looked over at Rico again. "You're sure this is going to work?" she asked.

"No problem. Now, what would you like as the ship's temporary name? What did you tell Ducayne?"

"I told him the *Seraphim*," Jackie said.

"Interesting choice, but sure. Close enough to *Sophie* that if you react to that, you can pretend you misheard," Rico said.

"So how do I change the identification codes?"

"Well, there is a way to do it manually through the ship's computers and access to the circuits, but it's a pain in the butt. This is easier." He held up his omni. "I have a handy app. I just need to jack into a specific port behind one of the access panels. May I?"

"It *is* reversible, and it won't do anything that might strand us out here, right?"

"Yes, it's actually easier to reverse than to do. And no, it doesn't touch the drive systems. Much as I like your company,

I'm not ready for that kind of long-term commitment," he said, and winked.

"*Ahem*," Boutelle cleared her throat loudly.

"It wouldn't be that long," Jackie said to Rico. "If I didn't kill you first, and Avril didn't, we'd run out of life support in a couple of months."

"Ah, there is that. Not to worry, though. So?"

"I don't remember," Boutelle said, "but doesn't the ship have a name or number painted on the side?"

"A long time ago," Roberts said. "The markings have long since faded or burnt off. They were kind of irrelevant anyway. If you look closely, you can just make out an 'S' on the starboard side and part of a 'phi' on the port. That's one reason I chose the name *Seraphim*."

"Ah, clever."

"So," Rico said again, "shall we make the change?"

It was probably safe. Rico had enough sense of self-preservation to not do anything deliberately suicidal, and Ducayne's team had made modifications to the *Sophie* beyond just the auxiliary antimatter power. "All right. Which panel?"

Rico examined his omni's screen. "Charlie-Papa-one-four." He turned the screen so Jackie could see it. It showed a diagram of a Sapphire cockpit, highlighting one of the portside access panels, marked CP-14.

The panel was near the deck in a position that would be awkward to reach under gravity, near one of the control panel supports, but by flipping herself upside-down, she put it at comfortable face level. She had the panel off a minute later and handed it to Boutelle.

"Now what?" Jackie asked.

Rico showed her another diagram on his omni. "Maintenance port to your right." He handed her one end of a cable. "Plug that in."

She found the port, and did so. "It's in."

"One moment." He tapped out a sequence on his omni's screen. He muttered a bit, tapped it a few more times, then undid the cable. "There, done. You can unplug."

"That's it?" Jackie said as she passed back the cable.

"It won't stand up to a detailed search of your logs, that's more complicated, but yes," Rico explained while Jackie replaced the panel. "Your transponders will squawk with the new number —still a Sapphire, registered out of Sawyers World with the name *Seraphim*—and that links to a new private key for your ship's encrypted messages."

"Sawyers World, not UDT? Does their government know about this?"

"If someone checks their database, they'll find a Sapphire registered under that number, with a name either 'not given' or 'Seraphim' if Ducayne updated it. It's a legitimate entry." Rico said. "Well, sort of. At least, that's what they told me in the briefing."

"What about my courier data?"

"What courier data? The *Sophie* was never going to Delta Pavonis. There's a flight plan for the *Seraphim*, or at least her new registration number. But don't worry, the data is still there; when we revert her back to the *Sophie* it will be like nothing ever happened."

"Handy, that."

"I think so. There were a few times I could have used that in a previous life."

Jackie shook her head and smiled to herself at that. *I'll just bet.* She finished her position check and adjusted the course directly for Delta Pavonis.

"All right, gentles. Secure from zero-gee and prepare for gravity. We're going to warp."

∞ ∞ ∞

"We should change your identity too, Jackie," Avril Boutelle said when they were under-way. "You're known as the pilot of the *Sophie*. Someone might wonder if you show up flying another ship."

"I assume you have something in your bag of tricks to change the ident on my omniphone," Jackie said.

"Sure, but you should also change your appearance. I assume you had that green hair last time you were there?"

"Of course, but—"

"Time to change it up then. What color was it originally?"

"Green," Jackie said wryly. She'd had conversations like this before.

"No, before that. Do you dye it or take pills?" Some people changed hair color like they changed clothes, although most spacers left it natural. One less thing to worry about.

"No, it's naturally green," Jackie said, and smiled at Boutelle's reaction. "It's a mutation."

"What? How?"

"How does any mutation occur? It was probably radiation-related, although it might have been something my mother ate before she realized she was pregnant. I'm lucky that was the only effect it had. You knew I was born on the Eta Carinae deep-space expedition, didn't you?"

"Oh, right, somebody mentioned that at the dinner at Rick's Place. But kids have been born to moms exposed to radiation before and since, I never heard of green hair."

"Apparently, it's some kind of structural change in the pheomelanin, and since Mom's naturally blonde, I don't have enough eumelanin to make my hair black or brown. And that's about as much biology as I know. At least it doesn't turn my skin green."

"Oh, wow. But still, if we can change the color, so much the better. I guess we can dye it. How do you feel about being a brunette?"

"You brought hair dye?"

"Part of my standard kit. You never know when you might want a quick change."

"That means rinsing it into my hair and dumping the excess, right?"

Boutelle nodded. "Yes. That's the usual way. We can just brush it into your eyebrows. Why?"

"Do we have to? I don't want to get any crud in the ship's recycling systems that they're not designed for."

"Oh. Good point. Crap."

There was an alternative. Jackie wasn't crazy about it, but it was preferable to getting dye in the ship's gray-water system. "There is another way. But don't you dare tell Rico or anyone else about it. And especially not Carson."

"Okay," Boutelle said, mystified. "What?"

"The ship's blackwater system goes to a holding tank that I just dump when I'm planetside. But that means we can't use the sink."

"Then what . . . oh. *Oh.*" Her eyes widened. "Yes, you have my word. Not a soul."

"Then let's get it over with." The ship's plumbing fixtures were all stainless, and Jackie knew she kept all parts of the ship impeccably clean, so in theory, it would be no different than dying her hair over the sink. But she'd never until now considered the idea that she might have to stick her head in the toilet bowl.

Chapter 20: Carson Attacked

Sawyer City

It had been a long day, and Hannibal Carson looked forward to getting home. Work always seemed to pile up toward the end of term, and his discussion of the pyramid with Matthews hadn't helped. It was a pleasant enough evening, and Carson had walked the two kilometers from campus to his apartment building.

He unlocked the door and had just entered his apartment when he was suddenly shoved from behind. Two large men pushed in, one grabbing Carson as the other slammed the door shut behind him. Carson tried to react, elbowing his first attacker in the gut and twisting away, but the other was on him and dealt him a staggering blow to the head.

Dazed, Carson stumbled forward, reaching for the omni on his left wrist with his other hand, trying to make a call for help, or at least activate the mic so he could tell it to. The first man, behind and to the right, grabbed his arm and pulled it away before he could activate the omniphone. The other grabbed his left arm and wrenched the omni off his wrist.

"Oh no you don't," the man growled as he tossed it aside.

Whatever these thugs wanted, it couldn't be good. Held now by both arms, Carson tried desperately to sweep his opponents' legs out with his own. They sidestepped, and Carson's own legs were knocked out from under him. He sagged but was still being held up by the thugs. One hit him, open handed, hard across the back of his head.

"Stop struggling before we have to hurt you. We just want to talk."

"Bullshit," Carson snapped. "Then make an appointment. My office hours are posted."

The thugs dragged him over to his desk chair and forced him to sit, still holding him. As the bigger of the two held him down in the chair, pushing on his shoulders, the other produced a zip-tie from a pocket and strapped one of Carson's legs to the leg of the chair, despite his struggles. The man tried to grab Carson's arms and pull them behind the chair back, but between Carson's struggles and the big thug holding him down, it wasn't working.

"Fuck this," the man said, and pulled out pistol. He stepped to the side where Carson could see him and pointed the weapon. "Freeze, asshole."

Carson stopped struggling. The man had angled himself so that his buddy wasn't in his line of fire, and Carson had no doubt he'd shoot. If they really just wanted to talk, he could hear them out. It wasn't like he had a choice.

"Fine, what did you want to talk about?" he said through clenched teeth. The man behind him tugged his arms back and got his wrists tied together, then stepped around in front of him, still out of the gunman's line of fire.

"Just a couple of questions, and a message," the gunman said.

Carson had a bad feeling about what the message might involve, but didn't see what he could do about it. "Message from who?"

"Someone you met a couple of weeks back. You interrupted his work. He doesn't like when somebody does that."

What was this guy talking about? Someone I met? Work? Oh. "You mean Reid?" The flicker of acknowledgment in the guy's eyes was all Carson needed. "He interrupted my work first. Tried to hijack it in fact. So, he's still alive? He didn't stick around to be patched up. We thought a leopard might have got him."

"One did. Tore his arm off, but he got away," the bigger man said. He seemed amused. Carson suppressed a grin.

"Shut it," the gunman told him.

"You said you had questions?" Carson said. If these were Reid's men, he wanted to deflect attention away from any feelings of vengeance they might have. Although from his amusement at the loss of Reid's arm, the big guy might be on Carson's side.

"What was in the pyramid?"

"What pyramid?" Carson asked.

The big man slapped him across the face, hard enough to dazzle Carson's vision momentarily. Carson shook his head to clear it and worked his now aching jaw. "Don't act stupid," the man said.

So much for him being on my side, Carson thought.

"Oh," he said, "that pyramid."

"Yeah, *that* pyramid. What was in it?"

"Mud."

The big man raised his arm again and Carson flinched. "No, I mean it. It was filled with dried mud. That's why Reid couldn't get the door open."

The big man lowered his arm and traded looks with the gunman, who shrugged. "Could be," the latter said.

"Didn't you dig it out?" he asked.

"I tried." Carson didn't see any point in hiding the truth, and it might encourage them to leave. "Got about a meter in, and it just kept going. It's going to take a major excavation to go any further. The government took over, I don't know what they're planning."

"You don't? You're the archeologist."

"And I hope they invite me in for the dig. But you know governments, they never do anything quickly. Sorry to disappoint, but if that's all you wanted to know, you can let me go now."

"Oh, we're not done yet."

Crap. He'd been afraid of that.

"Where's Rico?"

"Who?" That earned him another slap, and Carson felt his teeth loosen and tasted blood in his mouth.

"Let's try that again. Where's Rico?"

"I honestly don't know. I haven't seen him since he was medevac'd out by Space Guard, along with the rest of Reid's gang. He'd been shot, so maybe he's still in a traumapod." While that was all true, Carson knew Rico wouldn't have needed more than a day in the traumapod to treat his wound. He thought Rico might be off-planet with Jackie, but he didn't know that for certain, and he wasn't about to tell it to anyone who might be connected with the Velkaryans.

"After this long? I doubt it. Where is he really?"

"I told you, I don't know. I'm not his boss. I've been working at the university ever since I got back. I haven't seen him or heard from him."

"Is he off-planet?"

"How many times do I have to tell you, I don't know. Maybe. For all I know he's off smuggling illegal artifacts. Or maybe enjoying the sun on a Kakuloa beach. *I. Don't. Know.* Why do you care so much, anyway?"

"Reid wants him. He has a score to settle."

Carson could imagine. If those two ever met again, odds were that only one would walk away from it. Well, maybe not walk. As far as Carson knew, both their previous encounters had ended with them shooting each other.

"Sorry, I can't help you there."

"All right. Sorry to hear that," the gunman said, and gestured at the bigger man. "Okay let's do it."

"Do what?" Carson asked. It didn't sound good.

"I told you, we have a message to deliver. You've been a real pain in the ass, Carson. You need to stay out of our way." He raised his pistol. "If it were me, I'd just shoot you and be done with it, but Reid said he owes you one."

"So, what, you're going to torture me and then kill me? Just get it over with."

"No, Carson, you got it wrong," the gunman said, but did not lower his weapon. "Reid figures you saved his life. That bandage you put on his shoulder kept him from bleeding out when the leopard ripped his arm off. So, he owes you a life. That's now been repaid, so don't cross him, or us, again. Just to remind you —"

There was a *BANG*, and Carson felt a searing pain in his right forearm. He'd been shot.

"Reid said that's where you shot him. So now you're even." He looked up at the bigger man. "Let's go."

"Wait," Carson gasped. "Cut me loose at least. You just shot me!"

They were already halfway out the door. The smaller man had already reholstered his pistol, but turned back. "You'll live," he said. "I'm a good shot, that's just a graze. But it *will* leave a mark. Remember, stay out of our way."

With that, they were gone.

∞ ∞ ∞

Carson cursed. His right arm burned, and he was bleeding. He couldn't see the wound with his arms behind him. There was blood on the floor, but not a huge pool. He wouldn't bleed out. Probably.

He hoped someone had heard the shot and was doing something about it, but couldn't count on that. Where had his omniphone got to? He still had one leg free, and he managed to push himself around. The big guy had thrown it over in the corner. There it was!

Cursing the whole time, Carson shuffled and pushed the chair toward it. Then the chair snagged on the rug and toppled sideways, wrenching his left shoulder as it took the impact. He looked around to get his bearings and noticed that he'd left a trail of blood across the carpet. *That's going to be a bitch to clean*, the thought popped into his head.

Finally, he reached his omniphone. It appeared intact; he'd probably put it through worse in the field. But it was near his head, not his hands, still tied behind him. Twisting and turning, he managed to activate it with the side of his face.

"Emergency," he gasped. "Medical attention, this location." As the system acknowledged, he slumped back and relaxed as best he could to wait. Inside, he was still fuming over the attack. They'd picked the wrong guy to try to intimidate. There was no way he was going to stay out of their way now. He just had to figure out what he was going to do about it.

Chapter 21: A New Woman

Starship Seraphim, *deep space*

In the fresher aft of the captain's cabin, Avril Boutelle helped Jackie wash and rinse out the excess hair dye and do general cleanup.

"Okay, you're done," Avril said. "If you're worried about chemicals in your gray-water system, use a shower cap in the shower."

"And wash my hair over the toilet bowl again?" Jackie asked, not thrilled with the idea.

"That's up to you."

"Maybe I'll just flush the tanks when we get to Verdigris," Jackie said, unfastening the towel she had wrapped around her shoulders to keep them from getting dyed.

Avril, behind her, gasped and asked, "What happened to your shoulder?"

"What?"

"The scar on your left shoulder. Sorry, that's none of my business."

"No, that's okay. It's a bullet wound."

"Oh!" Avril sounded startled. "I didn't think . . . that is, it doesn't look like one. I mean, I've seen pictures, not actual. . . ." She trailed off, flustered.

"It was a ricochet. Messy but not deep, and I was too busy flying the ship to worry about it right away."

"You got shot on the ship?" Avril said, confused.

"No, just outside it. We were rescuing someone. Carson, as a matter of fact. Some Velkaryans objected."

"Velkaryans? Then it wasn't accidental."

"No," Jackie said grimly. "They were shooting at us pretty deliberately. Mind, we were shooting at them, too, but mainly to keep their heads down. I was a bit naïve. It was the first time I was in a shoot-out with Velkaryans." *Technically*, Jackie added to herself. In earlier incidents, she herself had been too busy getting to the ship to shoot back.

"The first time? There was more than once?"

Jackie saw something in Avril's expression, but couldn't identify it. Fear? Concern? Anticipation? "Yes. Velkaryans have a tendency to shoot first. Are you having second thoughts about the mission?"

"No, just . . . I don't know. I knew Rico had been shot, and more than once, but he's, well. . . ."

"He's a tough guy, the kind of man you'd expect to get involved in firefights. I'm just a pilot, and I still manage to get myself involved in them. You knew at a theoretical level that you might too, but this"—Jackie reached across with her right arm to pat her left shoulder—"makes it more real."

"Something like that. It's not the danger, though. On field trips I've faced plenty of things that might have killed me—no planet is tame—but that was impersonal; I was intruding on their territory, or potential prey, or just natural hazards of the environment. That's a bit different from people actively trying to kill you."

Jackie understood. She had visited enough wild planets in her life, starting in childhood, to be used to the idea that the universe might be a *dangerous* place, but it wasn't actually *malevolent*. The same couldn't be said for Velkaryans.

"Just be on your toes, same as any field trip. There's no reason for us to have any Velkaryan problems; we're just going to do a pick-up."

"Then why bring me and Rico along?"

Jackie didn't say anything. Despite any side missions Avril or Rico might have, she knew as well as Avril that the honest answer was "in case of trouble."

∞ ∞ ∞

"You look different," Rico said some hours later when he came out of his bunk space and into the galley where Jackie and Avril were watching an entertainment vid. "Did you do something to your hair? It looks shorter."

Jackie and Avril looked at each other across the table. Avril snickered.

"What?" Rico said.

"Nothing," said Jackie. "Different was what I was going for. Avril pointed out that I might be recognized as the owner of the *Sophie*, which could raise questions about the *Seraphim*."

"Ah. Smart move." He went over to the autochef and dispensed himself a coffee. He took a sip and turned back to them. "Although I think you should have gone with red instead of black. I've always liked redheads."

At their gasps, he winked and said, "I'm not as dumb as I pretend."

Chapter 22: Carson and Ducayne

Homeworld Security Headquarters, Sawyers World

"How's the arm?" Ducayne asked when Carson stopped by his office, and then, "I seem to be asking that a lot lately, between you and Rico."

"It wasn't much more than a graze," Carson said. "I'm glad the guy was as good a shot as he thought he was." Carson had given Ducayne the highlights over the phone before coming to see him. "And how is Rico? My visitors were very curious as to his whereabouts."

"Then I probably shouldn't tell you where he is," Ducayne said. "But he's fine too, last I heard."

"So, he's off-planet?"

"Why were they interested in Rico? And what else" Ducayne asked, ignoring Carson's question.

Carson took the hint. Ducayne wasn't going to tell him where Rico was, and he had to agree that was for the best. "Apparently Reid, the guy who bushwhacked us at the pyramid dig, managed to make it out alive despite his wound, although it seems a leopard tore his arm off."

"Oh really? We'll have to check into whose been buying prosthetic arms lately. So, it was a revenge call? And they didn't kill you?"

"Apparently, Reid decided he owed me one. The bandage I'd put on him helped keep him alive despite the torn arm. If they catch up with Rico, he won't be so lucky."

"Rico can take care of himself, but I wouldn't count on the gratitude of Velkaryans for long. Maybe you should get off-planet. Go visit your timoan friend. Maybe I can signal the *Sophie* to have it come back by way of Epsilon Indi."

Carson shook his head. "No. I can't be running off-planet every time somebody makes life a little rough for me. I've already done that twice."

"Those other times weren't exactly running away," Ducayne said. "You were on missions I gave you."

"Even so. Besides, it's almost end-of-semester, and I need to finish it up. That brings up what I wanted to see you about."

"Oh, not your evening visitors? Right, you had left me a message before that. So, what's on your mind?"

"The cat is out of the bag," Carson said.

"What cat, and what bag?"

"That Pete's Peak is a pyramid, and apparently built by space-faring aliens. The Velkaryans already know, that's one thing the thugs last night were asking about. But my boss, Dean Matthews, asked me about it after someone asked *him* about the 'structure' found in the Anderson Wildlife Preserve."

Ducayne frowned. "What did you tell him?"

"As little as I could, but probably more than you'd like." Carson recounted the conversation he'd had with Matthews, concluding with, "I don't know what you want to do in terms of damage control. Could we brief Matthews on the whole thing, or at least more of it, and swear him to secrecy? It would make my day-job easier."

Ducayne grimaced. "That wouldn't be my first choice. It might be better if the Sawyers World government did that; Matthews doesn't have the UDT connections that you do."

Ducayne referred to Carson's earlier days in the UDT military, before he'd left Earth, and the security clearance Ducayne had reminded him of when they'd first met.

"Of course," Ducayne continued, "I'd rather just keep the whole thing quiet, but that may no longer be an option. This isn't the first leak I've heard of, and not just here on Sawyers World.

That spaceship wreckage off Belize stirred up a mess of rumors, and the cover story is coming apart. Pictures of the alien writing on the instruments got out. The lowered classification on Elizabeth Sawyer's fifty-year-old close encounter report didn't help either. Too many people are becoming aware of too many pieces."

"And starting to put two and two together?" Carson said.

"Yes, but so far mostly refusing to believe that they add up to four, and settling for *pi*," Ducayne said. "So, we're trying to come up with an acceptable story to convince them, or at least the public, that it's really three."

Carson paused to wrap his head around that metaphor. "So, acknowledge that there's evidence of spacefaring aliens a lot more recent than the Terraformers, but not that they might still be active in T-Space today. Something like that?"

Ducayne nodded. "Yes, something like that. Thoughts?"

"I have to admit, I like the first part of that. I've been pushing that as a hypothesis for years, given some of the architectural similarities we've seen between neolithic sites on different planets. Too many pyramids, for one. Mostly that got me laughed at."

"And the second part?"

"That's probably close to the truth anyway, at least as far as the current edges of T-Space. Elizabeth Sawyer is the only person who has seen a Kesh—if that is what she saw—anywhere within twenty-five light-years of Sol, and the only other evidence we have is thousands of years old."

"You said Pete's Peak had only been buried a couple of hundred years ago, at most."

"I won't tell if you won't," Carson said, grinning. "But that's the point. If the Kesh are still active among the terraformed planets we're currently aware of, they're keeping very quiet about it. Whether for good reasons or bad, well, that's something you want me to find out, isn't it?"

Ducayne looked at him thoughtfully, then gave him a short nod. "I probably wouldn't have put it that way, but yes. Before that, though, if any of this information does get released, you're going to be in the spotlight. Even if we tried to keep your name out of it, someone is going to twig to your previous work and ask you questions about it."

"You're right, and I don't think I want my name kept out of it. I put up with a lot of ridicule over that hypothesis. It will be nice to be vindicated."

"All right. But I'm not saying we'll release anything just yet. It needs to be coordinated with both my higher-ups and this planet's government. And it will probably be best to trickle it out gradually rather than make a big splash, sorry."

"No, I get it. Let people get used to the idea. The fact that there are terraformed planets out here freaked out a lot of people when it was announced. Of course, most of them went right back to ignoring it when the hubbub died down."

"It did, but you know as well as I do, that fact isn't rubbed in everyone's face on Earth the way it is for those of us out here. People are happy to ignore it, and the government is happy to let them. Hell, even the Velkaryans get more traction on Earth from their other political agendas than from their 'terraformed planets for Terrans' nonsense."

Carson smirked. "So how do you think the Velkaryans will react to having news of spacefaring aliens made public?"

Ducayne looked thoughtful. "Hard to say. It might encourage some xenophobia, and swing folks to their side, but I'd like to think that it will encourage most people to see them for the idiots they are. On balance, I don't think they'll like it."

"Then I *definitely* want the word to get out," Carson said, grinning despite the throbbing of the wound on his arm.

PART III
VERDIGRIS

Chapter 23: Vaughan

New Toronto, Verdigris

Vaughan glanced up from his data terminal to his assistant chief of production. "Is there any *good* news in this, Cardigan? It's good that the tank pressure test cell is back in operation, but it should never have exploded in the first place." He was sure that the facility had been sabotaged somehow—there had been an uptick in suspicious incidents since Burnside had killed two of his men—but there was no clear evidence. If Burnside was involved, he covered his tracks well.

"Yes sir, there is. If you'll read a bit further. . . ." He broke off at Vaughan's glare. "Well, bottom line is that even with the setbacks, production is up seven percent this last quarter."

"Up seven percent?" It should have been double that, with the extra shifts and mandatory overtime, but there had been supply line problems. Shipments had been late, or showed up with more-than-usual numbers of defective parts. Again, nothing he could prove was deliberate, but there was an old saying that concluded, "three times is enemy action." But that wasn't his assistant's fault. "Good work, Cardigan."

"Thank you, sir. But it brings up a new problem. We're running out of parking space for all those ships. We'll have to step up ferry runs, although 784 Base is nearly at capacity already. Should we expand it, or activate 832?"

"I think we'll leave 832 alone. We can expand 784, although I don't like the idea of having everything tied up there either. I'll take it up with the council. But don't let that slow down production; we'll find somewhere to put them. There are other options, just not as convenient."

Vaughan dismissed Cardigan and turned his thoughts back to the matter of Burnside. He had no doubt the man was working for Homeworld Security. Fortunately, the UDT only had a small contingent on this planet, mostly concentrated in Verdigris City, and involved with administration. Still, he had to assume that Burnside was, somehow, sending them regular reports, and it would only be a matter of time before Homeworld Security sent more agents, both overt and covert, to investigate and disrupt Velkaryan plans.

He couldn't wait for a decision from the Velkaryan Council. He'd send them a report, and it was their privilege to reverse his decisions if they chose, but Burnside had been running around loose for over a month now. If he had gotten a message out to Sawyers World, the response could be arriving at any time now. It was time to move more ships off-planet, some to the base at Gliese 784, some to the Velkaryan base on *Bleu de Gex*, this planet's big moon. It was also time—past time—to get serious about finding and eliminating Burnside. There had been surreptitious monitoring programs scanning citywide video feeds for his face, and checking credit transactions for odd patterns, but the fact that those programs tried to keep themselves hidden limited their effectiveness. It was time to step up the game. He reached for his omniphone.

Chapter 24: Arrival

Nearing the Delta Pavonis system

"All right, people," Jackie Roberts announced. "We're approaching Delta Pavonis. We're going to drop out of warp, but it's not going to be what you're used to."

"What do you mean?" Boutelle asked.

"I'm going to shut down the warp field slowly, rather than all at once. It's going to feel a bit like going over the top of a roller coaster."

"But why?"

"Stealth move," Rico said. "Collapsing the warp field suddenly sends out a pulse of gravity waves that detectors can pick up. So does doing it slowly, but they're weaker and a different wavelength, so we won't be detected entering the system."

Jackie stared at him, surprised that he knew. It wasn't something most ships could do; it had been one of Ducayne's modifications. "Is that something you learned about recently, or are you speaking from experience?"

Rico grinned. "I didn't know the technical details before, but yes, we had occasion to do that in my, uh, previous job. The *Starhawk*"—that had been Hopkins' ship—"had some special modifications itself."

"Like missile launchers," Jackie said, frowning. "I remember."

"Yes, those too."

"Anyway," Jackie said, turning back to Boutelle, "he's right. I don't want anyone to know we're in the system until we've taken care of a few things first. We *could* still be detected by someone doing gravity research, but even then, they probably wouldn't realize what they were seeing.

"So, strap in. This might be a little uncomfortable."

∞ ∞ ∞

Normally the drop out of warp is like stepping off a high-diving board, or when the thrusters cut off after a launch. Weight just goes away instantly, all at once. By the time the body registers what's happening, it's over, except for the weightlessness. This time, as Jackie had said, it was like going over the top of a hill on a very large, very fast, roller coaster. Or perhaps like the beginning of a trip on a very fast down elevator. Gravity took a couple of seconds to go away completely as the warp field faded out, and they all felt a bit like they'd left their stomachs behind.

"Whoo!" Boutelle said. "That was actually kind of fun. Can we do it again?"

Jackie grinned at her. "We will. There are a couple more jumps to make before we officially announce our presence." She turned back to where Rico sat. He was gripping the chair arms, not looking nearly as thrilled as Avril had. "Are you doing all right?"

"I'm fine," he said grimly. "I've just never been a fan of that particular maneuver."

"Could be worse," she said. "Do you remember Marten, the timoan?"

"The one with you at Chara? Yeah, why?"

"He hates microgravity at the best of times. I think I'd have to sedate him before putting him through that."

"I'll settle for a stiff drink. Got any aboard?"

Jackie considered the request. *Sure, why not.* "I normally keep it locked up in flight," she said, but tapped a sequence on her control panel. "But go ahead, the autochef will dispense one for you."

Rico reached for his seat belt, but then left it alone. "Nah, I'm good. Keep it for if we have to do a bunch of those in short order. But thanks."

"No problem," she said, touching the control to re-lock the autochef.

Chapter 25: Burnside Undercover

New Toronto

Jordan Burnside had been living in New Toronto as Jean Lefebvre, among other names, for over a month now. He had a one-room apartment in an area of town with a high transient population. Not the seediest part of town, but enough to discourage attention from either the locals or the cops. The really bad areas were prone to having gangs of Velkaryan thugs come through to "clean the place up." Often, those raids went unreported in the local media. When they did make the news, the reports were couched in terms that made it seem they were doing everyone else a favor by removing criminal and other "undesirable" elements. Never mind that some of those undesirables ended up being recruited into the Velkaryan patrols themselves, and most of the others found their way back within a few days. While they were still building their support base, the Velkaryans didn't actually want to solve the problem, just appear to be solving it.

Meanwhile, Burnside had been scouting the city, largely on foot, always disguised, and analyzing the economy of the city, with particular attention to anything that might have Velkaryan connections. In short, spying. At irregular intervals, but roughly weekly, he managed to send a report to the UDT office in Verdigris City.

What he had discovered alarmed him. As far as he could tell, companies like Green Sky Armaments or Hansa Astrospace were buying far more raw materials and components than could be accounted for by what they sold. Either they were the planet's most inefficient industries, or their extra output was being quietly diverted to . . . somewhere. Since he didn't have the ability to run a full forensic accounting trace on everything they did, it was entirely possible that he was missing some innocent explanation. That's what Henry Prentiss had thought when his previous agent had reported some of the same things. Without some hard evidence to justify an investigation, neither the UDT nor local Verdigris authorities could launch the kind of forensic audit to prove anything. Even if they could, Burnside suspected that the Velkaryan books were sufficiently cooked to hide anything they wanted hidden, short of an inspection team looking over the shoulders of everyone on the factory floor.

Burnside had, in fact, made a couple of visits to Velkaryan-owned factories, in the guise of a salesman, or a repair technician, or riding in a trash disposal truck, or other subterfuges, but the last time he'd almost been caught. His disguise hadn't been sufficient to fool the automated recognition system the factory cameras were using. Fortunately, he'd noticed the sudden hyper-alertness of those near him in response to some signal, and had escaped before armed security showed up.

He had also engaged in a little sabotage. Nothing too dramatic, although there was that one time where he'd managed to hack the control system for a pressurization test facility, and the resulting tank rupture had caused damage that had taken two weeks to repair. The tweak to the computer responsible for controlling the propellant mixing at the Green Sky ammunition plant had been the opposite of dramatic: the resultant batch might have been useful for starting campfires, but not for anything more energetic. A round made with that would have been lucky to get the bullet out of the barrel of a gun. Alas, they had caught the problem in testing before that batch had made more than a few cases of ammunition.

Burnside knew that it wouldn't take Vaughan long to guess that a sudden increase in accidents and quality-assurance failures was the result of deliberate action rather than happenstance or worker fatigue. Already he was seeing increased vigilance around the plants, and new layers of software security when he tried to hack into their systems. He had collected a lot of information, some of it in isolated snippets that made little sense. What was "784," for example? He hoped that Prentiss, or Ducayne when the information was forwarded, could fit it into a larger picture. But his game here was almost up. If he didn't get a pick-up signal soon, he would make his way back to Louisbourg and then to Verdigris City.

Chapter 26: Carson and Proxima

Carson's Office, Drake University

Carson's omni chimed with its "unknown caller" tone. Carson looked at it, annoyed. It was supposed to block unknown calls. He checked the ID—"Office of Technoarcheology." *Ducayne.*

"Carson here," he said.

"Do you have anything scheduled for the next three days?" Ducayne asked immediately, without greeting.

It was a Friday afternoon, and Carson had no classes to teach on Monday. "No," he said, "but you probably already knew that."

"There's something I'd like you to look at. Come on down to the office and I'll explain."

"Why would it take me three days to look at something in your office?"

"It's not here, but I don't want to explain it on the phone."

Ducayne was being his usual mysterious self. Carson sighed. He did have some work to do, but it could all be done on his datapad. "All right. When?"

"As soon as you can get here. See you then." The connection clicked off.

Carson sighed again and began collecting his things.

∞ ∞ ∞

Ducayne's office, Homeworld Security

"Take a look at this," Ducayne said, sliding a datapad across his desk to Carson. An image filled the screen.

Carson examined it. It showed an outdoor scene, part of a landscape. The colors were a bit off, but it showed a mostly flat plain, broken up by what seemed to be, except for their dark purple coloring, patches of scrubby vegetation. Several low, straight features criss-crossed it, each protruding no more than a few centimeters above the surrounding surface, if Carson judged the scale correctly. It looked like any of dozens of archeological sites Carson had visited, the low features being the remains of old walls or building foundations.

"An old building site," Carson said. "Without a good scale reference, or some surrounding context, I couldn't say where or what culture. What's wrong with the color?"

"Nothing," Ducayne said flatly. "You're sure it's not a geological feature?"

"Not a hundred percent sure, no. It could be some kind of intrusion into cracked bedrock that's eroded away, but I'd expect more randomness. This looks too regular. Have you asked a geologist?" Carson wondered where the picture was taken but knew better than to ask. If Ducayne wanted him to know, he'd tell him.

"I have. He said pretty much the same thing, except to ask an archeologist. That's why you're here. I want you to go look at it in person, see what you think, figure out what you can."

"Okay, but—"

Ducayne cut him off. "It's about seventy kilometers from Grainger Station, on Proxima-b. The *Lark* leaves in two hours. It's a four-hour trip. The pilot's name is Joe Riley."

"Wait, what? Proxima doesn't have any terraformed planets; it's a red dwarf." Red dwarf stars weren't suited to terraformed planets. The habitable zone was so close to the star that any planet orbiting within it would settle into a low frequency tidal resonance, if it didn't lock completely, within a few million years. But it would explain the odd coloration.

"You understand my concern. You'll be briefed on the way, not that there's much to brief. Grainger is mostly a research station. They stumbled across this a little while ago. If it is ruins, I want to know how long ago it was built, and even more so, why it collapsed and what happened to the builders."

"I can't do that in just a couple of days," Carson protested.

"No, but you can tell if it's artificial or natural, and if it's worth further exploration."

"I'll need equipment."

"What you'll need for a preliminary survey is already being loaded. Brown made a list." Ducayne referred to Malcom Brown, one of his staff with some kind of archeological training, although Carson had never quite learned exactly what.

"Is he coming too? Why do you need me?"

"Proxima-b is a higher-gravity world, and you'll probably be working in a suit. Brown isn't up for that on short notice. Black"—the other archeologist on Ducayne's staff who Carson had met, and he remained sure that neither was their real name —"has other commitments."

"All right," Carson said, nodding. "That's certainly better than anything else I had planned for the weekend."

∞ ∞ ∞

The starship Lark

The layout of the *Lark* was very similar, although not identical, to that of the *Sophie*. Hardly surprising, given that they were both Sapphires, although the *Lark* seemed a little newer and roomier than the *Sophie*.

"I don't have the range that most Sapphire's have," the captain, Joe Riley, explained when Carson commented on it. "Mostly I just do runs in the Alpha Centauri system, occasionally to Sol, so I converted some of the fuel tankage to cargo space and moved some of the bulkheads."

"Is this Proxima thing a regular run for you?"

"Yep, except for a couple of weeks ago. The *Lark* was due for maintenance. In fact, the *Sophie* took the run for me that time. So, you know Jackie Roberts?"

"Yes," Carson said. "She and I go back a way."

"A fine pilot," Riley said, "and a smart young woman. I knew her when she was just young."

"Really? How?"

"Second Eta Carinae expedition. You knew she was born on the first one, right?"

"Yes, but you said the second?"

"A few years later. It was a follow up to the first, revisiting some of the same planets and exploring a few places they didn't the first time. Jackie was no stranger to starships. She must have been four when the first one came back, so she and her parents had no problem going out again. She would have been eight when she came aboard. I was part of the crew on *Deepstar Three*." Riley paused, looking around the cabin. "Of course, those Deepstars were a lot bigger than this tiny thing."

"I would hope. I can't imagine living aboard ship for five years, even on something the size of a passenger liner."

"Oh, it's not like we were in space the whole time. We'd travel for a few weeks between stars, then stay planetside for a couple of months while the scientists did their work before going on to the next system."

"Still, it must have been rough on a kid. Were there others?"

"A few, yes. There were five ships in the exploration fleet."

Carson shook his head. His own youth on Earth had been very different, ultimately joining the military to pay for college. "Is that where she learned about ship systems?"

"Some, yes. Everybody got drilled on ship systems in case of emergencies, and as I recall, she had both an aptitude and an interest. Heck, most of the kids didn't mind getting their hands dirty, often literally. They were always checked by regular crew, of course, but by the end of the voyage, they were experts."

Carson had only heard bits of the story from Jackie, and was curious to hear more, but he also had a mission brief to read. Also, he wasn't sure how Jackie would feel about his discussing her past with someone without her knowledge. He knew he'd made blunders before in their relationship, and with how things had been going recently, he didn't want to blow it again.

∞ ∞ ∞

Proxima-b, Grainger Station

A light snow was falling as Captain Riley landed the *Lark* at Grainger Station. Carson watched the falling flakes as the transfer bus rolled out from the base toward the ship. Sawyer City rarely got snow, and here it fell strangely, more quickly. The gravity was higher here, and while on a terraformed planet the air might also be thicker, here the air was thinner, stripped away by the wind from the red star the planet orbited so closely.

The bus nudged up and sealed against the *Lark*'s airlock, and a few minutes later Riley introduced Carson to Tony Mazzone and Jennifer Rudloe, part of the station crew.

"Welcome," Mazzone said. "So, you're here to shed some light on our little discovery, eh?"

"If I can," Carson said. "I saw the pictures. To be honest, my first thought was that it was a natural formation, but your geologist says otherwise."

"I do," Jennifer Rudloe said. "I'm the geologist in question. Brad Simpson is the other one, but he hasn't been out to the site yet. He'll be coming with us this time, but he's seen the pictures too, and the samples I brought back. He's the one who suggested calling in an archeologist."

"You'll meet everyone shortly," Mazzone said, "but first, let's get the supplies unloaded."

∞ ∞ ∞

The trip out to the site was in an oversized aircar. It had additional rotors to compensate for the higher gravity and thinner atmosphere, and had been stripped to a bare frame to reduce weight. It reminded Carson of a kind of bizarre flying spider. He, Rudloe, and Simpson were in suits, both for warmth and breathing air.

"I don't imagine you've done any archeological digs in a suit," Simpson said, making conversation as they flew. "An occupational hazard for planetary geologists, I guess, but I can't imagine that's something you face."

"You'd be surprised," Carson said. In fact, just a few months earlier, he'd been examining an ancient spaceship wreck while wearing a suit, coincidentally also on a heavy planet orbiting a red dwarf star. He wasn't about to tell anyone that, though, so he added, "there are archeologists who specialize in relics of the early space age, a hundred, hundred-fifty years back. They'd be working on the Moon or Mars."

"Oh, I didn't know that."

"Not a huge field. But while I haven't done any digs on non-terraformed worlds"—that was technically true—"I have helped out with refueling operations on ice moons, for example, so I'm comfortable in a suit."

"Hah," Rudloe exclaimed. "*Nobody* is comfortable in a suit, but I know what you mean. They wouldn't have sent someone who wasn't."

"You've got a point," Carson agreed.

∞ ∞ ∞

The craft set down on a broad plain, dotted here and there with dark purple scrubby vegetation. There was no sign of snow here, although the ground was damp in places.

"From the surface, it sure looks like some kind of magmatic intrusion to fractured rock," Carson said.

"That was my first thought when we spotted it," Jennifer Rudloe said. "Unusual, because you don't normally get cracks running at ninety degrees like that, but not impossible."

"Have you excavated at all? These walls, or dikes, or whatever they are, how far down do they extend?"

"Only a little, through the loose rock at the base. Not far enough to find the bottom, so it could be a meter, could be hundreds of meters. Except the walls don't look igneous."

By then they had reached one of the so-called walls, and Carson knelt to examine it, and then the fragments at its base, picking through the chunks. "Really?" he said. "Some of this looks melted." He held up a piece a few centimeters across. The edges mostly looked fractured, with some erosion on the corners, but one side had a glassy appearance.

Simpson took it and held it close to his helmet visor, examining it. "Yes," he said, "but look at the grains. This is more like sandstone or even concrete. If that were igneous melt, it would have cooled slowly, leaving larger crystals."

"Not if it were something like agate or obsidian," Rudloe said.

"Well, no, but then it wouldn't have grain at all," Simpson said, passing the sample to her. "See?"

"You're right. This looks more like an impact melt, or maybe a fulgurite."

"Fulgurite?" Carson asked.

"Sand fused by a lightning strike," Rudloe said. "Except that the shape is wrong."

"Does this planet get lightning?"

"Yes, but not often."

     Alastair Mayer

"All right," Carson said. "I'm going to do a walk-through of the site, take some measurements, collect a few samples. If this is a ruin of some kind, there ought to be something other than just walls left. If anyone lived here, there should be other artifacts. Let's spread out and look. If you do find something that looks artificial, give me a holler."

∞ ∞ ∞

After an hour of wandering the site in higher gravity that he was used to, and in a suit, Carson called a halt. The others, being more acclimated to the gravity, were willing to keep going, but Carson didn't see any need.

"It's almost certainly artificial," he told them. "The wall thickness is too constant to be a natural phenomenon, there's almost no variation. I am surprised we've found no artifacts, but probably the place was abandoned long before it started to decay. We need to come back with metal detectors, ground-penetrating radar, that sort of thing."

"Artificial," Rudloe said. "Built by who?"

"I have no idea," Carson lied. In fact, he had three possible suspects, but not enough data to pick one, and none of which he was prepared to discuss with anyone but Ducayne just yet. "It's too old to have been anything built by humans, and nowhere near old enough to have been left by the Terraformers."

"So, aliens? We haven't seen anything more evolved here than this scrubby vegetation," Simpson said, gesturing around him, "and some primitive animal forms. How old do you think it is?"

"I'd need to get data on local erosion rates, then look at isotope dating and things like cosmic ray flux or anything else that can affect dating before giving a proper estimate. But, going on my gut feel, I'm guessing maybe one or two thousand years. Just don't quote me on that."

"A thousand years," Rudloe repeated. "So, built by some other spacefaring species. But why, and what happened to them?"

"I didn't say that."

"You didn't have to," she said. "The questions still stand."

"Maybe so," Carson allowed, "but I don't have the answers."

Chapter 27: Approach

Approaching Verdigris

"I'm going to put the *Seraphim* into orbit at the Verdigris-Gex L4 point," Jackie announced, referring to a point as far away from both Verdigris and its moon, Gex, as the moon was from the planet. "I want to be far enough away that we can't be spotted from either the planet or the moon. At least not until we're ready to land."

"Right," Rico said. "We need to contact Burnside first."

"And how do we do that?" Boutelle asked. "We can't use radio and there's too much damned skyweed to use a comm laser reliably."

Rico grinned. "We send down a signal flare."

"What?"

Jackie had already discussed this with Rico, so she explained: "We drop a meteor on New Toronto. We'll coordinate it with one of Burnside's prearranged time slots. If he is anywhere near there, he'll know about it."

Boutelle wasn't buying it. "As will everyone else. And just how big a rock are you talking about? Isn't that going to cause a lot of damage?"

"Everyone else will just assume it's a random bolide," Jackie said. "They happen. And no, it will be a small one, and detonate high in the atmosphere. A big flash and a loud bang. It will rattle a few windows, but it shouldn't break any. It won't really be a rock; it will be mostly ice."

"So that's another reason you topped up the tanks."

"Exactly."

∞ ∞ ∞

Fabricating their artificial meteoroid took a while. Because they were orbiting in the habitable zone—of course—the water didn't want to just freeze without a lot of it boiling off into the vacuum first. Jackie worked out a way to pre-chill their stored water to the slush point using the store of liquid oxygen, a waste product from pulling hydrogen out of the water to run the fusion reactors.

They filled a fabric bag with the slush, keeping it in the *Seraphim*'s shadow to stay cold. They mixed regolith into it re-trieved from a couple of small bodies drifting at the L4 point.

"I hate being here," Jackie said, midway through the process.

"You picked it. What's the problem?"

"The L4 and L5 points tend to collect dust and debris, at least temporarily. That's one reason we're here, it's semi-stable and anyone does look in this direction, we're just part of the debris. But that also means space is crowded here. I can't go to warp without worrying that we might hit something big enough to be a problem. Even something pea-sized would be nasty and possibly wreck the ship."

"Seriously?"

"As much as ten percent of the mass would convert to energy at the warp boundary. You do the math."

"No wonder you get claustrophobic."

"Yeah."

A while later, the "iceteroid"—as Jackie insisted on calling it, much to Rico and Avril's disgust—was ready. A ball of dust, cel-lulose fibers, and ice several meters in diameter. The fibers, from the ship's fabber stores, were to reinforce the ice so it didn't break up too high in the atmosphere.

"Are you sure they won't be a problem?" Avril asked. "I'd hate for that to reach the ground."

"No problem. Even pykrete—which has a lot more cellulose —isn't much stronger than concrete. A concrete meteor would break up in the atmosphere. It takes a nickel-iron or a really big stony to survive to the ground."

"And if they send up a sniffer and detect cellulose?"

Jackie just looked at her for a moment, not sure if she was serious. "We're talking about Verdigris? The skyweed planet? Tell me you didn't just ask that question."

Boutelle had the grace to blush. Of course, the air was already full of cellulose. "Ah, what question?"

"Exactly."

"Okay," Boutelle said. "So now what?"

"Now I work out some orbital mechanics. We want it to hit over New Toronto at a particular time, and it has to come from a direction that nobody would normally be looking. Out of the ecliptic. And *then* we have to get it into position and give it a push."

"So . . . ?"

"Give me a bit of time to work out the numbers, and we'll be on our way. There may not be enough time to get it there tomorrow night, more likely the night after."

"And in the meantime?" Boutelle's voice lacked enthusiasm.

"As I keep telling Carson, spaceflight is *supposed* to be boring. That's why there's a ship's library. Now, I have to go math."

Chapter 28: Signal

Interplanetary space, near Verdigris

Aboard the *Sophie*, or rather, the *Seraphim*, Jackie Roberts had positioned the ship well out from the planet so they could watch the entry of their "iceteroid" without any question of a connection between them and it. Jackie had oriented the ship so that its main telescope, normally used for navigation, was focused on the area around New Toronto.

"How long to impact?" Rico asked her.

"*Entry*. It's five minutes, thirty-two seconds to entry. It should take about another ten seconds after that to get deep enough into the atmosphere to explode. It had better not actually impact."

"Yeah, entry, that's what I meant," Rico said, then he added, "No, wait, I meant explode."

Jackie just sighed. She knew, or hoped, that Rico didn't mean any harm by it, but he did seem to have a fondness for blowing things up. It reminded her of Carson. *Is it just me, or are all guys like this?* She tried to think of some men she knew who didn't like explosions, but none came immediately to mind. Come to think of it, she didn't mind watching a good explosion either, as long as it was nowhere near her ship, or anybody else.

"Hey, Avril," she called back to the galley where Boutelle was seated. "Do you want me to pipe the telescope feed into the monitor back there, or are you busy with something else?"

"Are you kidding, and miss the fireworks? Of *course* pipe it back here!"

"Okay." Jackie touched the controls. "There you go." *Okay,* she decided, *I guess* everyone *likes a good fireworks show.*

She checked the clock. "Atmospheric entry in ten seconds." The seconds ticked over. "We should see something in three, two, one, now." She watched the screen intently, waiting for the first glimmerings of entry heating.

"Nothing's happening!"

"Wait for it . . . ." At plus-three seconds, the image showed a faint orange trail that rapidly grew brighter, leaving a trail of smoke and condensation.

"Is it going to hit?" Avril's worried voice called from the galley.

"No, watch," Jackie said. The trail grew brighter still, small sparks shedding from it, then suddenly it brightened, lighting up the sky around it with a mottled pattern of whites and greens where its light reflected off sky weed, and even a brief glare as the light bounced off nearby Lac Quebec. Then the screens quickly faded to blackness.

"Very nice," Rico said. "Too bad we can't hear the bang. That must have been loud."

"I hope we didn't break too many windows," Jackie said.

"What took it so long?" Avril said. "I was sure it must be about to hit the city."

"My fault," Jackie said. "The countdown was in realtime, but we're three light-seconds away. It just *looked* like it took longer."

"Now what?" Rico said. "Do we just hope Burnside got the signal and will make the rendezvous, or will he let us know somehow?"

"I don't see how he could miss it," Avril said. "Even if he were in a basement or cave, that meteorite will be in the news, probably for days. I wonder what the natives will make of it."

"I don't think he will have missed it. His message did specify a signaling window, after all. The question is whether or not he is in any position to acknowledge the signal. Unless we hear otherwise, we plan to be at the rendezvous spot in four days. That's the plan he set up, so we follow it."

"Okay," Rico said, "that brings us back to my question. Now what?"

"Now," Jackie said, "we warp out to a reasonable distance and then call back to Verdigris Space Traffic Control like we just got here. Let's get things secured for gravity."

∞ ∞ ∞

Planet Verdigris, New Toronto

Burnside checked his omni. It was time for his evening walk. He had cultivated a habit of going for evening walks. Exercise value aside, if anyone *was* watching him, then an established pattern made it less likely to arouse suspicion if he had another reason to be out. Sometimes he did, but tonight it was just a walk.

The moon cast a glow through the thin overcast, tinged a pale green from a scattering of skyweed. The hydrogen cells in the weed lofted it higher in the cooler night air. Burnside wandered the streets, taking right and left turns at random intervals. He tried not to repeat the same path from one night to the next. As he walked, he considered that it had been more than five weeks since he'd sent his message to Ducayne. A follow-up mission should be arriving soon. He'd managed to get messages out to Prentiss more or less regularly, but getting anything back from him was problematic. Burnside had deliberately made himself hard to find.

As usual, the streets were dark. This area of New Toronto had few streetlights. Illumination came from the occasional lit window and from what moonlight penetrated the clouds.

As he walked, some subtle change in the light caught his attention. A flickering? His shadow, cast in front of him, was now pivoting from left to right. *What the . . . ?* He turned and looked up. A light, brighter than the moon, moved above the clouds, flaring and dimming. It was only for few seconds, then it suddenly bloomed to daytime brilliance and went out. Burnside looked around quickly, checking that he was well clear of any windows, and counted the seconds.

. . . fifty-five, fifty-six, fifty-sev—

An ear-splitting *CRACK-BOOM* shattered the night; Burnside felt it as much as heard it. It echoed and reverberated like an enormous thunderclap. Somewhere in the distance an alarm began to sound. His eyes were still somewhat dazzled from the flash, but from what he could see of nearby windows, they had survived intact. He checked the time. Ten-fifteen, a remarkably precise time for a cosmic accident. He grinned.

It was possible that the bolide was just a random occurrence, but Burnside had asked to be notified when his ride arrived in the system, and the timing suggested that *someone* was trying to get his attention. They had succeeded. It was time to leave.

∞ ∞ ∞

New Toronto, Velkaryan HQ

"What the hell was that?" Vaughan demanded as the echoes faded. It had felt and sounded like an explosion. "Get me a report! Lieutenant, contact the munitions factory!" He thought for a moment. What else? "And man defensive positions." It was unlikely they were under attack, not without some kind of warning, but if nothing else, the drill would do the men good.

A few minutes later, the reports were coming in.

"Numerous sightings of a probable fireball above the clouds, followed by an explosion. So far, no reports of major damage or injuries, beyond a few cracked windows or people being startled."

"What was it? A ship?"

"No traffic reported in the area. Best guess is a large meteor."

"A meteor? That seems unlikely. Why wasn't it detected?" Anything large enough to pose a serious threat should have had its orbit calculated and catalogued long ago, and there were observation satellites in place in case of long-period comets or objects being disturbed by space operations—although the latter were supposed to be reported as they happened.

"It must have been a small one, below detection threshold. It never reached the ground."

"But it happened to enter directly over the city?" That seemed an unusual coincidence.

"Not directly. It could happen. Chelyabinsk, back on Earth, about a century ago—"

Vaughan waved a hand in dismissal. "All right, it happens. Have the factories inspected for shock-wave damage. And get a drone or something up there to sample the air. If it was a meteorite there should be dust traces. If they find anything that *doesn't* look natural, I want to know."

"I . . . Yes, sir."

Vaughan didn't think it likely that anyone trying to infiltrate via reentry pack would make it so obvious—and if somebody had been trying that, it had apparently gone very wrong—but on the other hand, that might be just what they'd want him to think.

∞ ∞ ∞

New Toronto

Back at his tiny apartment, Burnside went through his things. He already had a bug-out bag packed in case he needed to leave in a hurry, that was a basic precaution, but now he had time to be more methodical. He also wanted to be sure he left nothing behind that might give him away.

It didn't take him long to clean things out and finish packing. Burnside had always made it a point to not keep anything incriminating in his room in the first place. Most of his tools of the trade were dual use. Each had an innocent explanation beside that for which he used them. There were, however, still the leftover components specific to the various bugging devices he'd made. With a sigh, he began crushing those with pliers into mostly unrecognizable piles of ceramic, silicon, and plastic dust and bits of metal, then flushed the debris down the toilet.

What else? He went through his dresser drawers, bottom to top, pulling out a few things and tossing them on the bed. Looking at the resulting pile, he decided against the change of clothing. He'd be travelling through the forest—he sighed—again. It would only be three days, and he didn't need to look nice. He'd be better off trading the weight for extra food bars.

The room didn't have a kitchen as such, but one corner held a sink, a cooking unit too simple to qualify as an autochef, and a pantry cupboard. He raided the latter for any kind of easily portable food.

Anything else? As he looked around the room, his mind flashed back to his hasty departure from Tanith at 82 Eridani a few months earlier. He hoped these hasty departures weren't going to become a permanent part of his lifestyle. At least he'd known when he arrived that he wouldn't be staying long on Verdigris.

Satisfied that he had taken care of everything that needed to be packed or disposed of, he went to bed. There was no point leaving before morning; he would need light to take out the boat he had already secured. He might as well enjoy sleeping in a bed under a roof while he could; the next time wouldn't be until pick-up, a few days hence. He had no idea what the shipboard accommodations might be, but it didn't matter. *Just so long as there's someone there to meet me*, he thought as he dropped off to sleep. He'd feel silly if the meteor had just been random, and he found himself waiting at the rendezvous with nobody expecting him. He could find a way to deal with it if that happened, but contrary to what he'd told Tevnar, he'd really rather not try to steal a Velkaryan starship.

Chapter 29: Landing

Approaching Verdigris, again

"We need to land at one of the cities first," Jackie said to her passengers. They had spent a day riding the roller coaster of stealthed-warp to just outside the system, then coming back in, dropping out of warp abruptly as if just arriving. The ship was now on a normal approach path to the planet, and it was time to let Space Traffic Control know their destination.

"Why don't we head straight for the rendezvous point?" Rico asked. "That's what Hopkins would have done."

"Hopkins had a tendency to operate outside the law. I don't know if his ship—the *Hawk*, wasn't it?—had disabled its transponder, but he might have been bribing someone in the local traffic control. Regulations call for landing at an authorized spaceport first, unless your ship is already registered as local."

"I think the *Hawk* was registered on Verdigris. And probably a half-dozen other worlds," Rico said. "It's easier to bribe someone in the records office once than to keep bribing people in traffic control. Although some places we just came in on an odd vector where nobody was looking."

Jackie shook her head. She understood what he was talking about, but it went against her nature. She had grown up on a ship; ignoring the rules could get someone killed. Plus, those were all sure ways to lose her courier's license. *Like changing Sophie's registration wasn't?* she thought. At least that had a much lower chance of detection, if Ducayne was to be believed. She squelched that train of thought.

"Well, this ship is going to at least pretend to be doing things above board. But New Toronto is out as a landing site, so that narrows it down to Verdigris City or Louisbourg."

"I vote for Louisbourg," Avril said. "I've been there before."

Louisbourg was the oldest city on Verdigris, near the original landing site of Paul Fabron's ship, the highly modified *Jules Verne*. With the same wry humor behind the naming of the planet and its moon, Louisbourg was named for the old French fortress on Île Royale, now Cape Breton, Nova Scotia.

"That works for me," Jackie said. "I've been to Verdigris City in *Sophie*. There's a small chance somebody might recognize me, even with the new hair, and wonder about the ship, so Louisbourg is preferable. Rico?"

"No, that's fine. As far as I know nobody there is out to get me," he said and grinned.

"Is that often a problem for you?" Jackie asked.

"Once or twice. More often, a problem for the other guy though."

"All right. Louisbourg it is. Let me call that in."

∞ ∞ ∞

"Louisbourg Control, this is the *Seraphim* out of Sawyers World, inbound crossing Gex orbit, requesting vectors and clearance for landing."

The response came a few seconds later. "Seraphim, *this is Louisbourg. Welcome to Verdigris. Uploading vectors. Cleared to ten thousand kilometers at your discretion, then standard approach. Call in range.*"

"Louisbourg, *Seraphim*. Copy ten thousand at my discretion, standard approach, and call in. Roger."

The vectors were the orbital parameters of any known satellites or other spacecraft. As the one doing the maneuvering, it was Jackie's responsibility to avoid them. The clearance formalities dealt with, Jackie commenced final preparations for entry and landing.

∞ ∞ ∞

Louisbourg Spaceport

The landing was routine but not uneventful. The ride through the skyweed layer—thankfully thin today—was, as usual, accompanied by the occasional flare as some of the plants combusted with the heat of the ship's passing. But the *Seraphim* glided to an approach over the spaceport runway without damage, not counting the green and brown streaks left on her fuselage.

"Louisbourg Ground, this is the *Soph*—"

Rico darted a hand to cover the microphone, startling Jackie into realizing what she had almost done. She recovered quickly, "—*phim*, request temporary parking spot. We'll being going out again in a few hours."

"*Say again? Was that the* Seraphim*?*"

"Affirmative, Ground. *Seraphim*, requesting overnight parking. We'll be doing a hop to the interior once we clear the formalities."

"*Roger that*, Seraphim. *You're cleared to the ramp north of the terminal building.*"

"Copy north ramp. *Seraphim* out."

Jackie slumped back in her control seat, and looked over at Rico. "I almost blew it there. Force of habit. Thanks, Rico."

"No worries. I was ready for it. Just be careful."

"Roger that."

"What now?" Boutelle asked.

Jackie didn't answer immediately, instead spooling up the ship's lift fans to hover-taxi to the parking ramp. As she maneuvered, she began tapping controls with her left hand. "First I secure the ship from space," she said by way of explanation. "Then we report in. Just a formality, but the government here is trying to crack down on artifact smuggling, so they want visitors to check-in with the Bureau of Antiquities. Mostly that's just a matter of acknowledging that you've been informed of the penalties associated with smuggling, a warning not to buy anything from undocumented vendors, that sort of nonsense. You read through a multi-page document and acknowledge that you've read it. Heck, you've both been here before, you know the drill."

"Actually, no," Boutelle said. "As a xenoanthropology student we got to bypass a lot of that. It was all prearranged through the expedition organizers."

Jackie turned to Rico. "And I suppose you just landed somewhere else and ignored the whole process?"

Rico grinned at her. "Something like that, yeah. There may have been bribes involved. Not my department."

Jackie sighed and shook her head.

"All right, let's get this over with."

They exited the ship down the portside boarding ramp. As Jackie closed the hatch, she looked over the ship. It was a mess from its passage through the skyweed, but most of that would burn off the next time she entered atmosphere from space. She shrugged. It wouldn't affect the flight characteristics, although she should inspect the sensor ports to make sure none of them were getting clogged or obscured.

Rico and Avril were already walking to the terminal building.

Avril turned back and called to her. "Are you coming?"

Jackie jogged to catch up. "Just checking the ship."

"And?"

"She's fine."

They crossed the field to the terminal. The air was humid, with a thick, leafy smell, and just a hint of decay. It was slightly less inside the building, and by the time the trio had finished with the formalities, Jackie hardly noticed it.

∞ ∞ ∞

"Okay, you guys go into town to do whatever it is you need to do to make this all look routine. I need to flush the ship's tanks, top up the fuel, and do an inspection."

"Meet back at the ship when?" Rico asked.

"No, let's meet for lunch." Avril said. "I want a break from ship food. Anybody object?"

"Sounds good to me," Jackie said. "Any recommendations?"

"There's a place not far. *Le Chaudron Noir*, The Black Kettle. They do a wonderful onion soup, with a thick cheese topping and wonderful crusty bread."

"Stop, you're making me hungry already," Jackie said. She felt herself beginning to salivate at the thought. They had been eating shipboard food for the past couple of weeks. "Does that work for you Rico?"

"Sure. Food's food. I'm game."

"*Le Chaudron Noir* it is, then." Jackie tapped that into her omniphone to confirm the location and verify the local time. "Three hours, then?"

"Copy that."

∞ ∞ ∞

Old Louisbourg

Rico wandered the streets in an older part of Louisbourg, one of his old haunts. It had been a while since he was last here, and he wanted to get an updated lay of the land. This part of town was, well, not exactly a dive—as with most settlements on T-Space worlds less than a generation old, they hadn't had time to get as seedy as some of the places he remembered from his younger days on Earth—but it was the mix of warehouses, light manufacturing, cheap hotels and cheaper bars that seemed to go with transportation hubs almost anywhere.

Part of his mission was to find out from any of his old contacts just what might be going on here, and this was as good a place as any to start.

"Rico?" a call came from behind him. "Is that you?"

Speaking of old contacts. . . . Rico turned to see a wiry, rat-faced character dressed in shabby clothes. The man looked around furtively, then waved at him.

"Mikey?" Rico said aloud, adding "You old dirt-bag," under his breath. This was one old contact he could have done without. The guy was a sleaze-ball, as likely to rat someone out as not, if he thought there was personal gain in it. "It's been a while."

"Yeah, no shit. I haven't seen any of the old gang in a couple of years."

Yeah, thought Rico. *There's a reason for that. They don't want to see you.*

"Are you still with Hopkins?" Mikey continued.

"Hopkins? No, we had a bit of a falling out," Rico said, grinning to himself. "I've been doing some freelancing. You?"

"Oh, a bit of this, a bit of that. Freelancing, huh? How's that working out?"

"Could be better. You know of anything?"

"Business is getting tighter. I was in New Toronto for a while, but the damn Velkaryan government there is running a tighter ship. They've increased patrols, making random ID checks, that kind of thing. The locals seem to like it, petty crime is down, but it does make our line of business harder. The Velka-ryans really crack down on anything alien related."

"Are you still in the artifact game?"

"You're not?" Mikey looked at him slyly. "Did you come in on that Sapphire that just landed? What game are you playing now?"

Rico shook his head. "No game. I'm playing tour-guide and bodyguard to a xenoanthropologist."

"You, baby-sitting? Come on, you're too smart to just be hired muscle. What's the scam? I bet this xeno'pologist knows of a new area where there are fresh goodies to find, right? Are you going to let your old friend in on it?"

"No scam, just as it sounds. If there are any new ruins, I wasn't told about them. I think she wants to try contacting the natives."

Mikey laughed. "The snake-eyes? Good luck with that. They're like ghosts. But seriously, you're not holding out on me, are you?"

"There's nothing to hold out. Hell, half the reason I took this gig is to see if I could make contact with some of the guys that weren't part of Hopkins' outfit. How about it? Anyone still around, or have they moved on? I hear Ransom's Planet is one of the hot new spots these days, I just haven't made it out there."

"Yeah, yeah, a lot of them have moved on. A couple were arrested and doing time. Georgio was killed."

"What? How?"

"Being stupid. A jade ribbon snake got him. Dumb ass, he shoulda known better."

"Oh, I thought you meant somebody shot him, or something," Rico said. "So, nobody left here?"

"A couple of faces I know to see but never really hung with. If there are any new guys moving merchandise, I would have heard about it."

Or maybe you wouldn't, Rico thought. Guys like Mikey got a reputation that they were only ever half aware of.

"Okay," he said. "Listen, Mikey, it was good to run into you. I've got a meet-up in about an hour"—it was more like two —"and I want to hit a couple of the old haunts. See you around, okay?"

"Sure, Rico, sure. Don't forget, if something is up, I want in on it. I've got local contacts you don't know about."

"You got it. Cheers." Rico turned and continued in the direction he'd been heading, waving as he left, and thinking about what he'd learned from Mikey, only a little of which had been from what Mikey had actually said. He wondered if the man had, despite his complaints, any contact with the Velkaryans, and how soon he would try to sell Rico out. Not that any of them here were likely to care. Velkaryans on Earth probably thought him dead, and there wouldn't have been time to get word here from Alpha Centauri even if they'd known he was coming.

∞ ∞ ∞

Louisbourg University

The university in Louisbourg was small compared to Drake University back in Sawyer City, but it had a well-regarded faculty of xenoanthropology. It was to this building—or rather, this floor within the main university building—that Avril Boutelle now made her way.

"May I help you?" the young man at reception asked as Boutelle stopped at the desk.

"Yes," Boutelle said, "I was wondering if Professor Carter was in, and if he still has the same office. I did some field work with him a couple of years ago."

"Ah. Well, his office hasn't changed, but I'm afraid he has a class at the moment. Was he expecting you?"

"No, I just wanted to say hello. What time does his class end? I can wait. I wanted to use the library anyway." While it would have been nice to see Carter again, it wasn't essential.

The receptionist checked his computer. "Not until eleven, but that close to lunch he may not come straight back to his office."

"*Pas de problème*," Avril said. "I'll just message him. *Merci*." So saying, she walked off down the hall to where she knew the library was. The room did have a few shelves of books, but more importantly it held a sophisticated repository of data about known Verdigran tribes, including their known geographic ranges, languages, trading patterns, and the like. It also held a collection of both modern and ancient Verdigran artifacts. The data was available over the network, of course, but accessing it directly from the library bypassed a lot of the associated logging and gateways, and would let her use the more-powerful index systems tailored to professional users.

She was primarily interested in the yeushpent tribes living in and around the planned rendezvous area. Academia preferred the term to "snake-eyes," although it was derived from the French words for the same thing: *les yeux du serpent*, as mispronounced by a native. She was also savvy enough to extend her searches to the entire Lac Quebec region, and a few scattered others, to mask her main focus.

In an hour she had downloaded language modules for all the regional dialects to her omni. She had also refreshed her memory on inter-tribe trade customs and communications. Different groups had their own methods of signaling each other through the jungle, many of which were not revealed to outsiders, but there were methods of communicating between tribes without face-to-face contact. She made a few notes in her omniphone, then went to look at the exhibited artifacts, where she took a few pictures.

She checked the time. Boutelle had what she needed from here, and there was just time to make a quick shopping trip before meeting the others for lunch.

Chapter 30: Heading for Rendezvous

Verdigris, a creek feeding Lake Quebec

By the second day, Jordan Burnside was having second thoughts about his choice of rendezvous spot. The designated pick-up point was a small lake some two-hundred kilometers north-east of New Toronto, four days after he'd received the signal. That had to have been the meteor dropped over the city, it seemed just the sort of thing someone Ducayne sent would do. When he had arranged it with Tevnar, looking at the maps, it had seemed simple. In the worst case, he could cover that two-hundred kilometers in three days of walking, or so he had thought. His trek to Verdigris City from where he'd first landed, and again to Fayetteville after escaping from Vaughan's thugs, had shown him that his estimate of travel speed through the Verdigran forest had been wildly optimistic. On the other hand, the area along this shore of Lac Quebec was largely agricultural, cleared of jungle and so more easily walkable. But Burnside wasn't walking.

The other thing that the maps had shown was that downstream—if lakes could be said to have a downstream, but toward the lake's outflow to the New Lawrence—there was a much smaller river flowing into it, and upstream from that was the small lake, Buckhorn, he had designated as the rendezvous point. Travel by water had seemed much easier than trekking overland. That was how much of the interior of North America back on Earth had originally been opened up, traders and trappers following the water routes. So Burnside was paddling a canoe toward the rendezvous.

Not that he'd planned on paddling. The canoe had been equipped with an electric outboard and a battery pack sufficient to cover the 250 kilometers—by water—to his destination. That was before the propeller had become hopelessly fouled in an old fishing net, late on the first day.

Even that wouldn't have been a problem if he'd named the rendezvous point as somewhere nearer to Lake Quebec. Paddling a canoe on still water was a fairly efficient mode of travel. Paddling upstream was significantly less so, depending on the speed of the stream, and Burnside hadn't taken into account the change in elevation between his Buckhorn Lake and Lake Quebec. It was rough going. Not for the first time, Burnside wondered if it would be quicker to get out and walk.

He had been hearing a faint roaring ahead for a few minutes now, but couldn't see what it was because of bends in the river. But he had a bad feeling about it. At least he was headed upstream; he wouldn't find himself unexpectedly at the *top* of a waterfall. He had passed into a low canyon about a kilometer back, as the surrounding land was cut by a ridge ten meters tall, crossing the river at an angle. The stream had cut the canyon into the terrain. But it might only be rapids upstream, or if he was lucky the canyon might cut completely through whatever had caused the uplift, and it would widen out again on the other side.

He rounded another bend in the river, and his fears were confirmed. A few hundred meters ahead was indeed a waterfall. It was not large as things went, perhaps ten meters high, but he would have to portage around it. He scanned the banks on either side of the river. The ground sloped steeply upward, more of a cliff in some spots. The rock was somewhat layered, but it wasn't limestone or shale, although it might have been shale at some point. It had metamorphosed into, what was it? Not gneiss . . . *schist,* that was it. Some of the layers were flaky; it wouldn't make for very solid footing. He could probably climb that himself, but there was no way he could drag the canoe up while doing that.

So, abandon the canoe? Or head back downstream to where the escarpment started and do a long portage? Not that there was

 Alastair Mayer

any guarantee he would be able to drag the canoe up there, either. He sighed.

He could manage the paddles, but it looked like he was going to be up schist creek without a canoe.

Chapter 31: Louisbourg

Louisbourg

Jackie Roberts, Rico, and Boutelle all arrived outside *Le Chaudron* at about the same time. Boutelle carried a small shopping bag.

"Buying souvenirs?" Jackie asked her.

"Of a sort." She reached into the bag and pulled out something that resembled an ocarina, made from a dried gourd, painted, with finger holes and a mouthpiece.

"What's that?" Jackie asked.

"If you wanted artifacts, I could probably find you better fakes than that," Rico said.

"Oh, I know it's fake," Boutelle said. "But, it's functional." She held it up to her lips one-handed and blew a quick sequence of notes. The tones were clear, sounding something like an owl's hoots, but louder. "See?"

"I've heard worse," Rico said.

"But what's it for?" Jackie was still mystified. Boutelle wouldn't buy a fake artifact just as a souvenir.

"Loosely speaking, it's a signaling whistle. These tones carry a long way in the jungle, like bird calls. We probably don't need it, but it helps my cover. If I'm going off in search of natives, I'd want something like this."

Jackie shrugged. "Okay, you're the expert." She gestured to the restaurant door. "Shall we do lunch? I'm starved."

∞ ∞ ∞

Le Chaudron Noir

As Avril had promised, the French onion soup at *Le Chaudron* had been excellent. Rico had made a more complete meal of it with a steak cut from one of the local game animals.

"I think I'll finish off with coffee and a pastry," Jackie said when the waiter came over to ask them if they'd like anything else. "What do you have?"

The waiter recited a short list of pastries, all of which sounded delicious.

"That all sounds wonderful. It's hard to choose."

"May I particularly recommend the *Gâteau St. Honoré?*" The waiter said.

"What is that, exactly?"

"Aah. It begins with a ring of light *pâte à choux* on a base of puff pastry. This is then filled with pastry cream. Finally, it is topped with delicate sugar-dipped cream puffs."

It was all Jackie could do to keep from drooling at the thought of it, although she wondered if it would live up to the description. "Wonderful, I'll have that."

"Excellent. And to go with it? Perhaps an expresso?"

Do you happen to have Tau Cetan coffee?"

The waiter, who had been leaning forward solicitously, jerked back, as if offended. "I think you'll find our Verdigris coffee even better. We get ours from the Collignon plantation on the mountain slopes of St. Thomas. It has been compared more than favorably with Kona or Jamaica Blue Mountain from Earth."

"Oh?" Jackie said. "Well, that sounds excellent then. Whatever you think goes best with the patisserie."

"*Ce bien, mam'selle.* And the other gentles?"

When the waiter left with their orders, Avril and Rico looked hard at Jackie. "What was all that about?"

"Just curious as to the demand for Tau Cetan coffee here. Last time I was on Skead, someone suggested that Verdigris coffee, if they had any at all, couldn't be as good as theirs."

"He was just trying to sell you some," said Rico.

"Quite possibly," Jackie said. She decided not to mention that her old crewmate's ship had been destined for New Toronto with a full cargo of Tau Cetan roast, nor her and Ducayne's conversation about the possibility of smuggling critical warp drive components in sacks of said coffee beans.

The waiter returned shortly with their coffees and Jackie's pastry—the others had foregone any—and appeared to be hanging near the table to catch Jackie's reaction to her first taste.

The coffee certainly smelled good. It had a not-too-robust aroma with vague cinnamon hints. *Interesting.* She took a sip. It actually wasn't half bad. Not, in her opinion, as good as her home Tau Cetan and certainly not up to the Jamaica Blue Mountain she'd had the first time she met Ducayne. But it was more than adequate. She smiled and looked at the waiter. "That's quite good," she said.

He grinned, nodded, and left.

"So?" Avril asked. "How is it really?"

"It's actually better than I was expecting. Probably enough so that the cost of shipping coffee from Skead would be hard to justify unless it was some of the best."

"Some people are wine connoisseurs, some coffee, I guess," Avril said. "But I also think there's something you're not telling us."

Jackie took another drink from her cup before answering. She kept the cup up in front of her mouth, holding it with both hands, as she answered. "Need to know," she said quietly. *Let somebody try to lip-read that*, she thought.

∞ ∞ ∞

After lunch they made their way back to the *Seraphim*.

"Rendezvous isn't until tomorrow," Jackie said. "It's about six hours flying time if I keep it in-atmosphere and subsonic. What do you want to do in the meantime?"

"Personally, I'm still wondering about what was up with that coffee," Avril said.

"She was wondering if somebody was smuggling something in coffee shipments," Rico said.

"How did—" Jackie began, and then, "I can neither confirm nor deny anything about that."

"Did Ducayne brief you?" Avril asked Rico.

He shook his head. "I'm guessing, but having had, ah, a vague acquaintance with smugglers in the past, it would fit. There are basically only a few ways to smuggle something successfully, at least on a regular basis. One, you can bribe officials to look the other way. That's unreliable, and risks leaving a money trail that can be used as evidence. We, I mean, my acquaintances, would almost never do that. Blackmail would work better than bribes, but still unreliable.

"So, two, you could land your smuggling ship in some out of the way spot and hope you either weren't tracked, or you could get in, unload, and get out before any authorities caught you. That works pretty well with some cargos and some destinations. It works better with commodities than specialty items, usually."

"Commodities? You mean like drugs?" Avril asked.

"Yeah, that's one example. It's not the end of the world if you lose a shipment, unlike if you were trying to get a particular rare artifact to a specific buyer. It also works for things like exotic pets. Animals are hard to smuggle any other way."

"You trafficked in alien animals? Do you know what that can do to an ecosystem?" Avril demanded, her voice rising.

"Whoa, calm down." Rico held up his hands placatingly. "No, I was never involved in that. The guys I knew who did made sure the animals were sterile. For one thing, that reduces the chances of competition; also, the penalties are lower if you get caught. But yeah, there are others who don't. Idiots."

"What's the third way?" Jackie asked him. "Hide the contraband inside something else?"

"Exactly," Rico said. "Of course, it has to be inside something that won't likely be searched. So, bulk agricultural goods that have been treated, so they aren't likely to carry pests are a good prospect. Roast coffee is one of those things. Bulk manufactured goods are another, but machine parts are tricky because they can attract attention, and something common like, say, bolts or fasteners are more likely to be manufactured locally, although that can work too."

"So when I mentioned coffee. . . ." Jackie said.

"I wondered, yeah. I have no idea what you might think is being smuggled, or by who, but given why we're here, I could make some guesses."

"Don't bother. It was something I discussed with Ducayne after a recent trip, but he told me to drop it. I was just curious."

"You want to be careful about doing anything that might arouse suspicion," Boutelle said. "Here, it probably doesn't matter. If you do that in New Toronto, the wrong people might start paying closer attention to us."

"You're right," Jackie said, realizing that if Avril and Rico had picked up on it, she hadn't been as subtle as she thought she was being. Well, the damage, if any, was done. "It's a good thing we're not planning on going to New Toronto, then, isn't it?"

"I thought that's where Burnside was?"

"It better have been, or he won't have got our rather attention-getting signal. But that's not where we're picking him up. No, tomorrow we're going to someplace called Buckhorn Lake."

Chapter 32: Up the Creek

Schist Creek

Burnside paddled the canoe around the edges of the waterfall's plunge pool, looking for the best place to beach it and climb up out of the gorge. He was mindful to keep clear of the falls themselves; if he got too close the current could pull him in and the canoe would be swamped instantly. He finally found a spot thirty meters downstream, where a shelf of harder rock had left a flat spot along the creek bank big enough for the canoe.

He hauled the boat up onto the ledge and considered his next move. The cliff face was steep but not vertical, with its top about eight meters above the ledge where he'd dragged the canoe. It was weathered stone, layered, which made for ready hand- and foot-holds. He tested the rock, checking to see if the fractured layers would crumble under his weight. Some layers had more shiny material—*mica?*—than others. Those were slick and uncohesive, but the other layers would take his weight. Okay, so he could climb up here, but then what?

He inventoried the gear he had. The canoe had a line attached to the bow, perhaps he could haul it up the side of the cliff that way? He measured the rope against the span of his outstretched arms, estimating it at five meters long. That wasn't enough. Could he climb up, to the length of the rope, and then pull the canoe part way up before continuing? The cliff had handholds, but nowhere he could brace himself, nor anywhere to rest the canoe while he climbed the remaining distance. That wasn't going to work.

Burnside checked through his gear again, looking for something he could tie on to the bowline to extend it. There was nothing.

Crap. He sat down on the rocky ledge to think. Did he really need the canoe? He could continue on foot, just as he had twice before. That had been slow going, though. Not being able to travel by water, as he'd originally planned, would add at least a day, more like two, to his travel time. What if he travelled at night too? No, in this jungle that was asking for trouble. Damn it.

He stood up and dusted his hands off on his trouser legs, looking around again. He really needed a way to get the canoe up that cliff. *Wait, would that work?* It just might. With a sigh, Burnside began stripping off his shirt and pants.

In a few minutes, now down to just his undershorts and boots, Burnside had tied one pant leg to the canoe's bowline, and the other to one sleeve of his shirt. With the stretched-out pants and shirt sleeves, he estimated he had enough length to reach the top. He pulled on the loose shirt sleeve experimentally, testing to see if his impromptu rope was strong enough to lift the canoe. The fabric was a strong synthetic; it held.

He looked up at the cliff, absently slapping at a mosquito that had settled on his bare shoulder. *That's going to get annoying*, he thought. He tied the loose shirt sleeve around his ankle, giving it a few tugs to make sure it wasn't going to slip off, then faced the cliff again. A few more mosquitoes were starting to buzz around him, and he felt one alight on his back. *All right, the sooner I get to the top, the sooner I can put my clothes back on. Damned bugs.* He started climbing.

After ten minutes, twice that many mosquito bites, and a couple of scrapes from when he'd slipped, Burnside reached the top of the cliff. He lay back on the ground, the leg with the tied-on shirtsleeve still dangling over the edge, his back on the cool ground. It felt good; the insect bites had started to itch. *I just hope I'm not lying on an anthill.*

He sat up and grabbed the shirt sleeve. The front of the canoe was at the base of the cliff, his improvised rope was just barely long enough. At twenty kilograms, the canoe's weight was manageable, even hauling it almost straight up. But it was also big and bulky, and it kept banging against the rocky hillside. Halfway up, it flipped around completely, and the stern hung up on a rock outcrop. Burnside laid down on the edge of the cliff, kicking the rope out with his leg to free it. It came loose, and the canoe flipped around again, the hull slamming back against the rocks with a bang. *That better not have cracked it*, he thought.

Finally, the canoe was at the top of the cliff. Burnside was sweaty, dirty, scraped, and bug-bitten. Worse, the haul up the cliff had so tightened the knots in his clothing that one of them proved impossible to undo. Desperate to get some clothing back on to shield him from a fresh onslaught of biting insects, he ended up cutting out the knot tying a pant leg and shirt sleeve together.

When he finished dressing, his left sleeve and right trouser leg were each about twenty centimeters shorter than the other leg and sleeve, with ragged edges, but at least most of his body and limbs were better protected. *I must look like I've been lost in the jungle for months*, Burnside thought, *not just a couple of days*. In his eagerness to travel light, he hadn't brought spare clothing. He hoped whoever picked him up would have something that fit, although at this point, as long as he could use their fresher, he'd be okay with making the trip back to Sawyers World in the nude if he had to.

He gathered up the rest of his gear, lifted the canoe up over his head in the usual portage position, and began the trek upriver. It was slow going, pushing through the vegetation with a canoe on his back, and thirty meters upstream from the falls he gave up and put the canoe back in the water. He tied off the canoe to a tree at the creek's edge, and took a few minutes to dip himself, still fully clothed—minus what he'd had to cut off—in the cool water, being careful not to let himself drift downstream.

Finally, and mindful of the waterfall downstream, Burnside climbed into the canoe, cast off, and paddled furiously. He planned to put at least a kilometer between himself and the falls before relaxing to a more leisurely stroke. By his reckoning, he was still some thirty kilometers from Buckhorn Lake, the designated rendezvous point. That was seven or more hours of steady paddling, assuming there were no more waterfalls, rapids, or anything else he'd need to portage around, and assuming the stream-flow stayed as it was. By now, there were only two or three hours of light left. Burnside wasn't about to try navigating the creek at night. *I am really starting to hate this planet*, he grumbled to himself as he paddled hard.

Chapter 33: Velkaryans

Velkaryan HQ, New Toronto

Klaus Vaughan was in his office reviewing production reports when one of his men, Horowitz, tapped at the door. Vaughan's head snapped up. "What?"

"Sorry to bother you, boss, but I had a call from one of my old underworld contacts. He has some information he wants to sell."

This caught Vaughan's interest. "Information? Something about Burnside?" Production had been experiencing a high number of apparent accidents and mishaps recently. There was nothing Vaughan could prove, but he was convinced that sabotage, instigated by Burnside, was behind it.

"No, at least, he didn't mention Burnside. He said Rico."

"Rico?" The name sounded familiar to Vaughan, but he couldn't place it. "Who the hell . . . ?" Then he remembered. The name had been mentioned in a message, along with the starship *Sophie* and her pilot, Jackie Roberts, as possibly on the way to Verdigris. "Do you mean Rico as in Hopkins' enforcer?"

"I don't know about enforcer, but my guy, Mikey, did say that Rico used to be with Hopkins."

"What else did he say?"

"That was it. He said he had more information, but he wanted money for it. The guy was always a bit slimy."

"Do you trust him? Maybe he's just making this up. And where is he?"

"He's in Louisbourg. I'm pretty sure he actually ran into Rico. How much other information he really has is another question."

Vaughan considered this. If Rico—and Roberts—was on planet, it was worth finding out whatever they were up to. Probably here to rendezvous with Burnside, in which case they would bear watching. That they were in Louisbourg might also explain why there'd been no alert from the New Toronto spaceport that a ship named *Sophie* had asked to land.

"All right. Go meet with him and offer to pay for his information. It's not worth much, make sure he knows that. Was he a friend of yours?"

"Friend? No, just someone I knew. I don't think the guy has any friends."

"Good. If this Mikey isn't cooperative, offer to pay him for the information with his life. Get it?"

Horowitz grinned. "I get it, boss."

"Then go. Take the *Carcharodon*; tell Stinson I said so." That was overkill for the 1200-kilometer trip to Louisbourg, but the ship was just using up parking space. "Let me know what you find out, soon as possible. Also, keep an eye out for a female pilot with green hair."

"Green hair. On my way, boss."

As Horowitz left the office, Vaughan was already dialing his omniphone. When it was answered, he said, "Get me a list of all starships landing anywhere on the planet in the last week. ASAP."

It was possible that Rico had come in on another ship. The message from Sawyers World, via Earth, had only speculated that he might be aboard the *Sophie*. The message hadn't explained the Velkaryan interest in Rico, but if he had arrived on Roberts' ship, could Hannibal Carson be far behind?

Chapter 34: Leaving Louisbourg

Louisbourg Spaceport

"Louisbourg Control, this is the *Seraphim* requesting clearance for takeoff and climb-out to the north. Remaining in atmosphere."

"*Roger* Seraphim. *You're cleared for immediate lift, otherwise wait pending inbound traffic from the southwest.*"

"Thank you, Louisbourg. *Seraphim* lifting now."

"*Roger that. Maintain northerly heading and report clear of the zone.*"

"Copy that." Jackie clicked off and spooled up the lift fans, feeding enough thrust to lift the ship before applying horizontal thrust to reach aerodynamic flying speed. This time, the fan gates cooperated in latching shut when they were supposed to, despite flying through a layer of skyweed as it climbed out.

"Louisbourg, *Seraphim* is clear to the north."

"*Roger* Seraphim *clear. Have a great flight.*"

The formalities dealt with, Jackie would keep the ship on a northerly course for about fifty kilometers before banking and arcing west toward their destination. She checked the charts she had uploaded before leaving. The terrain to the west was higher than here, with hills surrounding the lake she was headed for. At some point, she'd have to descend through the skyweed layer, but it would loft to a higher altitude as the day wore on. Good. Despite her radar, lowering down through a cloud layer that might intersect the terrain was always tense.

∞ ∞ ∞

Fifteen kilometers to the south, Captain Stinson watched as the glow of a ship's thrusters faded into the distance. His own craft was lined up now with the Louisbourg Spaceport's main north-south runway, on approach.

"Carcharodon, *this is Louisbourg Control. You are cleared to land.*"

"Roger that, Louisbourg. *Carcharodon* thanks you."

Chapter 35: Burnside Again

Verdigris Jungle, Schist Creek

Burnside woke on the fourth morning and crawled out from under the overturned canoe he'd used as a shelter. It wasn't much, but it helped slightly to shield him from flying insects. It didn't do anything about crawling insects though, so he'd spent the night on a stretch of bare rock, which helped. Well, helped with the insect problem. It hadn't done anything good for the muscles that had already been feeling the effects of three days of exerting themselves in ways they weren't used to. He ached all over.

He had also overslept. The sun, Delta Pavonis, was already above the horizon. He had wanted to set out as soon as there was enough light to see by, at the first rays of dawn. Moving quickly in defiance of his aching muscles, and hoping the movement would help them loosen up, he ate a nutrition bar and chugged a half-liter of water, then righted the canoe and dragged it back to the water's edge.

Burnside paddled his way upstream, checking his progress against the banks. The instructions he'd left for his pickup had said not to wait more than a day at the pickup point. Observation satellites would spot whatever ship was waiting for him, their radar penetrating the almost constant skyweed haze layer. The idea was that whoever was picking him up would land and depart between passes of those satellites. Their orbits would be known to anyone arriving from space.

The odds were low that anyone would happen to see the ship in a timely fashion even if it were imaged from orbit, but a record of the ship would put the Velkaryans on notice that something was up. There were no archeological sites in that area. A rogue ship was unlikely to be tomb raiders, although it might be animal collectors, if there was anything here worth collecting. Furthermore, even if a human wasn't scanning the images in real-time, computers almost certainly were, and a difference from one day to the next was exactly the sort of thing they were looking for. Even more so if that difference was something with straight edges or a geometric shape. The outline of a ship would be guaranteed to trigger whatever detection algorithm the computers were running, and that would bring it to somebody's attention.

Attention was the last thing he wanted.

All of which meant that Burnside had to reach the lake before dawn tomorrow, that in reality meant he had to reach it before nightfall.

He paddled on, ignoring the aches in his shoulder and arm muscles, and trying to ignore the swarms of mosquitoes attracted by the smell of his breath and sweat. Burnside wasn't normally one to complain—he'd run several kilometers with a gunshot wound once—but he was beginning to hope that whoever picked him up had a full-fledged autodoc; generally a mere traumapod didn't do much for muscle aches or insect bites.

∞ ∞ ∞

He forced himself to take a five-minute break every hour, to re-hydrate and eat an energy bar. So far today the stream had been slow-flowing, and he had been making good progress. He had seen various animals coming to drink at the water's edge. The smaller ones had startled and shied away as his canoe passed, the larger ones eying him warily but otherwise ignoring him. He wondered what might prey on them. He was fairly sure there was nothing like crocodiles or alligators in this area, the winters were on the cool side. He had certainly seen no signs of them, and most of the riverbanks had seemed too rocky to make good nesting spots. Did this planet have anything like hippopotamus? He hadn't seen anything like that, either, and surely this river was too shallow for them anyway.

As he rounded a gentle bend in the creek, the river widened and grew shallower. Water plants, something like rushes, grew along the edges, and there was a large creature standing knee-deep in the water, munching on the plants. It was bigger than a horse, with thicker legs and mostly bare, grayish, skin. It had a wide head and mouth that could chew through a wide swath of vegetation, or, he thought, noticing its tusk-like teeth, almost anything else. It lacked horns or antlers—it might have been female —and Burnside thought it looked something like a cross between a moose and a hippopotamus. He didn't know what it might actually be called, but the term "hippopotamoose" fit.

He and the animal eyed each other. It could easily topple the canoe even if it just wandered over in curiosity. Burnside paddled the canoe in a wide berth around it, close to the other shore. The "hippopotamoose" seemed to grow more agitated as he did so, taking a few steps in his direction and snorting. What was its problem?

He realized that the animal wasn't just watching him, it was also glancing at something on the opposite bank, the one he was closer to. He spared a quick look in that direction, but didn't see anything, just a few sparsely scattered trees and some low vegetation. He turned back toward the creature, who was now watching him intently. He paddled a few more strokes.

The hippopotamoose bellowed, and to Burnside's shock, there was an answering, higher-pitched bellow from the bank behind him. He looked again. A much smaller hippo, clearly a youngster, was in the vegetation near the trees. The larger animal —Burnside realized it must be the young one's mother—bellowed again. He realized he was directly between the mother and her calf and Burnside dug in and paddled for all he was worth. The mother hippomoose bellowed again and galloped toward him, the shallow water here no impediment to her long legs.

He hoped that once he was out of the direct line to her calf, the mother would ignore him, but apparently she was having a bad day. She caught up to the canoe and, leaning down, butted the stern, tipping it to where it took on water. Burnside grabbed his pack and jumped out, keeping low in the water and backing away from mother and child, watching in dismay as mother kicked at the canoe with her fore-hooves, ultimately battering it to the point where a rip opened up in the side. Now full of water, the canoe, its flotation compartments still managing to keep it barely at the surface, drifted slowly downstream.

"Aw, crap," Burnside muttered. He was going to have to hike the rest of the way anyway, and now he and his gear were soaking wet. Mother hippomoose walked over to her calf and nuzzled it, and the two stood placidly munching vegetation on the far side of the stream as Burnside crossed back and dragged himself out.

Chapter 36: Rendezvous Point

Lake Buckhorn

The *Sophie*, still masquerading as the *Seraphim*, descended from just beneath the cloud-and-skyweed layer toward the lake. Jackie flew a circuit around it, looking for a landing spot. Mostly the trees came down to the shoreline, but there was a beach up ahead.

She overflew it, estimating its width and the nearby trees and rocks. The beach itself wasn't very smooth and in places the trees came right to the water.

"That looks pretty narrow," Rico said. "Can you land there?"

"I have my doubts," Jackie confessed. "It doesn't look very flat. The only place wide enough for the ship looks like it slopes too much to make a good landing spot."

"So now what?"

Jackie glanced at the side-view screens. "Any sign of Burnside?"

"I've been scanning the surface and shoreline," Avril said, "looking for anyone trying to catch our attention, or a boat, or whatever. I haven't seen anything. Did his instructions give a time?"

"No, they just said four days after contact, not a time of day. We may be early."

"I'm still wondering where you're going to land," Rico said. "Do you have something to blow a hole in the trees?"

Jackie grinned to herself. Carson had done something like that with an improvised bomb the last time they were here.

"Sorry, not this time, and the ground isn't flat anyway. But we don't need to. I'll just land on the lake."

"Excuse me?" Avril said.

"It's a ship. It floats," Jackie said, hiding her grin at the expressions on Avril's face. Rico didn't seem concerned.

"All right," she relented, "S-class ships are designed to be flexible. They're exploration ships, Sapphires in particular. You never know when the only place to land and refuel is an open body of water, so they're designed to be amphibious."

"Copy," Rico said. "When was the last time you did a water landing?"

Jackie thought for a moment. It *had* been a while. "Um, about two years ago. But it's just like a ground landing . . . I just have to remember not to lower the landing gear. Oh, and the fans will kick up a bit of a spray."

Rico and Avril looked at each other, exchanging looks that said, "are you okay with this?" Then Rico shrugged.

"I've seen her fly," he said. "There was some fancy maneuvering on Chara III. I trust her."

"Okay," Avril said. She turned to Jackie. "Anything we should do?"

"Just make sure everything's stowed. I'm going to make a couple of low passes to check for hazards."

Avril heaved a resigned sigh. "Aye aye, Captain."

∞ ∞ ∞

Jackie ran a systems check on the seals on the ships lower hull. There were a lot of potential openings—landing gear, lift fans, refueling scoops, inspection hatches—although all were designed to seal both against water and against the heat of reentry. They had been through that last just yesterday, when they arrived, so there should be nothing wrong with them. But setting down on the surface of a lake was a bit different, although, as she'd told the others, she *had* done it before.

The more interesting part would actually be take-off. It was theoretically possible to do a vertical lift-off with the fan outlets underwater, but the preferred way was to power the ship along like a boat until the nose lifted clear, much like a conventional runway takeoff.

That was the other thing Jackie had to check for. Was this lake even long enough to do that?

It was, just. She would have preferred a few hundred meters more, but it would do. With any luck she'd have a headwind.

"All right, folks. Strap in. I'm taking us down."

∞ ∞ ∞

The surface of the lake had a slight chop, which both helped and hindered. It helped, because it made it easier to gauge both her height above the water and the wind direction. It hindered, because landing on a constantly moving surface was not what she was used to.

Jackie played it by the book, easing the ship's trailing edge onto the surface first. It shuddered and bounced slightly as it hit the peaks of the low waves, then settled and slowed abruptly as the nose came down, slamming into the surface harder than Jackie had intended and sending up a spray of water. It slowed to a halt some fifty meters offshore, bobbing and rocking gently with the waves.

"Sorry about that," she said. "A little rougher than I'd expected."

"Are we okay?"

Jackie had been scanning the instrument console as she talked and secured the ship. One caution and warning light flickered yellow and then went back to green like the others. She would double check that later, but for now . . . "We're fine. No problems. I'm going to pump some water into the tanks to help stabilize us, so don't be alarmed when you hear water rushing in."

Jackie activated the appropriate controls. The sound of pumps and gurgling water announced the tanks filling. Even though she had refueled at Louisbourg, their long flight in atmosphere had depleted some water. Warp travel was much more efficient than pushing air out of the way.

"What now?" Avril asked.

"If Burnside is around, he can't have missed our landing," said Rico. "I don't see him on any of the screens, though."

"If you want," Jackie said, "you can use the topside hatch and see if you can see him from the upper deck. There are binoculars in locker number seven. You'll have a better view from up there."

Rico looked hesitant, and Avril said, "I'll go. I could use some fresh air."

A scowl flashed briefly across Rico's features. "Do you have another pair of binoculars? We can both go, check different directions."

Jackie suppressed a smile and nodded. "Yeah, same locker. I'll mind the controls."

"Yeah, do that," said Rico.

"Anything we need to be careful of up there?" Avril asked.

"Stay toward the middle where it's flattest. Also, avoid any areas marked *NO STEP*."

"Got it," Avril said. "Don't fall off, and don't step on the no step."

"Exactly."

"And it's up to you, but I'd recommend you use a safety line. There's an attachment point just outside the hatch."

∞ ∞ ∞

A few minutes later Avril Boutelle climbed out of the dorsal docking hatch atop the *Seraphim*'s fuselage, with Rico just behind her. The top surface of the ship was largely featureless white, with a few green and brown streaks from the skyweed. Forward of the hatch were the cockpit windows, largely redundant given the much better view the navigation screens gave, and forward of that was the outline of the forward fan intake—surrounded by a black and yellow striped line and clearly marked NO STEP.

Aft, the surface was gently curved, rising toward a rounded peak at the very back, between the two variable fins that were currently angled outward at a forty-five degree up-angle. The broad, rounded ridge between them covered the dorsal warp pod. Between that and the fins were additional louvered intakes, currently closed, and also marked NO STEP.

"Well, so this is what the topside looks like," Avril said. "You only ever see the sides and the bottom, usually."

"Just try not to fall off. It doesn't look like there's an easy way back aboard from the water."

"And here I was thinking it's a nice day for a swim," she said. "Don't worry, I'm not going anywhere." So saying, she clipped her safety line to the eye bolt by the hatch. Rico was already hooked in.

"Fine." Rico held his binoculars to his eyes and looked south. "If Burnside was coming up that small river, he'd be coming in at that end of the lake. I don't see anything."

Avril began sweeping the shoreline with her own binoculars, slowly turning around in a circle. There was nothing but lake, and rocks, and trees. "I'm not seeing anything either. Like you said, he couldn't have missed us landing if he's anywhere near the shore. He must not be here yet."

"Then, I guess we wait."

"How long?"

"Until he shows up," Rico said. "I don't know. Do you have somewhere else to be?"

"The longer we stay here, the more we risk detection," Avril said. "There's no reason for us to be here, there are no archeological sites nearby that I know of, and even less reason to be floating in the middle of the lake. Somebody will come to investigate."

"So, what do you suggest?"

"Hold on." Avril stepped back to the open hatch and called down to Roberts.

"Jackie, did Burnside's instructions say how long to wait for him? There's no sign of him yet."

"Just one day. But there's another problem."

"What?"

"The wind is picking up. If there's a storm coming, we need to get out of here before it gets too bad. I can't do a water take-off in that, and it will be unpleasant if we stay. We won't get huge waves on a lake this size, but this isn't a boat, either. I also don't want to get us blown ashore."

"Don't you have thrusters?"

"Nothing for in-water use that would hold us against a strong wind. The hydrojet isn't that strong, and the space thrusters are just that, for use in space."

"So, how long?"

"I need to check the weather. We've got a few hours, anyway. Maybe Burnside will show up by then."

"Okay." Avril turned back to Rico. "Did you hear that?"

"Only your side of it. What was that about thrusters?"

"The wind is picking up. There may be a storm coming. She's not sure she can hold the ship away from the shore if the wind gets too strong, and we can't take off in a storm either. Also, Burnside said to wait no more than a day."

Rico muttered a curse. "All right. If she has to take the ship out before Burnside gets here, we stay behind. We can wait on the shore there." He pointed to a short stretch of rocky beach that would have a line of sight to the lake's outflow, from where Burnside would be arriving.

"Are you crazy? Wait there in a storm? What good does waiting do?"

"When he shows up, we can let him know we're here and that Jackie will be back when the storm clears. Like I said before, do you have somewhere else to be?"

Avril muttered under her breath. She'd camped out under adverse conditions during class field trips, and it wasn't fun.

"What was that?" Rico asked.

"This isn't what I signed up for," she repeated, loud enough for him to hear.

"It never is."

Chapter 37: Waiting for Burnside

Buckhorn Lake, Verdigris

"No! A starship is not a submarine. I don't care how watertight it is, it's not designed for the outside pressure." said Jackie, her voice raised.

"I don't want to go deep, just under the surface. Surely a Sapphire can take that. It has to take dynamic pressures while flying in-atmosphere, and what about planets that have a higher air pressure?"

"Even if it's within specs for a new Sapphire, this is hardly a new ship. She's got a lot of years on her. And it's completely different for a little outside air to get into an inspection panel than it is for water."

"It's not like it's sea water. This is a lake; a little freshwater won't hurt anything. Are you going to tell me the ship can't stand a little rain?"

Jackie crossed her arms and glared at Rico. She knew he had a point, and in fact *Sophie*'s hull could easily withstand a full standard atmosphere of additional external pressure without a problem, and she could raise the internal pressure to counteract some of that. The main concern with getting anything wet was with seawater, far more corrosive than rainwater or fresh lake water.

The truth was, the idea of being in a submerged ship gave her the willies. Jackie had a tendency to claustrophobia. Being inside a ship was fine as long as the outside was air or space. But the idea of being underwater—or underground, as she had discovered in that cave on St. Jacobs—brought on an irrational feeling of near panic. The annoying thing was that she knew it was irrational, but it still took considerable conscious effort to overcome her feelings.

Rico had suggested submerging the *Sophie*, or rather *Seraphim*, to avoid detection by anything overflying while they waited for Burnside. Avril Boutelle had gone along with it, after initially suggesting they just follow the original instructions and leave if he hadn't shown up.

"Look, it's not even a deep lake," Rico said. "I know it can be done. A guy I worked with before Hopkins had a Sapphire. He would hide it that way to avoid pursuit."

"It must have had special mods," Jackie said, knowing that was possible, but probably not the case.

"If it did, then this ship has the same. Maybe something the previous owner did?"

"How would you know that?"

"I was into the ship's systems when I modified the registry, remember? Options are coded as part of the serial number string."

"You just happen to know how to decode that off the top of your head?"

"No, but the program on my omni does. Of course, things like the antimatter mods don't show up there."

Jackie cursed under her breath. Still, it was her ship, and the previously agreed upon protocol had said nothing about playing submarine. And besides, "There's still that storm coming. I doubt we can go deep enough to ride that out underwater, and I don't want to risk wave action slamming our hull against the bottom. We don't know what's down there. It could be rocks, sunken trees, whatever."

"Soft mud?"

"Do you want to get stuck in the mud? Anyway," Jackie continued, "it's not dark yet. Burnside may still show."

Avril Boutelle had been listening to the conversation, and finally spoke up. "Can you put me ashore? I want to try to contact the yeushpent."

"The snake-eyes?" Rico said. "Why? And how?"

"If Burnside is anywhere within thirty kilometers of here, they'll either know or can find out quickly. If he isn't, there's no point waiting for him."

"How would they know? And how would you contact them?"

Boutelle held up the ocarina she had purchased in Louisbourg. "This is used to signal between tribes and clans, both to demark territory and to arrange meetings. The parallels to bird calls are fascinating. There's no guarantee that there are any natives within range, but I'm betting our landing would have attracted attention, and somebody is watching the lake, probably from the hills a couple of kilometers to the north."

"So? Would they hear you? And would they even come if you called?"

"They have very good hearing, and if I call from topside, the sound will carry a long way over the water. I'll need to go ashore to talk with anyone who shows up, though. Most clans honor the 'invitation to parlay' signal, so yes, they'll probably show up. What have we got to lose?"

"You, if they're hostile," Jackie said.

"I'd worry about that if we were closer to New Toronto. Who knows what effect proximity to the Velkaryans has had on the locals? But out here, I should be fine. This won't be the first time I've interacted with yeushpent."

"It's your first time with those indigenous to this area, though, isn't it?"

Boutelle paused, then nodded. "Technically yes, although from what I could gather, their trading range overlaps with that of clans I met a couple of years back near Louisbourg. I'm willing to chance it."

Jackie looked at Rico, who shrugged. "If she's willing, it's worth a shot," he said.

"Okay. Avril, go on up top, and start signaling. Rico, come on back to the cargo bay and give me a hand with the inflatable raft.

I don't know how close to shore I can bring the ship without running aground."

∞ ∞ ∞

Atop the Seraphim

Boutelle climbed up out of the topside hatch and clipped her safety line to the cleat. She felt a bit silly, wondering if she had promised something she wouldn't be able to deliver, but it was worth a try. The challenging part would be making face-to-face contact ashore, if there were any natives in the vicinity, and if they wanted to talk. But, first things first.

She stood and swept her gaze around the lake. There was no way she would spot any natives; even if they were down at the shore, their ability to blend into the background was uncanny. Rather, she was looking for the most likely spots they might have an observer watching, and trying to estimate the acoustics of the lake.

Finally, she held the alien ocarina to her lips and gave it a few practice puffs. Then, holding her fingers over the holes just so, and taking a deep breath, she blew a long, loud, high-pitched note, followed by two shorter tones, falling and rising. The signal for, roughly, *let's talk*. She paused to listen, and faintly, over the lapping of wavelets against the hull, heard the echo of her own tones. She waited a minute longer, but heard nothing. Well, she hadn't really expected an immediate response.

She turned slightly, took another breath and repeated the tone sequence. Again, she heard nothing but the waves and her own echoes in response. She tried again, with similar lack of results. Maybe this was just a waste of time. Her deep breathing had made her a little dizzy. Verdigran air was perfectly breathable, but hyperventilating even Earth air could do that.

Boutelle looked around the lake again. She was sure that her signal was audible anywhere near the shore, and even atop some of the tree-covered hills. She faced another direction and tried again. A long, high-pitched tone, a shorter, lower note, then another short note midway between the first and second. Again, faint echoes came back to her. She took another breath and raised the instrument to her lips. A faint whistle, rising then falling, sounded in the distance. Had she imagined it?

It came again. Two rising notes then a falling one. Loosely speaking, it meant *acknowledged*. Boutelle stifled a shout. *Yes!* It was virtually impossible for her to tell what direction the sound was coming from, but it didn't matter. Boutelle was sure they had eyes on her. Snake-eye vision wasn't optimized for distance, the natives had little need of that in the jungle, but it was certainly good enough to make out the strange white ship floating near one end of the lake, and they'd see her as she paddled the raft ashore. Wherever they were, they could make good time through the forest; they'd meet her wherever she landed.

She raised the ocarina again and this time blew the same two rising and one falling notes, acknowledging the acknowledgment as it were. A final call came in response. Three short notes, all the same pitch. *Roger, out.*

Boutelle stepped back across the hull to the open hatch, and leaning over it, yelled down. "I made contact. They've agreed to meet. Where's that raft?"

∞ ∞ ∞

Avril Boutelle was more than a little nervous as she stepped out of the raft and waded the last couple of meters to the shore. Rico had come with her to help paddle the raft, but they had agreed that he would then back off and leave her to meet with the yeushpent, the snake-eyes, alone. Rico could be intimidating enough to other humans, and the natives averaged smaller than humans.

One native stood near the trees at the edge of the short beach, but Boutelle had no doubt there were others hidden from view among those same trees, probably with bows or blowguns aimed at her. She had interacted with yeushpent in the wild before, as part of her xenoanthropology studies, but that had been with different tribes, and she hadn't done it alone.

She held her hands away from her body, palms facing the yeushpent, showing that she was unarmed. "*Alschoaa,*" she said, a word that meant "greetings" in many yeushpent dialects. She hoped it was at least understood here.

The native likewise spread his hands to her, and said, "*alshoa*".

Okay, Avril thought, *so the dialect is a little different. Or perhaps the accent.* Between her own knowledge, and the translation programs on her omni, she could deal with that.

After a few false starts, she and the yeushpent set to discussing why she had wanted to meet. A few others stepped out of the trees, weapons in hand but not at the ready.

"I was expecting to meet another human here, but he is late. I wondered if you knew of any in the area."

"Not in our territory. We would know."

"He would be coming from the south." She pointed toward the lake's outlet. "Probably up the stream, maybe overland."

"That Uktapi range. Ask them."

I would if I could, she thought. "I don't know how to find them. If I travel from here, I might miss him. Can you ask them?"

Her contact turned to the others, and they spoke between themselves for a minute, too quickly and quietly for her or her omni to follow.

"Why would we? We don't want humans here."

"When Burnside gets here, we will take him and leave."

"Burnshide?"

"That is his name, the man I am waiting for."

This triggered further hushed discussion between them. Finally. . . . "We will tell Uktapi you wait for Burnshide. You leave when he gets here. If we have news, we will signal you." He made a gesture to one of the others, who held up an ocarina-like signaling flute.

"Thank you." Avril said. The yeushpent, except for their spokesman, faded back into the trees. She turned to signal Rico to come back to shore. At his wave of acknowledgement, she turned to thank the yeushpent again, but she was now alone.

"Well?" Rico said as she climbed back into the raft. "Any sign of him?"

"I'm not sure. They said they'd talk to the tribe to the south, where he'd be coming from. It was odd, though, almost like they knew his name."

"The Velkaryans may be looking for him. Perhaps they heard it from them."

She shrugged. "Maybe, but I got the impression they wouldn't cooperate with Velkaryans, and were only cooperating with us to get us out of here faster."

Rico grunted an acknowledgment. "I hope for all our sakes that you're right. Let's report back and see if Roberts wants to stay or leave."

Chapter 38: The Hunt for Sophie

New Toronto

Vaughan banged his fist on the desk. It was as though Burnside, and now Rico, had vanished off the face of the planet. Of course, it was entirely possible that they had; perhaps the ship Rico had come in was here to pick Burnside up, but there was no record of the *Sophie* landing at any spaceport on Verdigris, no green-haired pilots, and no unaccounted for warp signatures. Horowitz's pal Mikey hadn't had any useful information.

He mulled it over. If Burnside had been responsible for the sabotage—and Vaughan was sure that he was—and he had left the planet, then the sabotage should stop. As far as production, that should be all Vaughan cared about, but that was too many what-ifs to be comfortable. Besides, Burnside couldn't be allowed to get away with the damage he'd already caused, and it would be useful to interrogate him, if he could be taken alive. But how had Rico gotten on-planet, and could he get Burnside off the same way? Was there even a connection?

Rico had worked for Hopkins, a notorious artifact smuggler both on Verdigris and elsewhere. And while smugglers would usually just conceal their contraband in some other shipment, or bribe a spaceport agent, they'd also have their own ways of getting on and off a planet. There was no reason they had to have landed at a spaceport.

Vaughan summoned his assistant.

"Soleck, I want a scan of all planetary surveillance satellite data for the last week."

"Looking for what, sir?"

"Ships out of place. Anything capable of getting to or from space that isn't parked at a spaceport. I think Rico must have used some smuggler trick to get here, and may do the same to get Burnside off."

Soleck looked doubtful. "There'll be quite a few. A lot of companies have their own ships. Mining sites, large farms, prospectors. . . ."

"And they should all be registered. Have them cross-checked. Especially look for anything in an unusual place."

"Not all that data is public. We'll have to go through channels. That will take a while."

"Then why are you wasting time making excuses? Get on it!"

"I. . . . Yes, sir."

As his aide beat a hasty retreat, Vaughan thought about it. Yes, there were a lot of privately held ships. Even though Burnside's "Mr. Fisher" had been fake, Otani Biochemicals was one such example. Vaughan knew where their ships were, he'd had them checked out. They'd never heard of a Mr. Fisher, didn't understand why Hansa Astrospace was asking, and weren't looking to replace their ships just yet . . . unless Hansa was offering a deal?

Still, Verdigris was perhaps the third most populated planet in T-Space, not counting Earth itself. Not quite as busy as Sawyers World or Kakuloa, but busy. Once Soleck got the "channels" set up, an automated comparison of orbital scans against registered ships should turn up any anomalies within a few hours. It occurred to him that UDT law enforcement probably had something like that already—but he also knew that such computerized systems could be made to ignore anomalies, either by subverting flaws in the algorithms, or by hacking, or by good old fashioned bribery or blackmail. That was the advantage to an ad hoc query like what Soleck was arranging; it couldn't be anticipated and evaded. If Rico's ship was still anywhere on the planet, it would be found.

Chapter 39: Encounter in the Jungle

Verdigris, somewhere south of Lake Buckhorn

Burnside pushed his way through the dense bush. This was as bad as the jungle he had made his way through after landing. The going was even slower than the canoe had been. What he wanted to do was rest, but he had to make it to the lake by nightfall. Assuming a ship was waiting for him, it wouldn't wait past tomorrow dawn, and might even lift during the night. Not that it would make a difference, there was no way he could make any progress through this in the dark. If one could call what he was making now "progress."

He slogged on, forcing his way through the brush, hoping that there was nothing venomous living in the vegetation he was shoving aside. Did jade ribbon snakes live this far north? Probably not, but Verdigris, like any other untamed planet, had plenty of other nasty critters. He just hoped that he smelled different enough from native animals that nothing would want to take a bite of him, although that wouldn't help if something were just trying to defend itself from the big strange creature lumbering through its habitat. For that matter, he realized as he slapped at an insect that had just landed on his arm, it wasn't helping against the mosquitos, either.

Burnside became aware that he wasn't alone. Aside from the insects, something large was stalking him, behind and to the right of his trail. He paused for a moment, silent. There was something to the left, also. He tried to remember what predator in these parts hunted in packs. Most were solitary hunters. Unless this was a mated pair; those might hunt together.

He went forward a few more meters, listening as carefully as he could to whatever was behind him. Were there more than just two?

He slid his pistol from its holster, thumbing the safety off. He took two more paces, toward a large tree, then turned quickly to put his back to it, raising the gun. "Hello?" he called loudly, then "*Alshoa?*"—the equivalent in the Verdigran dialect he'd learned a few words of.

There came a rustle from the bushes a few meters in front of him, and then a voice, Verdigran, called out, "Burnshide, *alshoa.*"

A snake-eye stepped out of the bushes to his right, holding a bow with a nocked arrow, aimed at him. It was not the one who had spoken.

"Friend," Burnside said. He slowly lowered his pistol. The alien lowered the bow and relaxed the tension on the string. Two others stepped out of the bushes. He didn't recognize any of them, but one of them had known his name.

He holstered his pistol, then activated the translation program on his omni. Eventually, between the translator, the few phrases in the local Verdigran dialect that he knew, and a few English or French words the Verdigrans knew, he learned that they had been following him for some time, and had heard a story through the native trade network of a strange human, not one from the big village, who had been wandering alone in the jungle to the south some weeks ago. From what he could make out, these snake-eyes either thought he was the same person, or that *Burnshide* had become a general term for such idiots. The latter would not have surprised him.

By now, Delta Pavonis was settling on the western horizon. Not that they could see the horizon through the trees, but it would explain how dark it was getting. Burnside tried to get the idea across that he needed to get the lake to the north before sunrise. The snake-eyes could see in much lower light than humans. He didn't know the evolutionary biology behind it and didn't really care, but it helped explain the slit-pupils that Verdigran natives normally showed in daylight. Right now, from what he could tell in the fading light, the pupils were wide, although not yet perfectly round.

"Can you guide me to the lake? I cannot see in the dark as well as you can."

They looked at each other, as though puzzled or amazed. "It ish not dark yet."

"It is to me. Not as dark as it will be soon, but dark enough."

"No wonder the big village has so many lightsh. You are night-blind, like"—and here he said a word the translator didn't recognize. Burnside assumed it was some diurnal animal.

"Perhaps," Burnside said. "but the night skies are brighter where I come from." That was true enough. Between the light pollution on Earth, and the two suns in the Alpha Centauri system, nights were brighter, although on either Kakuloa or Sawyers World there was half the year where only the moons lit the night sky, not the other star. But in that system, neither planet had a blanket of skyweed blocking the sky.

"We are going that way. You come with ush."

∞ ∞ ∞

Even with their help, the going was difficult. Two led the way, with the third following behind him to ensure he managed to stay with them. He did that mostly by sound, the Verdigrans no longer trying to remain silent. The occasional gleam of Gex-light through the skyweed and the trees also helped, and after a half-hour or so, Burnsides vision had become more dark-adapted. That didn't prevent him from occasionally tripping over a root or blundering into a low branch, much to the amusement of the Verdigran behind him, but he wasn't going to give up now.

It took several hours to reach a spot where the sky grew a little brighter, and Burnside realized that the trees had thinned out, and they were now closely paralleling a stream. He assumed it was the same one he had been paddling up earlier, and after a few more minutes, the ambient sound changed, as though there were a large empty area ahead. Then they broke out of the bush altogether and Burnside found himself standing on the shore of the lake. At last!

"This is lake," the Verdigran leader said.

"Yes, it is." There was enough glow from the moonlight through the overcast and skyweed that he could make out the lake's surface, and the shoreline for a few hundred meters in either direction. He caught more of that out of the sides of his vision than when trying to stare directly at it. It was a trick he'd used before; the human eye was least sensitive to light at the point of best focus, because of the difference between rod and cone cells, but he wasn't biologist enough to explain it. "Thank you for your help," he said, turning to the others.

There was no reply, and Burnside realized that they'd quietly slipped back into the forest, leaving him alone on the shore.

∞ ∞ ∞

Burnside shook off his initial dismay. It was fair enough. The snake-eyes had brought him to the lake, and that was all they had agreed to. Now he just needed to contact the ship, or vice-versa.

He peered out into the darkness. It was a big lake, and he hardly expected the ship to have its running—or mooring—lights on if it was trying to be stealthy. But they should be looking for him, and would have night-vision gear. He just had to make himself seen in a place they would be looking. There were waves lapping at the shore, not big ones, but more than Burnside expected given the current lack of wind. There had been a light rain earlier, and he'd heard distant thunder, but if a storm had hit, things would be wetter and the lake surface more roiled. The storm must have bypassed the lake. What would a waiting ship have done? *Probably left early*, Burnside realized. That made more sense than risking damage in the confines of a lake during a storm of unknown intensity, but they should return when the storm passed. Could the pilot land on a lake at night? It shouldn't make a difference with a light-amplifying viewscreen, but for all his joking about stealing a Velkaryan ship, Burnside was not an experienced pilot. He knew *he* wouldn't want to try it.

He could try walking around the lake. The shoreline should be reasonably clear, and he could see enough of it in front of him that he could walk. The small beach here was just gravel, small rounded stones and sand, but if the trees came down to the waterline somewhere, he'd be stuck. Besides, every muscle in his body ached, and all he wanted to do was lie down and sleep.

No, he thought. *They'll never see me if I just lie down*. He had to build a fire. Not too big, but they'd be able to see almost any fire from clear across the lake. Besides, it was getting cold. He could use the warmth.

He forced himself to trudge up the beach to the tree line, gathering scattered driftwood as he went, although there wasn't much of that. He found a few downed branches and old logs without having to go too far into the trees. He couldn't afford to get lost now.

Chapter 40: Moby Dick

Lake Buckhorn, next day

Burnside woke at the first glimmers of dawn the next morning, his muscles aching from the previous day's exertions and sleeping on the hard ground. There was a chill in the air, and the lake's surface was hidden beneath a blanket of mist. There was no ship anywhere in sight. He picked up a stone and tossed it out into the lake, where it splashed with a *kerplunk*. The disturbance cleared a small circle of the mist, enough to tell him that it rose less than a meter above the surface. So much for it hiding his ride.

He poked at the remains of the fire; it had died down to a few glowing coals. He put a few more sticks on it, blowing to encourage them to light. As the flames flickered higher, he put on a larger stick. The warmth was good. He wasn't worried about being observed. The natives already knew he was here, and to any passing observation satellite, it would just register as another snake-eye campfire.

The question was, now what? He was now a day late for his designated rendezvous, and if whoever had come for him was following instructions, they should have left. He looked out at the lake again. The mist was thinning, but that only confirmed that there was nothing there. Maybe he'd have to steal a Velkaryan ship after all. He almost relished the idea; it would really piss Vaughan off. What he didn't relish was the trek back to New Toronto.

He turned back to the fire and his backpack, and began digging through that for something for breakfast. Behind him, he heard splashing from the lake, and idly wondered if he had something he could improvise a hook and line from. The thought of fresh-caught fish roasted over hot coals made his mouth water.

The splashing grew louder, accompanied by a gurgling and bubbling sound. *What in the world?* Burnside turned to look out at the lake again. There, perhaps eighty meters offshore, a great pale shape, like the back of a white whale, was rising from beneath the water. As the fins broke the surface, he realized what he was seeing. *A ship.*

∞ ∞ ∞

Fifteen minutes later, Burnside had his gear packed and the fire extinguished, and was greeting the man who had paddled ashore in an inflatable raft deployed from the ship that now floated on the lake's surface.

"Are you JB?" the man called as he hopped out of the raft and pulled it up the narrow beach.

"Were you expecting somebody else?" Burnside asked. "Yes, I'm Jordan Burnside. And you are?"

The man stuck out his hand. "I'm Rico. Just Rico. I'm here with Jackie Roberts. She tentatively ID'd you from the ship, but she says the beard is new."

Burnside grinned and stroked his chin. Yes, he had several days growth there, as well as otherwise being considerably more bedraggled than the last time Jackie had seen him. "I guess it is," he said. "I'm looking forward to getting cleaned up, and I'm certainly glad to see you. Let's get out of here."

"Works for me."

Burnside threw his pack into the raft, then the two of them pushed it out into the water and climbed aboard.

Rico handed him a paddle. "It will go faster with two," he said.

Burnside took the paddle with a sigh. "I had hoped I was all done with paddling for a long while, but you're right." Over the protests of his aching muscles, he joined Rico in propelling the inflatable craft toward what he assumed was Jackie's ship, the *Sophie.*

They reached it in a few minutes. A young woman Burnside didn't recognize, obviously not Jackie Roberts, stood topside. A rope ladder hung down to the waterline, and he and Rico maneuvered the raft alongside it.

The woman tossed another line down. "Rico," she called out, "attach this to the raft and we'll haul it out." Then, "Mister Burnside, I'm Avril Boutelle." She reached down. "Hand me your pack."

Burnside did so, saying, "Call me Jordan," and climbed the ladder while Rico finished tying the raft to the extra line. Then Rico started up the ladder too.

Avril started to haul the raft up as soon as it was empty, and Jordan Burnside stepped over to help her. Rico began gathering up the rope ladder as soon as he was topside.

"I take it we're in a hurry?" Burnside said.

A voice came from below, Jackie Roberts's voice. "You tell me, Jordan. Your instructions said not to linger more than a day."

He checked the time on his omni as Rico and Avril finished deflating the raft and stuffing it down the open hatch. He called down after it, "We've got forty minutes before the next satellite pass. Can we be out of here before then?"

"We can if you guys get your butts down here," she called back.

"You heard her," Rico said. "Go on down, Boutelle and I will finish securing things up here."

Burnside took the hint and clambered down the hatch that opened into the ship's airlock. Jackie Roberts was pulling the deflated raft out of the way and pushing it back toward the galley. He lent a hand, while wryly saying, "Request permission to come aboard?"

They got the raft out of the way, and Jackie stepped around it. There was something different about her. "You changed your hair," he said.

She smiled, and looked him up and down. "So did you. You look pretty scruffy."

"A few days in the woods will do that. It's good to see you again."

"Likewise, and, permission granted." At his puzzled look, she added, "To come aboard. Welcome to the *Seraphim.*"

"The *Seraphim*? A new ship?" It didn't look any different from the *Sophie* he remembered.

She shook her head. "No, just changed the name. We're travelling incognito."

"Ah, hence the hair," Burnside said. "But from that white whale act you pulled this morning, you should have named it *Moby Dick*."

"Playing submarine wasn't my first choice. Thank Rico. But we can talk about that later."

Avril and Rico were already in the airlock, with Rico checking the hatch. "All secure topside, Captain," Avril said.

"Roger that. You and Rico finish stowing the raft while I finish getting us ready for takeoff. Jordan, I'm sure you want to hit the fresher, but let's get out of here first. Stow your gear in the upper starboard bunk and get yourself strapped in. We'll talk more when we're in the air."

This was the no-nonsense Captain Roberts that Burnside remembered, quite distinct from the "Queen of Diamonds" role she'd been playing when he first met her. It fascinated him how she could switch that on and off as the situation demanded. "Aye, aye, Captain," he said, and went to make it so.

∞ ∞ ∞

Lake Buckhorn

The *Sophie/Seraphim* had a small hydrojet thruster to maneuver the ship in just the event it had touched down on water. Jackie Roberts used it now to maneuver the ship out away toward the center of the lake. Near the shore, trees interfered with whatever wind there was, making it difficult to tell the best direction for her takeoff run. She hoped there was more of a breeze in the middle. She could see ripples, but not clearly enough to tell the wind direction.

Rico came forward and sat down in the copilot's seat. "Everything is secured aft, Captain," he said. "What now?"

"Now, I figure out the best direction for takeoff while the tanks finish draining."

"Don't we need the fuel? Or are you just talking about the extra we took on for ballast?"

"We just need enough fuel to get airborne and fly a hundred kilometers or so. I don't want any more than that, or we might be too heavy to get out of here. It's not a very long lake, even shorter if there's a strong crosswind." She didn't think there would be much wind this early in the morning, but it remained to be seen.

"You can't just lift straight up?" Rico asked.

"Once we're clear of the water and the fan covers have time to open, yes. Until then, we have to rely on aerodynamic body lift, so the question is whether we can get clear of the lake and the hills on the far side in time. Didn't I mention this earlier? Or your friend who used to hide his ship underwater?"

"With him, we never discussed the details. If you did mention it, I missed it."

By now they were in the middle of the lake. The morning mist had cleared, and sure enough, there was a faint breeze blowing from the east. Unfortunately, the long axis of the lake ran mostly north-south, although with a slight curve to it.

Jackie brought up a topographic display on her main screen. What she had told Rico about engaging the lift fans had been true enough. Once they were at full thrust, *Sophie*—or *Seraphim*—could lift straight up. Until then, however, the ship needed enough forward airspeed to fly like any other lifting body, meaning fast. The transition from horizontal to vertical flight wasn't instantaneous, they'd be covering ground while that took place, and the trick was to keep or gain enough altitude *above* that ground at the same time. Given the size of the lake and the height of the surrounding hills, that would be a challenge. There were two other possibilities that she hadn't mentioned to Rico. If she could get enough up-angle by pitching the nose up after take-off, she could cut in the main thrusters and power out like any other launch. The trick there was to do that without pitching up too quickly—that could cause an aerodynamic stall, or complete loss of lift—before the thrust could even that out. Normally the lift fans helped there.

The other option, not normally used in-atmosphere, was to use the ventral thrusters *without* the fans. They could throttle-up far faster than the fans could spin up, and collectively their thrust came close to that of the main, aft, thrusters. The thing was, applying them at full thrust in atmosphere was incredibly loud—they normally operated only at partial throttle, with the fan downwash both providing extra lift and masking the noise produced by the shear of the thruster exhaust against the surrounding air. The aft thrusters generated the same noise, but the aerodynamics of the ship dampened that somewhat, and those thrusters were at the back, with meters of sound-deadening structure between them and the cabin. The ventral thrusters were right under the floor, both ahead and behind the cabin. In vacuum, of course, none of that was a problem.

It wasn't just the loudness she was worried about. Their ears might ring for a bit afterward, but noise was vibration, and this was an old ship. It shouldn't actually break anything, but the wear and tear meant an overhaul that much sooner.

She stared at the topographic display for a while, plugging several different takeoff scenarios into the computer. Finally settling on the least worst one, she engaged the hydrojet again and headed the ship back to her chosen starting point at the south of the lake.

"All right folks, listen up," she announced. "This takeoff is going to be interesting—"

"I hope you don't mean that in the 'oh god, oh god, we're all going to die' sense," Burnside interrupted.

"How would you like to swim back, Jordan? It would help lighten the ship."

"Sorry," he said. "You were saying?"

"Okay. Because we can't lighten the ship any further"—the tanks had been drained to the minimal fuel point Jackie was comfortable with—"and because *somebody* didn't pick a longer lake for us to land on, I'm going to have to use a few short-field take-off tricks to get us out of here. This may seem a little different from other take-offs you've experienced, including some rapid changes in attitude. Just remain calm, keep your seatbelts tight, and enjoy the ride. Trust me, I'm a trained professional. Do not try this at home. Everyone good?"

"Ah, okay."

"Roger that."

"We're good, let's go."

"All right. Oh, one other thing. It may get louder than you're used to. That's normal too. Here we go."

Jackie fired up the auxiliary thrusters mounted above the main thrusters at the back of the ship, and the *Sophie/Seraphim* surged forward, the nose dipping at first from the asymmetric thrust, then rising again as their speed through the water increased.

One of Jackie's screens showed the view from an aft camera, showing where the water came to on the back surface. As the ship accelerated, they rose higher in the water, raising fierce waves in their wake. Ahead, the curve of the lakeshore was threatening to intercept the straight path of the starship. This was the first tricky bit. Jackie angled *Sophie*'s fins to vertical as high as they would go, applying rudder pressure to help turn the Sophie to parallel the shore. As soon as they had curved enough that Jackie could see a straight shot to the furthest point in the lake, she dropped the fins back to a horizontal position to get the most lift.

She checked the aft screen. All thrusters were clear of the water now. She hit the control to open the forward fan vents, then fired the main engines. With a *BOOM* and then a sustained roar, the thrust shoved them forward, pushing the nose back toward the water before Jackie could compensate. She got the nose up again, and then they had flying speed. *Sophie* lifted from the water. Jackie slammed the control for the rest of the ventral fans, powering up everything *Sophie* had.

They weren't clear yet. The far shore was coming up fast, and they were still well below the hills beyond it. Jackie angled the ship toward their lowest point, but they weren't climbing fast enough. The display showed the aft fan vents open, but the forward vent was sticking again. *Damn it!* Without that, the unbalanced force would tend to push the ship's nose down. Screw it.

"It's gonna get loud!" she yelled back over the already loud roar of the main thrusters, as she reached to apply full power to all the ventral thrusters.

A high-pitched hissing scream, like a thousand steam-engines venting at once, came from beneath them as the ventral thrusters came to full power. The ship surged upward, shaking in the grip of the turbulent airflow around them.

And then they were clear of the hills, flying above them at fifty meters and still climbing. Jackie hastily throttled everything back to more reasonable levels for a smooth climb out, and as their airspeed increased, she cut the ventral thrusters and fans altogether. The sound subsided to reasonable levels.

She turned back to the others. "Everyone still good?"

Rico gave her a thumbs-up. Avril was rubbing her ears and shaking her head slightly as if to clear them, but nodded. "Yeah, I'm good."

Burnside also nodded. "That was even more fun than Tanith," he said. "But you looked a little busy at the end there. Couldn't the computer have done it?"

Jackie grinned. That had, in fact, occurred to her. "I offered," she said, "but it didn't even want to try."

∞ ∞ ∞

Aboard the Seraphim

"So, what now?" Burnside asked as Roberts leveled off at five thousand meters.

"Now we head for Lake Quebec," she said. "We're on minimal fuel at the moment. I assume you would rather I topped up on the lake rather than the New Toronto spaceport."

"Just so long as it doesn't involve another takeoff like that one, then yes I would."

"No worries. A hundred kilometers of runway, minimum."

"How long to get there?"

"Half an hour, less if we need to. Why?"

"No rush. That gives me time to use the fresher and find some cleaner clothes to wear. Uh, do you still have spares?" The first time he had boarded the *Sophie*, he had just suffered a gunshot wound and needed to replace his torn and bloody shirt. Jackie had given him a new one from ship's stores, that she'd had for her former co-pilot.

"We'll find you something," Avril said, "but please, do hit the shower." She waved a hand in front of her wrinkled-up nose.

"Yeah, sorry about that," he said, unstrapping and rising from his seat.

"Spare clothing's in the same drawer by the traumapod," Roberts called back. "Should be something left in there. Go easy on the water for now."

"Thanks." Burnside headed aft, stripping off what was left of his shirt as he did so. He tossed it in the trash disposal, then rummaged in the drawer until he came up with a tee-shirt and shorts, still packaged.

The small captain's cabin, behind the cockpit, had its own small fresher, but there was another midships for passenger and other crew use on the port side, forward of the galley. "Out soon," he said, and stepped inside.

Under normal gravity, such as now, shower acted as just that, a normal water shower. In zero-gee, it got more complicated. Burnside was glad Jackie hadn't climbed straight for space. He stripped off the rest of his tattered clothes, then stepped into the shower and turned on the water.

The hot spray felt so good on his dirty skin and aching muscles that he would have liked to stay there for a while, but he kept it short, just long enough to get clean. He looked himself over. His skin, in particular on his arms, was a mass of scratches and insect bites, now brought into prominence as the warm water flushed his skin. He shrugged; there was nothing bad enough for the traumapod. He'd had worse.

He dried off and donned the fresh clothing, disposing of the rest of the rags he'd been living in for the past few days, and returned to join the others.

"Better," Avril said as he came forward.

"Yes, thanks."

"That was more of a statement than a question," she said.

"Cheeky."

"All right," Roberts said. "Touching down in about ten minutes, you might as well get strapped in."

"You know you're a tyrant, Captain Roberts," Burnside said. "You probably all had coffee before you even surfaced this morning. I haven't had any in three days."

"Sorry. You'll have to wait just a little longer. You can have coffee and breakfast while we refuel. That, and tell us what we're going to do next."

Chapter 41: Side Trip

Aboard the Seraphim, *Lake Quebec*

The starship bobbed slightly on the surface swells of the lake, the sound of the tanks filling making a background gurgle as the team sat around the galley table.

Burnside had already consumed a cup of coffee and an omelette—or something that professed to be an omelette, despite being more of a rectangular slab—and was now working on a second coffee and the autochef's approximation of a raspberry danish.

"So, what's next?" Jackie asked. "Back to Alpha Centauri?"

"Eventually," Burnside said, "but there's something we need to check out in this system first. Also, why are Rico and Boutelle here? You didn't need their help just to pick me up, did you?" He looked at them both. "Not that I object to your company, of course," he said, focusing more on Avril as he said that. She ignored him.

"Ducayne sent us along," Rico said, "partially as a contingency. Avril and I both have previous experience on Verdigris that would give us some cover."

"Okay, I can see how that could be useful." "What are your specialties?"

"I'm primarily an analyst," Boutelle said. "And part-time, at that. I'm working on my masters in xenoanthropology, and I've got field experience here."

"Oh? I could have used your help earlier. I had a couple of encounters with the Verdigran natives. Interesting people. But I'm surprised Ducayne sent you out here if you're not a field agent."

"I've had the training," Boutelle said, her voice firm. "I can take care of myself."

"Okay," Burnside said, "no slight intended. It's just that most analysts aren't." He turned to Rico, wanting to change the subject. "What about you?"

"Oh, I'm definitely a field agent," Rico said, grinning. "I used to be a, let's say troubleshooter, for a shady character who was involved in artifact smuggling out of Verdigris and some other activities. Then I got involved with Roberts here and ended up working for Ducayne."

"Involved?" Burnside said, looking from Rico to Jackie.

"What he means is," Jackie said coldly, "that he was 'troubleshooting' for the guy who tried to interfere with Carson and me on Chara III"—she knew Burnside had been at least partially briefed on that encounter—"and we ended up rescuing his sorry ass from a crashed ship."

"Sorry ass?" Rico protested.

She grinned at him. "Of course, he did return the favor by helping to rescue me from some Velkaryans and blowing up *their* ship."

"I like him already," Burnside said, and gave Rico a thumbs up. "And what's your cover here? Back in the artifact business?"

"No, officially, I'm a bodyguard for Boutelle while she's in the jungle looking for natives," he said, "not that she needs one," he added hastily. "Although I did run into an old acquaintance from that business."

"Oh? Any problems?"

"He was down on his luck and wanted to know if I had something lined up. I wouldn't have told him even if I had. The guy's an untrustworthy rat. I just gave him the cover story."

"Where was this?"

"Louisbourg," Jackie said. "We landed there first to clear the formalities."

"Okay," Burnside said. "We should probably go there again to clear the planet. Otherwise, they'll eventually get around to wondering whatever happened to the *Seraphim*."

"What about Rico and me?" said Boutelle. "It seems kind of a waste to come all the way out here just to turn around and go back."

"I've kicked over a few hornets' nests lately. Was there some specific assignment you had?"

"Not as such, just whatever was needed to help get you out."

"And you've done that, and I thank you. There may be something else, but I need to think it through, catch up on any updates from Ducayne that you brought me, and probably have some more coffee."

The background gurgling of the filling tanks had stopped, as had the gentle rocking. With the added weight, the ship now rode lower in the water.

"Speaking of updates from Ducayne," Jackie said, "there's something I need to ask you. Come and join me in the control room while we secure the ship for takeoff." She looked at Rico and Boutelle. "Can you two take care of the galley and cabin area?"

The two glanced at each other, obviously curious but knowing better than to ask. "Sure," Rico said.

Jackie made her way forward and, as Burnside followed her into the cockpit, closed the hatch behind him.

"What's this about?" he asked.

"Remember the discussion we had on Tanith, about possible faster than light communications?"

Burnside thought for a moment. A lot had happened between then and now, but he remembered. "Yes, I do. We were talking about the anomaly you saw in the Zeta Reticuli system, and wondering if Tevnar's alien artifact might be related to something like that. Was it?"

"We don't know yet. We *did* find something to suggest that FTL comm is possible, and Ducayne wants to know if you heard or saw anything that might indicate the Velkaryans have an FTL link between here and Earth, or anywhere else for that matter."

"Okay, but do *you* need to know? And why now?"

"If it exists, the main relay is probably not here on the planet. Ducayne wants me to look for it if we can do so safely and covertly."

"Ah. I take it that neither Boutelle or Rico know about this, then. Hence the closed hatch," he said, gesturing behind him.

"Exactly, although I can brief them if you think there is something worth looking for. Do you?"

Burnside considered the question. "I'll have to give that some thought. Certainly, they have radio dishes suitable for deep-space communication, but that doesn't prove anything. My main focus was on their starship and weapons production, but I did gather some information that didn't quite add up. Let me get some more coffee in me and think about it for a bit."

"All right," Jackie said, "but we should get moving. I don't want to stay in any one spot too long." She touched a control, and the cockpit door slid open. She sat down at the main panel and began closing intake valves and otherwise readying the ship for takeoff. Before Burnside could leave, she turned to him and said, "Think about it while I fly us to solid ground somewhere. Any suggestions? What's our next stop likely to be?"

"Probably Louisbourg, although I'm not ready to go there just yet. Just find some clearing for now."

"Clearing, on this planet?" She was joking. Although the forests and jungles of Verdigris were extensive, any such would have some clearings where the soil was too thin or there had been a recent fire, and the planet was not without its deserts, although they too were often hidden beneath the airborne skyweed.

"A desert would be fine," Burnside said. "I've seen enough trees for a while."

Avril Boutelle had come forward at the opening of the door. "We'd stand out in the middle of a desert," she said. "Our cover has nothing to do with prospecting for minerals, or for ancient ruins. But what about the Nakamp?"

"What and where is that?" Jackie asked. She'd never heard of it.

"It's an area that is recovering from desertification. There's a strip of jungle on either side of a river that runs through it, and natives have been spotted in the area. The river is a transportation route."

"Kind of like the Nile in Egypt?"

"On a much smaller scale. We could land near the edge of the jungle."

"And where is it?" Jackie brought up a map of Verdigris on one of the control panel screens.

Boutelle pointed it out, an area to the east and south of them.

"That works for me," Burnside said.

"All right," Jackie said, turning back to the controls. "Jordan, grab yourself another coffee, and then you folks finish securing the galley while I get us ready for flight."

∞ ∞ ∞

Verdigris, Nakamp Desert

The *Seraphim* settled onto a low plain, sand and dust billowing out from her exhaust through the low scrubby vegetation. Fifty meters away, trees at the edge of the forest swayed slightly, settling as the ship's thrusters and lift fans came to a stop.

Jackie Roberts looked at the window screens and the slowly dissipating dust clouds beyond. "Well," she said, "that certainly raised a ruckus. I was expecting more sand than dust."

"This desert is more loess than sand," Boutelle said. "That's why it lofts so easily, providing nutrients for the skyweed. Will it cause a problem?"

Jackie shook her head. "No. I suppose if we stayed here long enough, we might get a drift forming over us, but that would take weeks or months."

"Barring a dust storm," Boutelle said.

"We're not staying," Burnside said. "I just wanted some time to plan our next moves without bobbing around on the lake, looking obvious."

"You mean like a fish out of water?" Jackie asked, her expression all wide-eyed innocence.

The others groaned.

Burnside shook his head and rolled his eyes. "Yes, exactly not like that. As I see it, there are three objectives. One, return to Louisbourg to let the *Seraphim* clear the planet. Two, after take-off, check near-space for some specialized communications gear."

"What kind of communications gear?" Rico asked.

"Specialized," Burnside said, his glare not inviting further discussion.

"Okay, okay. And third?"

"Third, do a flyover of the New Toronto spaceport so I can get a count of how many ships they have parked there. I wasn't able to get close enough lately to keep track."

"A flyover of a spaceport?" Jackie said. "That's going to have to be from space, or at least high enough to not be in controlled airspace, which is again, effectively, in space."

"That's fine. I just need to take a few pictures. From space should be fine."

"Skyweed?"

"Oh, crap. You're right. Any suggestions?"

"Let me think on it," Jackie said.

"What about the surveillance satellites?" said Rico.

"What about them?" Burnside asked, puzzled at the apparent non sequitur.

"That's why we're here instead of bobbing around on Lac Quebec, right? And why you were wanting to make sure we weren't still on Buckhorn Lake."

"Yes, but. . . ."

"I get it," Jackie said. "If we fly over the spaceport at the same time an observation satellite flies over, we can do a radar scan, and if anyone on the ground notices, they'll just assume it's the satellite. Is that what you were thinking, Rico?"

"Yeah, something like that."

Burnside nodded, smiling. "That should work. I assume you have imaging radar on the ship?"

"I do. It comes in handy for landings sometimes, and I've had clients who want radar scans. I'll have to reconfigure it to boost the signal to scan from space, is all."

"What about after that?" Boutelle asked. "Do you have a mission for us on planet, or do we head back to Sawyers World?"

"Right," Burnside said. "So, four objectives. Number four, we go home."

"That sounds good to me," Jackie said. The truth was, she was eager to get back. This back and forth with Ducayne's agents —and Avril and Rico were that, even if not as much so as Burnside—made her realize how much she missed Carson. With him, neither of them had to worry about "need to know" in their conversations. She wasn't cut out to be a spy, although she loved the investigative aspect of it, just as Carson did with his archeology.

"Before we take off," Rico said, "can I ask how we're going to look for this specialized communication gear?"

"What do you mean?" Burnside said.

"You said it was in space. Even near-space is big. Huge, depending on what you mean by *near*. So, what's the plan?"

"Okay, fair question. Jackie, you're the pilot, and you know what we're looking for. What do you think?"

Jackie thought the idea of looking for what was probably a spacecraft-sized needle in a planetary system-sized haystack might be a colossal waste of time, but there should be some way to narrow it down.

"Well," she said, "if we're right about some of our assumptions, this gear—call it a relay—may be somewhat sensitive to gravity waves and so would be out away from fast-moving massive bodies and ships going in and out of warp. It would probably be well beyond the orbit of Zeus."

"So, huge values of *near*, then," said Rico.

"Yes, although we can eliminate small values."

"So how do we find their relay if it has to be out beyond the gas giant?" Avril Boutelle wondered.

"They have to talk to it somehow," Jackie said. "There will be a local transmitter of some kind."

Burnside agreed. "She's right."

"Would they use a radio?"

"Probably," Jackie said. "They can't count on a laser getting through the skyweed."

"Okay," Boutelle said, "but they'd need a large dish, fifty meters or so. That should be obvious from orbit."

Jackie didn't agree. "Not through the skyweed."

"It would show up on radar." Boutelle said.

"That would certainly announce our presence," Burnside said, "just like scanning the spaceport. But anything that big would also be obvious from the ground."

"Of course," Boutelle said, "but how many people would know what it was for?"

Jackie shook her head. This was sidetracking the conversation. The answer was obvious, at least to her. "You don't need something big enough to beam a radio signal thirty AU," she said. "You only need to get it to orbit, or to the moon, Gex. A laser would work fine from there."

"Oh," Boutelle said. "You're right. So how do we find that?"

"They'd have a relay at one of the Verdigris-Pavonis Lagrange points, wouldn't they?" Burnside asked.

"Why?" said Boutelle.

Jackie had been thinking the same thing, so she answered. "They would if they want to use their relay when they're on the opposite side of Delta Pavonis as the planet orbits around it. Otherwise, there'd be a period of at least a couple of weeks or so when any signal would be lost in the glare. With a station elsewhere in orbit, they can relay through it and then on to the one out beyond Zeus."

"Right," agreed Burnside. "So, we look for *that* relay."

Jackie nodded. "Yes, and there are only two logical places to look, the L4 or L5 points. That's where I'd put it."

Boutelle nodded slowly. "Sounds reasonable to me," she said. "So how do we do that?"

"Very carefully," said Burnside. "If it were me, I would put detection gear on it so I could tell if someone were nosing around. Maybe even post a ship there. That way, they could keep intruders away and do any maintenance or re-pointing as needed."

"Wait," said Rico, who had seemed to be only half-listening while distracted by what looked like a game on his omni. "We were at the L5 point a week ago. We didn't see anything. Hopefully, it didn't see us."

"Different L5 point," Jackie said. "That was the Verdigris-Gex L5 point. We're talking about the Delta Pavonis-Verdigris points."

"Oh, right. Sorry." He turned back to his omni.

Jackie looked at him suspiciously. Had he really not been paying attention, or was this part of his perpetual "playing dumb" act to encourage others to underestimate him?

He looked back at her. "What?"

"Nothing," she said, but gave him a knowing grin.

He winked at her and returned to his omni, then raised his head again and said, "You guys were talking about them posting a ship?"

Jackie gave her head a slow shake. "Right," she said, turning back to Burnside. "Yes, they might post one if they were worried about intruders, but not likely for maintenance. Fully automated deep-space relays go back at least a century, to the early Mars missions. I don't think maintenance or pointing would be an issue, at least not worth keeping a ship on station. But yes, a sensor suite for intruder detection would make sense."

"How big would it need to be? The relay?"

Jackie Roberts thought for a bit. Power supply, station-keeping thrusters, probably a parabolic antenna for radio communication with Pavonis, and a laser and telescope for communication with the FTL relay. Electronics, thermal management . . . the usual. "A cubic meter or so. Maybe a dish on it a couple or three meters in diameter. Radiators, probably a solar panel for power. It wouldn't have to be very big. If they deployed it by just chucking it out the airlock of a ship, they'd want it small enough to fit."

"How hard would that be to find?"

"Probably the easiest way would for us to sit to sunward of the L4 or L5 point and look for hotspots against the cosmic background," Jackie said. "There will be some noise, and we might pick up the odd asteroid or two, but it would give us something to focus the instruments on. Then we look for something more artificial than natural."

"Would it be able to see us?" Boutelle asked.

"Not if I do the approach right. Come at it straight out of the sun, or rather Delta Pavonis. We should be lost in the glare."

"Then what?" Rico said, raising his head from his omni again. "We figure out where its comm laser is pointing and follow it from there? How far?"

"I don't know that we even need to do that," Burnside said. "The very fact of such an interim relay confirms that there's *something* of interest out there, that's valuable information in itself. We don't want to let them know that we know by being spotted chasing down their laser beam."

Jackie shook her head at all the double indirection. "That's fine with me," she said, "but I suggest we check out both Lagrange points even if we find a relay at the first one. If there is a second, we can calculate the intersection of the two comm lasers. We won't have to chase anything." As she finished, she noticed Rico giving her a knowing smile. She wondered how long ago he'd figured it out. The man was definitely smarter than he let on, and she was glad they were now on the same side.

"Excellent," Burnside said. "We'll do that."

"One thing, though," Jackie said. "With all this warping around in system, unless we want to be spotted by Velkaryan gravity wave detectors, we're going to have to do slow warp transitions. Avril and Rico know what I'm talking about. I hope you like roller coasters."

Chapter 42: Louisbourg, and Then to Space

Aboard the Seraphim

They had overflown New Toronto at an altitude of fifty kilometers, well out of the controlled airspace of the spaceport, and well below orbital space. As planned, Jackie had run a full instrument sweep, timed to coincide with the routine satellite scans. Unsurprisingly, most of the scans in the optical wavelengths picked up little more than the mottled green streaks of skyweed, but the imaging radar revealed plenty.

"The parking area is almost empty," Burnside said as he examined the pictures. "A few weeks ago, that was packed with ships, twenty at least. Where did they go?"

"Is that a hangar building?" Jackie asked, pointing at a large flat-roofed rectangle adjacent to the field.

"No, that's final assembly. They move the ships in there to fit out the interiors and such. There's probably room for a few more ships in there at any given time, but it would crowd the workers, and why do it?"

"So, they've gone somewhere else. Another field somewhere?"

"Not impossible, I suppose. There's cleared land south of the city that isn't being used for farming yet."

"Let me check the scans. We were flying high enough to cover a broad swath of the ground." Jackie accessed the raw radar image data, showing a wide strip that extended about ten kilometers on either side of their flight path over the city. She zoomed in on the area to the south, seeing a few scattered buildings, obvious farms, some forest, and yes, cleared fields. But no ships.

"You meant this area here?" she asked him, pointing. "I don't see any parked ships."

"No," Burnside said. "Okay, they could be anywhere. Dispersed in twos and threes, on the moon, maybe even sold to a big customer. All right, never mind. Let's get out of here."

"To Louisbourg, then," Jackie said.

"Do we have to? Why not straight to space?"

"We checked in," she said. "We should check out. You said so yourself, remember? It's not strictly required, but if we don't, there'll be a flag on the ship's name and registry, and that will invite extra scrutiny in the future."

"The *Seraphim*'s name and registry," Rico said, "not *Sophie*'s."

"True," Jackie said, "but there's no harm in clearing port. We just won't mention that we picked up an extra passenger. They're not going to search the ship. I'll just land, get the tanks topped up, and take care of the formalities. You can all stay aboard."

Rico muttered something Jackie didn't quite catch, but she could guess. "Yeah," she said, "your old boss probably wouldn't have bothered. Force of habit in my case; couriers follow the rules. Besides, after all this in-atmosphere flying, I really do need to make sure the tanks are full."

∞ ∞ ∞

Refueling and clearing port at Louisbourg had gone as smoothly as Jackie Roberts had expected, and now the ship was headed to space.

"Okay folks," she announced, "we're going to warp. This will be a short hop so say strapped in." She hit the control.

"What were you saying about roller coasters?" Burnside asked as gravity came back. "That was norm—"

Jackie cut the warp drive, fading it out to minimize the telltale gravity wave.

"—whoops!" Burnside said. "So *that's* what you meant. What are we doing now?"

"We want to look for the, ah, specialized communications gear, right? We're going to head to the Pavonis-Verdigris L5 point, or rather, considerably sunward of that. If there is something there, it won't see us against the glare. Meanwhile, anyone on Verdigris who cares will have seen the signature of our jump to warp, but not of us coming out of it, so they'll assume we're on our way to interstellar space. From now on, we do slow warp transitions."

"I can hardly wait," Rico said.

Jackie grinned to herself and began lining up the ship on their new destination.

Chapter 43: Looking for Relays

Orbiting Delta Pavonis

The *Seraphim* drifted a million kilometers to sunward of the Verdigris L5 point. Far enough from that point that they were unlikely to be detected by anything stationed there, and far enough from the star itself that the ship's cooling systems weren't overtaxed. The passengers were back in the galley area while Jackie trained the ship's instruments on the thin cluster of planetary debris orbiting L5.

Burnside glided forward to the cockpit and watched Jackie for a while as she went over the image data. "Well," he said, "is there anything that looks interesting out there?"

There wasn't, yet. The L5 region was home, at least temporarily, to several small asteroids. So far, they all showed up at the expected equilibrium temperature for a dark body that distance from the star, within minor variations. There had been no detectable electromagnetic signals, but they'd have to be lucky to intercept a radio beam at this distance.

"I've been doing spectroscopic analysis on our collection of bright spots," Jackie said.

"And?"

"So far, seven stony asteroids, two metallic asteroids, and three carbonaceous. Twelve down, another seven to go."

"Is that a lot?" Boutelle asked.

"Not really. None of them is even a kilometer wide, just a few tens of meters at most, spread out over a thousand kilometers or so. There will be more that are too small to see. That's why it's a good idea to avoid trojan points. Large rocks aside, there'll likely be dust associated with them."

"How much longer until you've scanned them all?" Burnside said.

"Maybe an hour. I need to bring the ship's targeting telescope to bear. It has the spectroscope." She had been doing that already, making tiny adjustments to the ship's attitude, but her passengers had ignored it as her doing "pilot stuff."

"All right. Can I get you anything from the galley?"

Jackie thought for a moment. Drinking coffee from a bulb wasn't quite the same as from a mug, but it was better than nothing. "Sure, a coffee, thanks."

"No problem," Burnside said, and propelled himself back aft.

∞ ∞ ∞

As it happened, it was only twenty minutes until Jackie called back, "I think I've got something."

"What do you have?" Burnside said as he came forward. Rico was right behind him.

"One bright spot. The spectrum looks very much like that of Delta Pavonis. Whatever it is, it's highly reflective."

"I wouldn't have thought that even polished metal would reflect everything equally."

"It doesn't. There are some dropouts. I just need to check a wider spectrum. Hang on."

She tapped at one of the monitor screens to the side of her main console, then nodded. "Confirmed. It's metal, mostly aluminum. Now what?"

"Send a drone in for a closer look?" suggested Rico.

"Wouldn't that tip our hand?"

"That depends on the drone," he said, and grinned.

Jackie looked at him quizzically. "What do you have in mind?"

"I'll need to borrow your fabber."

"Okay, but that didn't answer my question."

"I want to throw rocks at it. At least, they'll look like rocks."

"Seriously?" said Boutelle, who had also come forward.

"I think I know what he means," Jackie said. "This I want to see."

∞ ∞ ∞

Verdigris L5 position

The *Sophie* had moved closer to the suspect object, hanging in space two kilometers away. One of the ship's inspection drones, now cocooned in a fabricated shell to make it look like a rock—except for gaps over the sensors and thruster ports—drifted toward the device.

"How close do we want to get to it?" Burnside asked.

"No closer than a hundred meters," Jackie said. "More would be better. That thing may have proximity detectors. I've angled the path so we look like a rock just drifting by. Approaching it directly would trigger a collision alarm; we don't want that."

Jackie was piloting the drone, although most of the actual piloting had been to set it on course with a slow rotation so that the drone's sensors would stay focused on the target as it passed. She didn't know if the relay, if that's what it was, would be watching for a space rock to maneuver under its own power, but that would be a small subroutine to add to whatever debris track-and-evade software it did have.

"When can we get a good look?"

The current screen image showed the other satellite as a bright blob a few pixels wide, not enough to make out any detail.

"We're three hundred meters out now. Closing rate is just under a meter per second, and that will drop as we get closer because of the angles. The camera is designed for close-in work, so we can't zoom in. We're not going to see much until it's near its closest approach."

"Are you recording this?"

"Of course."

"Can you stack successive frames to get more detail?"

Jackie understood. Due to the movement of the camera, the image of the satellite would fall differently on the sensor's pixels with each frame. By overlapping successive frames, the computer could tease out details not obvious in a single frame. It was a technique used by astronomers probably since the dawn of digital cameras.

"Yes, just a moment." She tapped out a sequence of commands, and on another screen, a near duplicate image appeared, the satellite still a fuzzy blob. "Wait one." She tapped another control, and the few-pixel blob expanded to half the window size, but highly pixelated. Over the next couple of seconds, the image refined as the computer continued to process the incoming data. It was still pixelated and fuzzy, but it now showed more shape, angular, perhaps a hexagonal prism with flat ends.

"Well, that's either a huge quartz crystal, or it's artificial," Burnside said.

"My money's on artificial," said Rico.

"So's mine," Burnside agreed, "especially since quartz crystals don't look like aluminum on a spectrograph."

The image continued to improve as the drone drew nearer to the satellite, now showing rectangular panels, small projections, and several dark spots on the visible sides of the object.

"What are those features?" Boutelle asked.

"Could be almost anything," Jackie said. "The rectangles are probably solar panels. The other things might be stub antennas, sensors, control thrusters, and the like. But yes, it's definitely man-made."

"Could it have any purpose out here other than as a relay?" Burnside wondered. "I don't want to assume that it's what we're looking for just because it's in the right place."

"This would be a good location to monitor the sun—Delta Pavonis—for solar weather, watching for coronal mass ejections or the like. Of course, it could do that and serve as a relay too."

By now, the drone was nearing its closest approach, and the shifting perspective as it passed the satellite made it look like the latter was rotating. That may have been why Jackie and the others missed the fact that it had actually adjusted its attitude.

As they watched the image on the screen, it suddenly flashed and then went black.

"What happened?"

"We lost the signal. Checking." Jackie said as she checked another screen, then tapped several controls. "Damn it. I've lost all telemetry from the drone."

"That flash, was it from the satellite or because of the loss of signal?"

"I don't know yet. Let me try to reboot the drone." She tapped another sequence.

Rico, who had left the crowded control cabin at the LOS, came back in with a pair of binoculars. He went over to the window and peered out.

"I don't think that's going to work," he said. "I suggest we get out of here."

"What? Why?" Jackie said.

"Hard to be sure at this distance, but I think I see an expanding debris field where the drone should be. It looks like the satellite fired on it."

Chapter 44: Vaughan

New Toronto, Vaughan's office

Vaughan's omni chimed for an incoming call; it was the *UR-GENT* ringtone.

"Vaughan here. What?"

"Signal from Relay-two. It just fired on an approaching spacecraft."

"*What?* Give me the details."

"We're still downloading the full data dump, but it's programmed to fire on anything approaching too close that's either maneuvering or transmitting. It sent us a signal that it had just done that. We should have video and other details soon."

"Was it a ship?" Part of Vaughan's mind was exulting, *Got you, Burnside!* but there were other possibilities, including just a false alarm.

"Just a moment, we're checking."

While waiting, Vaughan considered the implications. Burnside or not, the chances that this was some innocent incursion were virtually nil. Somebody was curious about satellites stationed at the L5 position, and that wouldn't be idle curiosity. Did they suspect, or even *know*, about the FTL Communicator out beyond Zeus? That would be hard to find, but a fixed relay would be less so. If they suspected a need for such a relay, that meant whoever was looking didn't know any more about how the FTL comm worked than the Velkaryans did. The ancient aliens who had installed them in pyramids must have known how to make it work within a planet's gravitational field, but the Velkaryans hadn't figured that part out.

"Sir?" the voice came back over his omniphone. "Whatever it was, it was too small for a ship. Maybe a cubic meter, but it was emitting a radio signal. We're still downloading the video stream from the relay."

"A remote drone, then."

"Seems like it."

"All right. Continue to monitor the feed from Relay-two. Also, check Relay-one at L4. See if it's picking up anything unusual. And alert the FTL station. Somebody is poking around, and I don't like it."

"Okay, I'm on it."

Vaughan next summoned Soleck.

"Yes, sir?"

"Scramble three ships, armed, toward the Verdigris-Delta Pavonis L5 point. The *Sophie* might be there. If there's any ship there, I want it boarded or destroyed."

"Sir? Why would it be there?"

"We have special purpose equipment there, and it's detected something. Never mind the details, just get those ships there, fast." Vaughan's fierce expression didn't invite further discussion.

"I . . . okay, got it. Consider them on their way." Soleck beat a hasty retreat, already on his omniphone.

Chapter 45: Back at Alpha Centauri

Ducayne's office

"You wanted to see me?" Carson said as he entered Ducayne's office. There were two other people with Ducayne, Regina Elliot, his second in command, and a man Carson didn't recognize.

"I did. Take a seat. I believe you know Regina Elliot. This," Ducayne gestured at the other man, "is Anil Dejois, with the Sawyers World government."

The man reached forward, extending his hand.

Carson shook it, and said, "Dejois? Any relation to . . . ?"

"Yes," Dejois said, but did not elaborate.

"What's this about?"

"Good news," Ducayne said, "at least for you. I'm not exactly enthused about it, but Elliot and Dejois here convinced me, and my superiors concur. We—and by that I mean both the UDT and the Sawyers World government—are declassifying certain information regarding both the pyramids and your talismans. You can go ahead and write your paper."

Carson felt his heart beating faster. This was what he had been working toward for years. "That's fantastic, but you said *certain* information, so not all of it. Just what, exactly?"

Dubois spoke up. "As far as the pyramid in the Anderson Wildlife Preserve, we, the government, will reveal that it is in fact a pyramid, and that according to the archeologist in charge—that would be you—it is probably not connected to the native paleolithic spearhead makers. You're free to discuss your findings about that pyramid and how it may connect to whatever the UDT government is willing to let you reveal."

And there was the rub, Carson thought. "And just how much is that?" he said, looking to Ducayne and Elliot.

"You can talk about the pyramid on Verdigris," Elliot said, "including the fact that it was apparently damaged by illicit artifact traders before you found it. You can even mention the room you found, but avoid any speculation about what the missing equipment may have been."

"No problem. From an academic viewpoint, there's no basis to speculate about anything of the kind. What about Chara?"

"While I'd prefer you didn't mention it all," Ducayne said, "it seems that rumors of something on Chara III have been leaking out, and it's public record that you were gone long enough to have made a trip there, and while that covers plenty of other places in T-Space, you weren't seen at any of those. Thin evidence, but more than enough for conspiracy theorists."

"I've also published a paper on the primitive stone fences we found there," Carson pointed out. "I had to publish something."

"Right. Well, we might as well come out and admit it."

"You're saying I *can* talk about that pyramid?" Carson said.

Elliot provided the detail. "You can describe the exterior. We have a team in place there now, to discourage snoopers, but if you discuss what you found inside, it could start a rush on any other pyramids in T-Space. I'm sure you don't want that either."

"That's a good point. No, especially not if I'm going to be visiting those pyramids myself in the near future." Carson turned to Dejois. "What about the interior of the local pyramid? What are the plans to excavate it?"

"That's under discussion. Frankly, I think we'd all like to defer that for a while. If it were just another teaching museum like you found under the Chara pyramid, there wouldn't be a rush. But given the possibility of finding advanced alien technology within the pyramid itself. . . ."

Carson darted a glance at Ducayne and Elliot. He was sure they would have tried to keep that quiet. How had the Sawyers World government found out?

Ducayne guessed the reason behind Carson's questioning look, shrugged, and nodded. "Yes, they know."

Dejois nodded too. "The UDT and Sawyers World intelligence services have a special relationship," he said. "Even though we're independent of the UDT, we have common interests. And getting back to your question, one of those common interests is possible advanced alien technology. But if and when we go digging for that, it will have to be done carefully. Meanwhile, there's a Guard force in place to make sure nobody else goes digging for it."

"I see," said Carson. "That doesn't exactly leave me with a lot to write about. What about the talismans?"

"I think we've found all there are to find for the moment," Ducayne said. "At least, our network and catalog searches for any similar artifacts haven't turned up anything new in months. Barring a new find, or something in a private, undocumented collection like your most recent acquisition, that's probably it. You can describe them; you can even mention the embedded technetium battery. In fact, it's the battery's radioisotope dating that puts it safely far enough in the past for people to ignore."

It had been the radiation from the broken talisman Carson had found that first made him realize they were special. In fact, he had found a similar talisman on another dig a year before, but it had been intact, completely shielding the radioactive battery. The isotope itself, too short-lived to occur naturally outside of a recent supernova remnant, had been dated to fifteen thousand years ago, created at a time when humans hadn't even developed agriculture.

"What about the markings?" Each flat, stone-like talisman had a pattern of colored stones and lines, star maps. Not all had been deciphered, but those that had, each indicated a different planet where a pyramid had been found.

"You can describe them," Ducayne said. "There are on-line images of some of them already, so that reveals nothing. It would be best if you didn't discuss how to decode them."

Carson bit back his disappointment. That was one of the most convincing arguments in favor of the star-faring ability of whoever created those talismans, but he could see Ducayne's point. If other talismans were still privately held, why hand the owner a map to another pyramid? Especially since any such privately held artifact would almost certainly be in the hands of an illegitimate collector.

"All right. I assume I'll have to get any papers I write cleared for security first?"

Ducayne nodded. "I'm afraid so. Not that we don't trust you, but just to make sure something doesn't accidentally slip out."

"Of course." He turned back to Dejois. "Is there going to be some sort of advance publicity about the find here? That's usually the case on big finds; they don't just appear all of a sudden in an archeology journal paper."

"There is. The initial release will just mention discovery of the pyramid. Nothing about spacefarers, perhaps a hint that it was contemporary with the spearpoint makers."

"So, downplayed, but enough of a release that nobody can accuse the government of a cover-up," Carson said.

"That's one way of looking at it. We don't want to make too big a splash about it, of course, but there'll be a coordinated release between the Office of Land Management and the University."

"Does Dean Matthews know about this yet?"

Dejois grinned. "I thought you might like to be the first to tell him."

"Yes," Carson said, grinning himself. "I think I would."

Chapter 46: Busted

Aboard the Seraphim/Sophie, *near L5*

"Fired on it?" demanded Burnside.

"Hang on," Jackie said, "I'm moving." She was strapped into her seat at the controls, but the others were unsecured, loose in the zero-gee of normal space. She used the ship's maneuvering thrusters to put more distance between themselves and the mysterious satellite. It was probably armed and hostile.

"See for yourself," Rico said, handing the binoculars over to Burnside.

He looked, scanning the area. Against the starry black, it was hard to pick out anything specific. Then he found the expanding cloud of twinkling dots, each a fragment of the drone, flashing as their tumbling reflected the light.

"Something destroyed it, anyway." Burnside said. "If the satellite did fire on it, it will have sent a signal to its controllers reporting it. Yeah, we should leave."

"Already doing that," Roberts said. "Any sign of pursuit?"

"Not from the satellite. Verdigris could warp ships here in a matter of seconds if they had some waiting in orbit. Minutes if they had to take off from the surface."

"I know," Roberts said grimly. "And I don't want to engage warp until we're well clear of the crap floating around L5. Any thoughts on what destroyed my drone? Missile or laser?"

"Does it make a difference?" Burnside asked.

"I don't want to point the ship's telescope at anything that might shine a laser on it."

"Would you rather point your warp axis toward an incoming missile?" Rico said.

Roberts darted a glance at him, as if to ask *how do you know this stuff?* then turned back to her controls. "No," she said, and began pitching the ship up out of the orbital plane. That direction should get them to free space the quickest.

"Secure for warp. As soon as I think it's clear, I'm going to jump us a few million kilometers from here."

∞ ∞ ∞

New Toronto spaceport

Three Velkaryan ships lifted almost simultaneously from the field, their three-man crews—pilot, engineer, and weapons officer—having scrambled to them moments before.

Their state of readiness was something Vaughan had instituted some weeks back, prompted by the report of the Space Force war games in the Alpha Centauri system. Not that he expected anything soon; that exercise had been a fiasco, and Vaughan imagined it would be a while before the Space Force was ready to try anything in earnest. Nor had the local Velkaryans given them any reason to, yet. But that was coming. A declaration of independence from the UDT would almost certainly trigger a response, and it was better to be well trained for it than otherwise.

The crews of the three ships now climbing to space were sure this was just another drill, until the message came through.

"Clear atmosphere and warp to position PV-L5. Assume search pattern alpha, looking for a ship, possibly Sapphire class. Attempt to engage and board. Use of weapons authorized if met with resistance."

Warping there would take less than a second, but lightspeed delay between Verdigris and its L5 position was eight minutes each way. That was far too long to ask for additional instructions if and when they did spot the target ship. They'd been given their mission. Everything else was up to them.

∞ ∞ ∞

Aboard Seraphim

"What's our distance from the satellite?" Boutelle asked.

"Coming up on eighty kilometers," Jackie replied. "We're clear of most of the L5 asteroid cloud, but there might still be some dust." The L5 point wasn't so much a point as a region where gravitational forces between the star and the planet balanced with centrifugal "forces" to keep things together, but like an eddy in a stream, those things didn't stay fixed, but rather drifted around the point. A rock could wander many kilometers away from the geometric point and still be pulled back toward it. The further the ship got from that point the happier Jackie would be.

"It's been ten minutes since the drone was destroyed," Boutelle said. "Surely if the Velkaryans were sending a ship it would be here by now."

"It would take eight minutes for a radio signal to get from the satellite to Verdigris," Jackie reminded her. "If they had a ship on standby and react quickly, they could have it in the air in less than five minutes, and in space in another three. If they already had something in orbit, it could be coming out of warp any second now. There's no reason to hang around, so I would just as soon be elsewhere."

There was a general murmur of agreement from everyone else.

"Okay then. Everyone ready for gravity?" Jackie asked as she lined up the ship on empty space and made ready the warp drive.

"Yes, let's go."

"Engaging." Jackie hit the button. Gravity came back, then, with a flash, just as quickly went away, like hitting a bump on a road, and the shrill of the radiation alarm pierced the ship.

Chapter 47: Company

*Aboard Velkaryan ship, callsign "*Ripper*"*

The three Velkaryan ships had just come out of warp near the L5 position when an alert sounded.

"Radiation surge," the engineer announced, "not us, it came from outside."

"*Slasher* or *Arrow?*"

"No, they're fine. There was also a gravity ripple, separate from ours. I think another ship must have hit something in warp and dropped out."

"Our target? If it destroyed itself, that saves us some trouble."

"Might have been our target, but it was a small surge," the engineer said, reviewing the data. "It might be damaged, but it wasn't big enough to be destroyed."

"I can confirm," the weapons officer said. "I'm getting radar reflections now from one large object, Sapphire sized. Range 875,000 kilometers."

"Copy. Give me a bearing," the pilot said. "I'll coordinate with *Arrow* and *Slasher* to surround it at a thousand klicks."

"If there's debris in the area—" the engineer began.

"Radar isn't seeing anything else. Any debris is small," the weapons officer said.

"I'll make it two thousand. Weapons, warm up the laser."

∞ ∞ ∞

Aboard the Seraphim

Jackie swore as she slapped off the radiation alarm and scanned the instrument panel.

"What happened?" Burnside called from somewhere aft. "Are we under attack?"

"Maybe. We detected gravity ripples from ships coming out of warp about the same time we did. But no, I don't think so."

"Explain."

"We probably hit something," Jackie said curtly, "checking." As she scanned her panel, she added to the explanation. "If we had been hit by some kind of weapon before going into warp, we wouldn't have experienced that brief surge of gravity, and no energy weapon could touch us in warp. As for the ripples, most likely the wavefront just caught up to us when we dropped out. But it means there are other ships in the area, somewhere. We can't stay here."

A small rock fragment hitting the warp boundary was the most likely possibility. The resultant burst of radiation would automatically cut the warp drive, and Jackie couldn't think of anything else that matched the signs.

They were still alive, so if they *had* hit something, it must be small, but bigger than the dust particles the rad sensors were set to ignore. The question is whether it had damaged anything. If so, they were sitting ducks for those other ships. They would have detected her the same way she had detected them.

There were no red lights on the panel, other than the now mute radiation alarm. She double-checked the thruster subsystems, confirmed from forward scans that there was nothing big in their path, and commenced thrust. "Thrusting!" she hollered back to her passengers. "I want to get away from the immediate vicinity while I run further checks, but we look good."

They weren't far outside the L5 region, they must have hit some meteoroid fragment associated with it. For all she knew, it could even have been a fragment of their own drone propelled by whatever had destroyed it.

"How long before we can go back to warp?"

It would take her five minutes to finish resetting the systems that had tripped hard-off at the first alarm, but she wanted to put more distance than that behind them. "Call it ten minutes," she said.

"More than enough time for those other ships to get here if they warp," Burnside pointed out.

"Crap, that's right." Jackie had been thinking they'd be as cautious as she was about warping into an area where debris was likely, but they might not be. "Stand by." Jackie nudged the ships throttles higher, increasing thrust from 0.2 gee to a full gee. "That's acceleration gravity," she reminded them, "so stay strapped in."

In one corner of her panel, another annunciator lit up. Jackie glanced at it and swore. A number beside it incremented twice as she looked at it. It was the ship's short-range gravity pulse detector.

"Brace yourselves," she called back. "Three ships just came out of warp, and nearby. Looks like the Velkaryans are here."

∞ ∞ ∞

Aboard the Ripper

"Where's our target?" the pilot called out as they dropped out of warp.

"Scanning, wait one." The weapons officer wanted to be sure that anything he locked onto was the unknown ship, and not *Slasher* or *Arrow*. "Found it. Accelerating ecliptic northward at one gee, range six thousand meters." They should have been closer. Perhaps the pilot wasn't as good as he thought he was. He slaved the image to the main screen.

"Give them a warning shot. Enough energy so they know they've been hit, not enough to destroy them. I'll hail."

Easier said than done, the weapons officer thought to himself, as he adjusted the power setting on the laser.

"Firing."

On screen, the image of the unknown ship disappeared.

"Damnit," pilot shouted, "I said *not* enough to destroy them!"

"But I—" the weapons officer started, then he double-checked the power. "It wasn't. They must have gone to warp."

∞ ∞ ∞

Aboard the Seraphim

Jackie gave them a full minute in warp before dropping out to get her bearings.

"Okay," she said, "we're well out of the system, about sixty AU north of the ecliptic plane. Unless they've got some tech we're not aware of, we should be clear." As she said this, Jackie remembered the tests she and Black had performed, just a few weeks earlier, with an alien gadget right there on her galley table. The device had been retrieved from the Spacefarer pyramid on Chara III, and they'd suspected it might be related to the Velkaryan FTL communicator. It had proven surprisingly effective at detecting warp signatures in near real time out to a quarter light-year—so long as the detector was well isolated from any strong gravitational source. *So how did it work inside a pyramid on a planet?* Jackie wondered, not for the first time. But that didn't matter right now. If the Velkaryans had a similar gadget . . . but there had been no indication that her earlier "stealth" warp maneuvering around the system had been detected. Maybe they hadn't figured out the detector mode, just as Black and his team hadn't yet figured out the communicator mode.

In any case, the detector hadn't shown direction, it was just a raw signal. With any luck, even if they had detected the *Sophie*, they couldn't tell the Velkaryan ships where to find it. Jackie didn't intend to stick around to find out. "Let me get us lined up on Alpha Centauri and we can head home."

"Before that," Burnside said, "I'd like to know where the rest of their ships went. A fleet like that isn't to be taken lightly."

"What did you say their range was?" Jackie asked.

"Fifteen light-years. They need deuterium-rich fuel."

"Then they couldn't get to the Sol or Tau Ceti system, or even Alpha Centauri. The only habitable stars in range would be Epsilon Indi, and Zeta Tucanae, and . . . let me check." She brought up a chart on a nearby console. "Beta Hydri, p Eridani maybe. There are a couple of others, but they're out toward the edge of T-space. Even if they went to Epsilon Indi, they'd have to refuel before coming back, or going anywhere else, and it's a restricted system. You don't think they'd be so stupid as to try a raid on Taprobane, do you?"

"Not with just a dozen ships. That would turn UDT sentiment against them completely, and they'd have the Space Force and Peace Enforcers down their necks. It wouldn't be worth whatever damage they could inflict. At least, I don't think they're that stupid. Their rank and file, maybe, but not their leaders."

"Well, we saw no sign of them at Gliese 832, so they didn't go there."

"Gliese 832? What's there?"

"An old refueling station from back when all ships used deuterium-rich fuel. We stopped there before changing the *Sophie's* identity, part of our cover."

"That would be a logical place for them to go, then. You sure there was nothing there?"

"Very sure. We landed and checked out the base. There'd be nothing to stop them refueling, but it had been abandoned for years. We took a copy of all their data logs, though."

"Are there others like that?"

"A few, maybe. 832 was set up to avoid refueling stops at Taprobane, and then tech improvements rendered it obsolete. Let me check the database."

Jackie spent a few moments tapping at a keyboard and examining her screen. "Here's something. Gliese 784 is also in range. It has a hot Neptune and a cold outer planet. They started to build one a base there, then cancelled the project. It was never used, and it's not clear how much was actually completed."

"Did you say 784?" Burnside asked. "That rings a bell, something I overheard, but didn't know what it meant. Where is that?"

"About the same distance from here as 832, just 7.3 light-years, but it's further than 832 from anything else terraformed. I'm surprised they even began building a base there." She checked the chart further. "And again, with a fifteen-light-year range, they can't get anywhere from there that they can't get to from here."

"Where can they get to?"

"Just Epsilon Indi, and Gliese 832. Unless. . . ."

"Unless what?"

"There's a trick to extending the range of some ships, Sapphires for example. The aerodynamic shape leaves empty volume between the hull of the ship and the edge of a warp bubble. A properly fitted drop tank will fit in that space. I've done that once myself, for the trip to Chara." It had been an uncomfortable few weeks, knowing that her ship was cocooned between two large tanks almost flush with the warp boundary. She'd been happy to jettison them. "Depending on the ship, it could double the range.

But you have to install them in space; a ship can't transit atmosphere with them."

"What about on a moon?"

"An upper tank would be okay, depending on the weight and balance. You'd need a belly tank that didn't interfere with the landing gear or the thrusters. I'm not aware of any tank/ship combination like that, but if the Velkaryans are designing their own ships, it's not impossible."

"Okay, where could a ship go with a thirty-light-year range?"

"Half-way across T-space. Pretty much anywhere this side of Sol, and a bit beyond. Getting back would be problematic if they ditch the tanks."

Burnside rubbed a hand across his forehead. "Great. Well, something else for Ducayne and his bosses to worry about. Let's get back to Sawyers World and report in."

"Roger that." Jackie had been looking at the charts while they talked. Now she was curious. "Want to go by way of Gliese 784 just to take a look?"

"Can you do that? Do you have the range?"

"Either I use my own range-extender"—she still had antimatter left—"or we go by way of Epsilon Indi and refuel at Taprobane, the *Sophie* has landing permission there. So, yes."

"All right. Let's do that."

"Okay." Jackie raised her voice so the others could hear. "Listen up, folks. Side trip to Gliese 784. Prepare for warp in five minutes; get everything secured for gravity."

Chapter 48: Vaughan

New Toronto

Having lost their target, two of the Velkaryan ships remained near the L5 position, in case it returned, while the third warped back into orbit above New Toronto. It was the fastest way to report.

"Did you get an ID on the ship, at least?" Vaughan demanded over the comm.

"No sir. Its transponder was switched off, and it warped out before we got close enough for a good visual."

"Any idea where it went?"

"It was pointed north out of the ecliptic. There's nothing nearby in that direction. My guess is they just wanted to get away. They'll stop somewhere in deep space and reorient to whatever their destination is."

That could be anywhere, including back into this system, Vaughan thought. "Very well. You left two ships at L5, correct?"

"Affirmative."

"Then take up a position at L4, in case they show up there. I'll send another ship to join you. Vaughan out."

"Soleck," he said, turning to his aide, "dispatch another ship to L4."

"How long should they stay on-station?"

"We'll contact them. Probably a day, but let me give it some thought."

"Got it, sir."

As Soleck departed, Vaughan sat back to consider the problem. If Burnside, or whoever it was, thought that L5 was worth investigating, he might well decide to check out L4 also, except that the destruction of his drone and the follow up by three armed ships would make him wary. Perhaps he'd just head to Alpha Centauri, or Earth, or wherever he had come from, to report in. The next visit might be from the Space Force.

He must suspect the existence of the FTL Communicator, or at least some off-world installation. If his drone had gotten close enough to the relay at L5, he might have been able to tell where its message laser was pointing, but he'd have to triangulate that with the one at L4 to narrow down his search for it. That was now covered.

Where else might Burnside go? Given how much trouble he had been causing, Vaughan rephrased the question. Where else could Burnside cause him the most grief? Of course, 784 Base.

There was no reason Burnside should know about it, but then there was no reason he should have known about the relay at L5. Vaughan clenched his right fist and thumped it against the palm of his left hand. Security had to be stepped up, starting with a complete sweep of their systems for malware and bugs. He also had to report this to Headquarters on Earth. He grimaced. At least he had time to think about how to compose *that* message; it would get to Earth long before any ship could.

In the meantime, Cardigan had wanted to dispatch more ships to the base at Gliese 784. Fine. They would go in fully armed and weapons free. They might not beat Burnside there, if that's where he was headed, but they could make sure he didn't leave.

Chapter 49: Gliese 784

Gliese 784 system, aboard Sophie

The *Sophie* dropped out of warp well away from the red dwarf designated Gliese 784, with Jackie lowering the warp field in the same stomach-unsettling way she had while moving around in the Delta Pavonis system. The original base wouldn't have had gravity wave detectors; they were a more recent technology. But if there were Velkaryans using the base, they would have added the gear to detect the pulse of a ship's warp field collapsing, and Jackie wanted to avoid that.

"Now what?" Burnside asked. "We're too far away to tell if there are Velkaryans in the system."

"That's not what I'm looking for," Jackie said. "I want to see exactly where 784-b is in its orbit. Then I'll set up a jump to bring us out of warp near it. From there, I'll have good enough fix on 784-c to get us close."

"You said 784-b was a hot Neptune, doesn't that mean it's close to the star? Isn't that risky?"

"The term 'hot Neptune' refers to its mass. It's probably rocky. That close to its star, most atmosphere would be long gone. I'll take us away from the most likely orbital planes for dust or debris. There's still a risk, but if the Velkaryans do have armed ships here, I'd rather take my chances with the rocks."

Burnside nodded. "All right." He turned to the others. "Avril, Rico, any comments?"

"I've said it before, I trust Jackie's flying," Rico said. "We came here for a reason, let's get it done."

"Are we too far out to detect any radio chatter?" Avril said. "That would give us more information."

"It would," Jackie agreed, "but even if we weren't too far out —and we are, for anything less than a beamed transmission— there's no reason for them to be transmitting, unless they happen to have a ship landing or something. We can't assume that radio silence means there's nobody here."

"What about radar? If they're worried about visitors, won't they be looking?"

"They might not turn it on unless they detected a warp collapse signal, but you've got a point. A radar beam would be detectable much further out than a commlink." The receivers on the Sophie were normally configured to listen for communications signals. While it had a transponder—currently switched off —to detect and respond to radar, as a civilian ship it wouldn't normally care if it were being painted by a radar beam and wouldn't listen for one. With the transponder off, it would take a 300-meter dish, like the old Arecibo observatory on Earth, to detect the weak echo from the ship. However, if Jackie tuned the receivers, she should be able to detect the direct beam of a normal radar. She made the adjustments.

"Okay, we're now listening for radar. Even if there is one, it might take a while before the beam sweeps our position. Don't worry, our reflection will be too weak to detect. Meanwhile, I need to finish plotting positions relative to everything else in the system. Give me a half-hour."

Eleven minutes later, and again twenty minutes after that, the console emitted an urgent *CHIRP* as the sensors detected a radar transmission.

"Well," Jackie said after the second such chirp. "That confirms it. There is somebody home. All right, get ready for a short hop to 784-b, then to 784-c."

∞ ∞ ∞

Aboard Sophie, *near planet 784-c*

The *Sophie* lay in high orbit above 784-c, a thousand kilometers from the rock-and-ice world where the refueling base had been planned. The team had gathered in the galley, reviewing pictures taken with the ship's telescope.

"Well, well. Someone has been busy," Jackie said, looking at the images on the screen. The old spaceport field had been considerably expanded, and it was occupied by row after row of new ships. One side of the field was mostly new construction. The original, incomplete base itself had been added to. Several large tanks adjoined an older, original tank, and evidence of new construction and plumbing was clear.

"It looks like they've completed the base's refueling capability," Rico said.

Burnside nodded. "And then some. This must be where they've been hiding the ships that disappeared from the New Toronto field."

"Yes," Jackie agreed, "and with the refueling facility, it makes a good staging point."

"Yes, it does," Burnside said, his tone thoughtful.

Jackie looked at him. "What are you thinking?"

Rico answered for him. "Nice looking fuel depot they've got there. It'd be a shame if anything happened to it."

Burnside grinned fiercely. "My thinking exactly. Especially if the extraction gear went with it." He gestured at an area near the tanks that looked something like a small refinery.

"*Sophie* isn't exactly equipped for an attack on what is undoubtedly a defended facility," Jackie said. "No missiles, no bombs, no lasers, not even an autocannon. This is just a courier and light cargo ship. Let's get back to Alpha Centauri, and you can send the Space Force."

"Where's the fun in that?" Rico said. "I suppose Burnside and I could go in overland in suits. It wouldn't be the first time I've rigged explosives out of what you've got in your arms locker."

Jackie remembered. It had been on Dirty Snowball at Lalande 2285 on the way back from Chara, mostly as a distraction. "I thought Carson had rigged those."

"He's not the only one with previous experience. I imagine Burnside here also knows a thing or two about it."

"I do," Burnside said, "but that's the hard way. I seem to recall a pretty big bang over New Toronto a few days before you picked me up. How did you do that?"

"Oh, of course," Jackie said. "We threw a big block of ice at it, just like a meteor."

"Can we do that again? How good is your aim?"

"That depends on how far away we have to be to avoid detection. At least the air's thin." Jackie paused for a moment, thinking. "For that matter, we don't need a single big bang. A cloud of small projectiles, say a kilogram each, would get through. It will make a lot of holes in the tanks and plumbing." She paused, then added, "Also in the habitat, but not as much damage to that as a kiloton blast would. It should be survivable."

"Their survival isn't high on my priority list," Rico said.

"Maybe not," Burnside said, "and I'm inclined to agree, but we're not officially at war *yet*. It's better to minimize casualties for now. Unless they start shooting at us first."

Boutelle had her doubts about shooting at all. "Are we sure they're Velkaryan? The photos aren't clear from this distance. If it's some private company that's working on opening up some kind of cheap bulk shipping operation. . . ."

"Doubtful," Jackie said. "The economics don't make sense. Time is money. You want to carry as many cargoes as you can in a given amount of time to cover the capital costs of your ship, and having to refuel part way is going to kill you on that. Why hide them out here? Commercial competition isn't *that* cutthroat, and Gliese 832 is closer to everything."

"On the other hand," Rico said, picking up the argument, "we know that Velkarayan political competition *is* that cutthroat, and after that wargame fiasco back in the Centauri system, the Space Force could use all the time it can get to be better prepared."

"Wargame fiasco?" Burnside asked.

"The UDT Space Force decided to stage a mock assault on Kakuloa, with the Sawyers World Space Guard defending. It didn't go well for the Space Force."

"Interesting. All the more reason to do what we can to push Velkaryan plans back a few months."

During the conversation, Jackie Roberts had continued to review the other data they had recorded during their sweep over 784 Base. The images had been the main focus, but the *Sophie's* sensors had been recording across all bands.

"In answer to your earlier question. . . ." Jackie began.

"What question?"

"About our aim, and how far away we'd have to be to avoid detection."

"Yes?"

Jackie pointed to a display on one of her console screens. "It seems that among their other improvements, they've added high power search radars to the base's equipment. We detected their beams earlier. Even if we're far enough away that they don't see us pushing rocks around, they'll detect the incoming long before it gets there. Certainly, in plenty of time to intercept it if they have any kind of defensive capability."

"Huh," Burnside said. "And if they've got that radar, it's a good bet they've also got defensive capability."

Rico just grinned. "I guess we're going to have to do it the old-fashioned way."

Burnside nodded slowly. "I think you're right, Rico. But I also think that Jackie can give us an advantage. Maybe a little meteor shower to distract them."

"I can do that, but it means you'll be on the surface for a while. I'll have to set you down and pick you up far enough away to avoid detection."

"Do you have long-duration suits?"

"I do." Ducayne had provide those a while back, after she'd loaned—well, donated, now—a suit and reentry pack to Burnside back when he'd transferred to Tevnar's ship. "You might as well requisition a full set," he had said, "unless they take up too much cargo space." He had known they wouldn't. "You never know when something like that will come in handy." Yes, quite.

"Then that shouldn't be a problem," Burnside continued. He looked at Rico. "Agreed?"

"Wouldn't be the first time," Rico said, nodding.

"All right then. Rico, why don't you see about improvising some explosive devices, and Roberts and I will figure out where she's going to set us down."

"Is there anything you want me to do?" Boutelle asked.

Burnside glanced at Jackie, who shrugged. "Go over the photographs with an analyst's eye. See if we've missed anything at the base. Jackie and I will be looking at the ground approaches."

"Okay."

"I've got something," Rico said.

They turned to him. "What?" Jackie and Avril both said.

"If we're blowing up their heavy-hydrogen tanks, I can make a bigger bang by combining it with a pail of air, or rather, liquid oxygen. If you have a suitable pail, and LOX."

"You know I've got LOX, but for the same reason, those tanks probably aren't liquid deuterium. Heavy water takes up less volume than the equivalent amount of liquid deuterium." *Sophie* had plenty of LOX aboard, it was a byproduct of separating out the hydrogen—used by its own fusion reactors—from the water that carried it, and the oxygen couldn't be vented in warp.

"But the tanks at Gliese 832 contained liquid deuterium," Boutelle said.

"Older tech," Jackie said. "They didn't have efficient, compact electrolysis units back then. Even this ship didn't when it was first built, I had them retrofitted."

"She's right," Burnside said. "The Velkaryan ships will run on heavy water."

Rico looked at Burnside. "So, Operation Gunnerside? But we could bring some LOX along anyway. At the least, we could get some plumbing-rich combustion."

Jackie chuckled at this. "How about I give you a spare charcoal canister from the air system?"

"No thanks," Rico said to her surprise. "That combination is too unstable even for me."

Burnside shrugged. "Let's bring it along, we don't have to mix it."

"By the way, what is Operation Gunnerside?" Jackie asked.

"Historical reference," Burnside said. "I'm surprised he knows it."

Rico grinned. "When we get back, you can tell her about Operation Freshman, too."

She looked at the two men quizzically.

Burnside just shook his head slightly, grimly. "Don't ask."

Avril Boutelle turned to Jackie. "War stories aside, they'd need something to carry the LOX. Do you have anything like that?"

"I just might. There should be a couple of empty dewars in a corner of the cargo hold."

"Why do you have those?" Burnside asked.

"Usually for liquid nitrogen. Sometimes I carry biologists, and they use it to flash-freeze specimens. No reason the dewars wouldn't work for LOX, there's nothing reactive in them."

"I'll get them." Avril turned to Rico. "Is it safe building bombs in zero gee?"

He grinned at her. "Heck no, not at all."

The others darted startled looks at him.

"That's why I'm not going to do it," he continued. "I'll do what's safe, the tricky bits will keep until Roberts sets us down." He looked at Burnside. "So, don't be planning any touch and go landings. We'll need a few minutes, also to tap off LOX from the external drain. I'll build the bombs so we can do final arming on site."

Jackie shook her head slowly. "Boys and their toys," she muttered. Then she brought the terrain maps up on the big monitor. "Okay, Burnside, where did you have in mind?"

Chapter 50: Operation Gunnerside

On the surface, a kilometer from the base

Burnside and Rico approached the base with as much stealth as they could muster, keeping to the low ground behind rocks and low ridges, and with the tall deuterium tanks between them and the main base. That wouldn't help if there were outward-looking cameras on the tanks, but neither man could think of a reason, besides paranoia, why there would be. Rico dragged an improvised sled behind him, laden with the two oxygen-filled dewars.

Of course, they observed strict radio silence, but the suits had been designed with that possibility in mind, and had built-in short-range directional infrared transceivers. The old gimmick of touching helmets to talk worked in theory, but required a lot of yelling and was prone to scratching the visors. As a backup, they could just jack into each other's suits with a cable.

"They have more tanks than we have bombs," Rico said as they drew near. The photo images had been fuzzy. "How do you want to handle this?"

"We definitely want at least one for the refinery," Burnside said, "so to be sure, another one on the tank closest to it, with an oxygen booster. Maybe the other one on the opposite tank?"

"That works. They might even think something went wrong with the refinery, and the tanks were collateral damage."

"Exactly what I was thinking."

They had several explosive devices, improvised from the ammunition in the ship's weapons locker. Burnside had been surprised at just how much ammunition there was.

"Were you planning to fight a small war?" he had asked Roberts.

She had grinned at him. "Better to have it and not need it. Occasionally it comes in handy, especially on wild planets. I visited a *lot* of wild planets as a kid."

"I'm just glad there's no way to separate out a gram of the antimatter," Boutelle had said. "I'm sure Rico would love to play with that."

Burnside wondered if she were joking, but given Ducayne's resources, the *Sophie* might well have had a built-in antimatter "range-extender."

Rico shook his head. "No thanks. I'm not *that* stupid." He had paused, then added, grinning, "A milligram, maybe."

As he looked over the storage tank he was attaching the bomb to, it occurred to him that if this moon had had an oxidizing atmosphere, a tankful of deuterium—heavy hydrogen—might well make a blast equivalent to a milligram of antimatter. As it was, though, the tank would just rupture and spill, the heavy water boiling away, and any metal or organics reacting with the LOX until it was gone.

There was a fill-and-drain pipe at the base of the tank. Rico secured the LOX dewar atop it, the charcoal canister beside that, and wedged the explosives into the gap between it and the side of the tank. Most likely the tank was double walled, to help insulate its contents, but the bomb would at least crack the joint and split the pipe and dewar, and the result should cause more damage to the tank itself. The oxygen and charcoal should also react violently. Worst case, the remaining deuterium would quickly spill out of the tank, but Rico was expecting larger fireworks.

∞ ∞ ∞

Fifty meters away, on the other side of the refinery, Burnside had been doing the same thing to a tank there. Refinery was something of a misnomer; it was more a distillery. Heavy water had a slightly higher boiling point than normal water, and the water here was supplied by a nearby ice field. As the two men reunited amidst the plumbing of the refinery, Burnside pointed out an electrolysis unit, no doubt used to extract pure deuterium for the base power reactors. Heavy water distillation took a lot of energy. A bomb here would find oxygen and hydrogen to further react, and would be a logical place for an accidental explosion to start.

Rico nodded and went to place his remaining charges, while Burnside placed his to damage the pumps and other hard to replace components. Between this and his troublemaking in New Toronto, he was getting quite a bit of experience as a saboteur. The bombs themselves were to be detonated by radio signal, but had timers both to give them time to get away before listening for that signal, and as a last resort, to detonate if the radio signal hadn't been received within twenty hours. Rico had also added a shock switch, so that when one went, its blast would trigger the others.

"Okay, that's the last of the charges set," Rico said as he rejoined Burnside. "Let's get out of here."

"All right. Did you arm them?"

Rico held up the remote arming transmitter he'd rigged. The timer and radio lights were red, but the indicator for the shock switches was still green. "I want to put some distance behind us before I arm that last one, just in case."

"Good thinking." It wouldn't do to be too close if some random vibration triggered it.

With that, the two began to make their way back to the rendezvous with the ship.

∞ ∞ ∞

Aboard Seraphim, *in space*

"By the way, Jackie said to Avril after they were back in space, "do you know what Operation Gunnerside is?"

"I looked it up," Avril said. "It was a World War Two operation to destroy a Norwegian heavy water plant, disrupting Nazi nuclear research."

"Ah, so an appropriate name, then. And Freshman?"

"An earlier attempt. It went horribly wrong."

"Oh, ouch. I knew Burnside had an interest in that era, but I'm surprised Rico knew."

"Rico knows a lot of things," Avril said, with an odd smirk.

Oh? thought Jackie, and then, *Not my business.* But if it was what Jackie thought, she was surprised she hadn't noticed.

"Okay," she said, changing the subject, "now we just lob our sackful of rocks at the Velkaryan base, then swoop down and pick up the boys during the confusion." They had gathered rocks for just that purpose when they had dropped of Burnside and Rico. They were currently in the airlock.

"*Une morceau du gâteau*, right?" Avril said.

"I wouldn't call it a piece of cake, no, but not bad."

Just then a series of lights lit on the console and an alert tone sounded.

"What's that?" Avril asked.

Jackie silenced the tone and scanned the console, her expression changing to a frown. "Okay, this is bad. The cake is in the fire. Three ships"—the tone sounded again, and she silenced it once more—"no, *four* ships just came out of warp. We've got company."

"Could it just be coincidence? Another ferry convoy from the factory? They couldn't have followed us."

"We already know they have some advanced alien technology," Jackie said, thinking of the FTL communicator. "I don't know that they couldn't have, but it is unlikely. Let's just sit quiet and see what they do."

"What about throwing rocks at the base?"

There was that. Rico and Burnside were counting on the impacts creating enough of a distraction, and confusion about the cause of the explosions, to give them time to get away. In theory, *Sophie* could pick them up just as quietly as she'd dropped them off, but not with the inevitable search that would follow an obvious act of sabotage. On the other hand, with Velkaryan ships in space heading toward a landing at the base, radars on both the base and the ships would surely notice inbound meteoroids and take some kind of defensive action, and they might well spot the *Sophie*.

She made her decision. "We go with the original plan, otherwise, we'd be hanging the guys out to dry. I just have to be more subtle about it."

"Subtle? How?"

"Those ships are going to be focusing on their approach. They've still got a couple of small jumps in warp to get to the moon in reasonable time, so that will help cover anything we do."

"What *are* we going to do?"

Jackie hadn't finished figuring that out yet, so she talked while she thought. "I can't tell where they are just from the gravity waves from the collapse of their warp bubbles; my detector isn't directional. But if they follow the usual procedure, they'll have aimed just to one side of the primary and timed their warp jump to be well toward the outer edge of the system when they came out. Especially with four of them, they'll have agreed on location ahead of time. So that means we're well to sunward of where they are. Our thruster flare will be lost in the glare."

"And if not? Those ships are almost certainly armed."

"Perhaps. If it's a ferry run, they won't be expecting trouble." *I hope*, she didn't say out loud. "But we'll just have to take our chances. As soon as we get the projectiles on course, I'll warp to elsewhere in the system."

Boutelle looked unconvinced but didn't argue. "All right, I'll go suit up."

The plan was for Boutelle to literally just empty their bag of rocks out of the airlock while Jackie piloted the ship on a trajectory toward the base, then she'd peel off. The rocks would continue on their way to impact, while *Sophie* headed for deep space. With any luck, the Velkaryan ships would be none the wiser.

∞ ∞ ∞

Aboard Velkaryan ship AC-37, callsign Utahraptor

The engineer aboard the *Utahraptor* acknowledged the radio call and turned to the pilot. "That was *Atrociraptor* calling in, that makes four."

Attack Crafts 37 through 40, also known as *Utahraptor, Atrociraptor, Dakotaraptor,* and *Velociraptor,* had come out of warp, as standard procedure, in the outer reaches of the Gliese 784 system, distant enough to allow for any minor variances between navigation systems.

"Copy. Advise all ships, we want a standard tetrahedron formation centered on Base, twenty-thousand-kilometer radius. Weapons hot. Anything not us is a target; there's no reason for any of our ships to be in space."

The formation was one they had all practiced. It would place each ship at the corner of a triangular pyramid, like a four-sided game die, with the planet in the center and each of them far enough away from it to have a clear line of sight to all three other ships.

∞ ∞ ∞

Aboard the Seraphim

Avril Boutelle was at the open airlock hatch, suited up and secured to the grab rail. A small swarm of rocks accumulated just beyond, growing as Boutelle added to it, reaching into the bag beside her and letting the rocks go one by one just outside the airlock. Although she was being careful not to add too much sideways velocity, the swarm was inevitably expanding. That was fine; they wouldn't spread to more than a kilometer in the hour-and-a-half to impact.

The ship was on a high-speed trajectory toward the Velkaryan base, with Captain Roberts keeping it steady as Boutelle deployed the projectiles.

She released the last large rock and looked into the bag. There were a few handfuls of dust and gravel left. She gently shook them out, too. They wouldn't hit the ground, but the display as they burned up in the planet's thin atmosphere would add to the confusion.

"Okay," she signaled to Roberts back in the cockpit, "bombs away. I'm closing up."

"Copy that. As soon as the hatch closes, I'll get us out of here."

The door slid shut, and indicators both above it and on the main control panel turned green. Boutelle felt a violent shove, pushing her against the now-closed hatch, as Roberts fired thrusters to move them first away from the rock cloud, and then on a course away from the planet.

Nice of her to wait until the door closed, Boutelle thought as she pushed away from it and began to pressurize the airlock.

∞ ∞ ∞

Aboard the Utahraptor

"Message from *Dakota*, sir. They spotted what looks like a drive flare heading away from the planet. Radar says it's Sapphire-sized," the engineer reported.

"Tell them to pursue it. Get a bearing and see if we can spot it too."

As the *Utahraptor* began turning toward the *Dakotaraptor*'s position, the engineer broke in again, urgency in his voice. "Radar's showing a group of small objects heading toward the base at high speed, upwards of thirty kilometers a second." He paused, then, "They'll enter atmosphere in about five minutes."

"Damn it!" The pilot hailed the base himself. "784 Base, 784 Base. This is *Utahraptor*. Urgent. You have high speed incoming, secure the base. I say again: Incoming, secure the base."

"Say again, Utah? Did you say inco—Shit! Copy that, Utah, our radar just picked it up. Stand by."

By now, the *Utahraptor* was accelerating as hard as it could toward where radar showed the fast-moving objects-Missiles? Bombs? Meteoroids?—to be.

"Weapons, target those things with the laser, see if you can detonate a few." It was a long shot, they were thousands of kilometers away, but it was worth a try. "And call the *Dakota*. What the hell is going on out there?"

Far ahead and below, bright streaks appeared in the atmosphere as the first of the objects entered.

Chapter 51: Chaos

Aboard Seraphim

Jackie brought the Seraphim in low over the planet's surface, approaching the designated rendezvous from the opposite direction as the Velkaryan base.

"*We see you*," came Burnside's voice over the tight-beam infrared message laser. "*We're behind the rocks on your starboard side.*"

"Copy that," she responded.

That was good thinking. The rocks shielded them from the ship's downblast, and they'd be close to the airlock. Jackie hit the controls to extend the boarding ramp and open the hatch even before the ship had completely touched down.

She watched the starboard viewscreen as the two of them came out from behind the rocks, jogging toward the ramp. Then, in the distance, bright streaks of light appeared in the sky. That would be their meteors.

The original plan would have given them more time for the pickup before the bombardment started, but the sudden arrival of Velkaryan ships changed that. The rocks were now coming in much faster, and it had taken some fancy flying to get here ahead of them.

One of the figures was already coming up the ramp. The other—Rico?—paused for a moment and did something with a control box in his hands. Far ahead, from the deuterium refinery, came several bright flashes and a fireball. Then more flashes as the meteors hit.

Jackie heard the boarding ramp retract, and saw the airlock indicator turn green.

"*We're aboard,*" came Burnside's voice over the intercom. "*Let's go.*"

Jackie throttled up, and the ship climbed toward space.

∞ ∞ ∞

Aboard Utahraptor

"*Dakota* reports they lost their target in the confusion, but it's back, and they are in pursuit. *Velociraptor* and *Atrociraptor* are converging on the target's position."

"Copy that." The pilot had a screen zoomed in to view the base. Several of the fuel tanks were severely damaged, as was the distillation plant. The main building had some damage, and there were scattered craters all over the landing field, with at least one ship destroyed and several others showing damage. As he watched, another missile—or meteorite—flashed in and detonated beside another ship.

"734 Base, this is *Utahraptor*. We are prepared to land and offer assistance."

"*Negative*, Utahraptor. *It's too hazardous. Maybe when this bombardment stops. The base itself is holding. We have punctures and a few casualties, but I don't think you can do anything to help right now. But thank you.*"

"Copy that, Base. We have three other ships in pursuit of an intruder. We'll fly overwatch. Signal if you need us."

"*Roger that,* Utah."

∞ ∞ ∞

Aboard Seraphim

Jackie cursed as a stream of white-hot slugs streamed past her ship a few hundred meters to starboard. She had just jinked to port, or they might have hit.

"Strap in harder, and stay suited," she called back to her passengers. "This is going to get rough."

"Strap in harder?" Boutelle exclaimed. "I don't think I can." She was still suited from having tossed the rocks out, but her helmet was open. She closed it.

"I've seen this ship dodge missiles," Rico said. "Mind you that was in atmo. I guess the bad guys are giving her a hard time." He closed his own helmet, and Burnside did likewise.

Jackie wasn't rolling the ship with the turns the way she would if she were in atmosphere, she was firing the translation thrusters in random directions with random timing. It was less comfortable for all involved, but faster and less predictable. She had seen the railgun slugs, but she wouldn't see the beams if Velkaryan ships had lasers. She just had to make sure they couldn't line up a good shot until she was in clear enough space to go to warp.

And hope nothing hits the ship before that, she thought. Unlike the others, she wasn't wearing a suit. She hit a control to close and seal the cockpit doors behind her. They were airtight, so if the hull was holed aft of that, she'd be all right. She'd deal with getting *out* of the cockpit later.

The enemy ships were coming in from different directions, but two of them were much further away than the one firing on her. She angled her course away from them all, still firing the maneuvering thrusters randomly.

A little-used indicator lit up on her panel, indicating an electrical surge. Behind her, the pursuing ship erupted in a flash of light. *What the hell?*

The immediate area was clear. Jackie pointed the ship in the emptiest direction she could think of, and hit the warp button. She'd come back from a different direction to check out the damage to the base, but right now, *away* was the highest priority.

∞ ∞ ∞

Aboard Utahraptor

"What the hell was that?" The pilot had just seen the *Dakotaraptor* explode, and there might have been a streak of light hitting it just before that. The ship it had been pursuing, not the source of the light, had gone to warp seconds later. "Engineering, report!"

"Instruments showed some kind of power surge when the Dakota exploded."

"When it exploded, or before?"

"Uh, if it was before, no more than a fraction of a second. I'd have to replay the data recordings to tell."

"Any other ships in the area?"

"Just the *Velociraptor* and *Atrociraptor*, still over a thousand kilometers away, still on their intercept courses," the engineer said, then, "What the . . . ?"

"What?"

"*Velociraptor* just changed course abruptly, like it was hit by something. It's firing weapons."

The pilot got on the radio. "*Velociraptor*, this is *Utahraptor*. What's your status?"

"You're not going to get an answer. *Velociraptor* just blew up."

"*Fuck!*" He clicked the radio again. "*Atrociraptor*, *Atrociraptor*. This is *Utah*. Break off. Disengage and return to Base 784. Acknowledge."

"Utahraptor, *this is* Atrociraptor, *ackskiaasksssss. . . .*" the signal broke off with a burst of static.

"*Atrociraptor* just showed an abrupt change of direction," the engineer said. "No explosion as far as I can tell, but it seems to be tumbling."

"Shit!" The pilot scanned his panels. There should be enough fuel, but it would be close.

"Engineering, do we have enough fuel to warp back to Delta Pavonis?"

"What? Just a moment." Then, "Yes, although we may not have much to maneuver in-system when we get there. You're not thinking of leaving?"

"Somebody has to report this. We'll worry about maneuvering when we get there, we can always call for help."

"What about the base?"

"They seem okay for now. I'll apprise them of the situation. Prepare for warp."

"Sir, I'm seeing a charge buildup."

"Warping *NOW!*"

∞ ∞ ∞

Aboard Seraphim

As she had planned, Jackie brought the ship back toward Gliese 784-c from a different region of space, having made several jumps in succession to get around the system. They had done a quick pass by the base, with all sensors recording, then she had hopped the ship to near Gliese 784-b, the larger planet.

"Well, we sure made a mess," Rico said as they reviewed the images on the big galley monitor. "That ought to set them back a bit."

"Yeah," Burnside agreed. "The distillery totally out, most of the tanks destroyed, several of the ships completely destroyed, others damaged. The base itself seems mostly intact, but some of these other ships show odd damage."

"Let's see that," Jackie said. She had been nursing a suspicion since she saw that first ship explode.

"Here look," Burnside said, zooming in the image. "See those lines on the hulls?"

Jackie did. That was enough for her. "Standby for warp!" she shouted as she propelled herself toward the cockpit. "We're leaving!"

Her fingers flew over the control panel, reconfiguring the warp drives not to generate an artificial gravity field. She didn't want to take the time to secure anything or anyone that was floating around the cabin. The ship's bow was pointed away from the planet and its moons, and away from the orbital plane of this system. *Good enough.*

"Warping now." She activated the drive, and the scenery outside the viewscreens went away.

Burnside came forward. "What's going on, and why don't we have gravity?" he demanded.

"I want us as far away from this system as possible as quickly as possible. I've seen that kind of ship damage before. As for gravity, I'll get that restored as soon as everything is secure. I didn't want anyone falling and breaking an arm."

"I don't get it, what's the significance of the damage? Who attacked the Velkaryan ships?"

"The first time I saw damage like that it was just superficial, to Vaughan's ship *Carcharodon*, as a matter of fact. It had just taken a graze by a particle beam in the Zeta Reticuli system. The second time was on the hull of the wrecked alien ship at Kapteyn's Star where Tevnar found that artifact. You know the saying, 'Once is happenstance, twice is coincidence, three times —'"

"It's enemy action. Okay, you did the right thing. But who is the enemy? And why here?"

"How much were you briefed on what went on in the Zeta Reticuli system?"

"I was briefed, but I wouldn't know if they'd left anything out, would I? I know you met an alien—Kesh, was it?—do you think they did this?"

"I don't know who it was, but I don't want to hang around here to find out the hard way."

"I can't argue with that," Burnside said.

"There's another thing. This is the second time star I've seen beam-damaged ships at a red dwarf star. Maybe third, if the old Staravelle at Gliese 832 has beam damage. We didn't inspect it."

"Oh? There aren't terraformed planets around red dwarfs, surely?"

"No, they're too cool. But some red dwarf planets may have a common biochemistry with each other, Non-terran, but like someone did the equivalent of terraforming them."

"Seriously?"

"Just conjecture, but a guy I talked to at Grainger Station, at Proxima a few weeks back, seemed to think so."

"But not in this system, surely? There's nothing very habitable."

"I don't know what a red dwarf alien would consider habitable, but no, probably not. If it *was* the degkhidesh, maybe the Velkaryans disturbed some kind of automated listening post. Or maybe it wasn't them. We just don't know. Like I said, I didn't want to wait around to find out. Feel free to come back and check it out, but not with my ship. Speaking of, when we're well clear of the system, let's change her identity back to *Sophie*."

Chapter 52: Home Again

Sawyers World

Carson finished entering the last of his student grades into the system and closed the form, heaving a sigh of relief that it was complete. One less thing to worry about.

His omniphone chirped, and he answered it eagerly. He had been expecting Jackie back for several days now. This might be her. He glanced at the caller ID and was both disappointed and annoyed. Why would *Bruce's Bar and Grille*, whoever they were, be calling him? He was about to disconnect when a thought occurred to him and he answered anyway. "Hello?"

"Hannibal, it's Jackie Rob—" a familiar voice began.

He cut her off. "Jackie? Where are you calling from?"

"The spaceport, I just landed. You ought to come on down."

"Down where? I've never heard of Bruce's Bar and—"

"Our usual place, silly. You'll understand when you get here." The connection clicked off.

As far as Carson knew, there was no Bruce's Bar and Grille at the spaceport, and the only "usual place" there was either her ship or . . . of course, Ducayne's Homeworld Security offices. She and whoever was with her would have reported in as soon as they landed. Carson was already shutting down his desktop and gathering his things to leave.

∞ ∞ ∞

Briefing Room, Homeworld Security, Sawyer City
"*Bruce's Bar and Grille*, really?" Carson said as he entered the briefing room to which the guard/receptionist had directed him. Roberts, Rico, and Avril Boutelle were also there, as was another man who looked familiar, but Carson couldn't quite place him.

"Protective camouflage," Ducayne said, "It's automatic." He waved Carson to a seat. "I think you know everybody."

Carson looked at the fourth man. "I'm not sure I . . . Oh, of course, Jordan Burnside. I almost didn't recognize you."

"I decided to let the beard grow. I was getting pretty shaggy by the time Roberts here pulled me out of the jungle."

"That's it. I knew there was something different." There was something different about Roberts, too. He studied her for a moment. "Jackie, what did you do to your hair?" A hint of green at the roots of her now black hair made the answer obvious; his real question was why.

"I didn't want to be recognized too easily on Verdigris. It was Avril's idea. What do you think?"

"To be honest, I think I prefer the green, but on you, anything looks good."

She smiled at this, but before anyone else could say anything, Ducayne spoke up.

"Now that we're all caught up on personal matters," he said firmly, although that was hardly the case, "let's get back to the debriefing."

"I take it there's something of archeological interest," Carson said. "Or else why invite me?"

"Close," Ducayne said. "Take a look at these." He threw several images up on the main briefing room screen. "What do you think?"

The images were somewhat fuzzy and noisy, as if they had been highly compressed at some point, or taken from extreme range and blown up. It was an aerial few of several parked ships, all the same model. It wasn't one Carson recognized, although it was vaguely Sapphire-like, but he was no expert. Several of the ships showed obvious damage; a missing fin portion, explosion damage from where a warp condenser might have been located. Carson looked closer at the straight, burn-like lines across the surfaces of most of the ships, and felt the blood draining from his face. He'd seen damage like that before, twice.

The others had obviously seen these pictures before, because they were looking at him, not the screen. Ducayne spoke. "You look like you've seen a ghost. Burnside tells me that Roberts had a similar reaction. I take it you agree with her assessment?"

"If she said that this damage looks like it was inflicted by what might be degkhidesh particle-beam weapons, then yes, I agree. Where were these pictures taken? Not Verdigris, PBs don't work in atmosphere, do they?"

"Only at short range, and no, not Verdigris. Gliese 784-c, a small planet orbiting a red dwarf about seven light-years from Delta Pavonis."

Carson looked at Jackie. "What were you doing there? No, never mind, I don't need to know." He looked at Ducayne. "Do I?"

"Not right this instant. I'll brief you later; you might as well know. But, it brings us to why you're here. You're our resident degkhidesh expert. Who are they and what are they up to?"

"Me? I'm no expert."

"Do you know someone better qualified? Let's get them in here."

"I, no. No, I suppose not." Ducayne was right. As far as Carson knew, he and Jackie—and Marten, the timoan—were the only ones even aware of the degkhidesh, and that only from what little Ketzshanass, the Kesh individual, had told them, back at Zeta Reticuli. For that matter, they couldn't be certain that the particle beam weapons had anything to do with the degkhidesh. An active beam weapon in the Zeta Reticuli system had fired on the *Carcharodon*, damaging it enough to give Carson a chance to escape after Vaughan had grabbed him. Given Ketzshanass' concern over starships operating within the system, and the damage they had seen on ZR-III that Ketz had attributed to the degkhidesh—or 'enemy of the Kesh'—they had assumed it had not been a Kesh weapon. Then again on the planet at Kapteyn's star, the wrecked ship had instrument markings that resembled Kesh language. The surmised Kesh ship had suffered similar beam damage, presumably from those same enemies of the Kesh.

So yes, that made Carson an "expert" on a species and culture he knew almost nothing about.

"All right," he said, "let's lay out what do know, which isn't much."

"First, we know that the Kesh are not the Pyramid Builders. It's possible that these degkhidesh were, but I'm going to say not."

"Why? That means you're assuming a third spacefaring species in the last few thousand years: the Pyramid Builders, the Kesh, and whoever the degkhidesh are."

"All right, forget the pyramids for now. They were fifteen thousand years ago. Maybe the degkhidesh are biologically related, but I don't think they're culturally the same."

"Again, why not?" Ducayne said.

Avril Boutelle answered. "It's the simplifying assumption. Cultures change over time. Until we have some evidence that the two cultures are the same, or one strongly influenced the other, it's safer to assume that they were different. That way, we don't make misleading assumptions."

"Exactly right," Carson agreed. "We want to evaluate the degkhidesh as they are today, whether or not they're related to the Pyramid Builders."

"Okay," Ducayne said. "So, what do we know?"

"They fought a war with the Kesh, at some point after the Kesh had been fighting a civil war themselves."

"Cause of that war? Of either war?"

"The civil war seems to have been some kind of revolt against a priest class. Ketz was short on details. The degkhidesh war may have been them seeing an opportunity against a weakened opponent, or it may be that they simply wanted to stop the Kesh civil war because it was interfering somehow in what the degkhidesh wanted to do."

"You said the cities on Zeta Reticuli were abandoned." Ducayne said.

Carson nodded. "That's right, yes."

"So, the degkhidesh had no interest in occupying territory, then."

"Well, not in *that* territory, anyway," Burnside spoke up. "Maybe it wasn't strategically advantageous. It may be far to the rear of whatever the battle lines were. They took it out but didn't try to hold it."

"Then why wouldn't the Kesh reoccupy it?"

Carson knew the answer. "The degkhidesh left automated defense systems behind to prevent that. The Kesh seemed pretty nervous about them."

"Then why not just occupy it?"

"Maybe they don't like yellow suns," Jackie said.

"What?"

"The places where they attacked other ships, Kapteyn's Star and Gliese 784, they're both red dwarf stars. What if the degkhidesh evolved under a red dwarf? They wouldn't want to occupy a terraformed planet under a K or G star any more than we'd want to occupy a planet orbiting Procyon or Sirius."

"We have a station at Procyon, and a facility on the planet," Ducayne reminded her.

"It's an antimatter factory, like what we had on Mercury. Nobody tried to colonize that planet."

"Okay, but can intelligent life even evolve under a red dwarf sun?"

"There's life on Proxima-b, there was life on the planet at Kapteyn's star," Jackie said. "We know life can evolve there, or at least, under a red star, so why not intelligent life?"

"What about the archeological site on Proxima-b?" Carson said.

Ducayne may have winced, but the others all looked at him. "What archeological site?" Boutelle voiced the question everyone else wanted to ask.

Ducayne shrugged resignedly. "You might as well tell them. It's relevant."

Carson gave them a quick recap of the structure remnants that he'd been called in to look at. "It looked like the remains of buildings, like you might see on Earth at the site of an old Roman frontier town, although more like concrete than stonework. Not like anything designed to hold an atmosphere, so whoever or whatever built it may have been perfectly comfortable breathing the air."

"Or whatever they were using was lost," Burnside said. "How old were these ruins?"

"Maybe a thousand standard years. We'll know better when we're done with the isotope dating."

"About that," Ducayne said. "I have the results. I asked for them to be re-checked, with new samples."

Carson looked at him sharply. "You didn't tell me. What was wrong with them?"

"Possibly nothing. That's why I wanted them double-checked. The results we did get were consistent with the site being nuked."

There were several indrawn breaths at this. Carson frowned. "If it was, that messes up my date estimate. There would have been less to erode. Make it five hundred years."

"So perhaps the war wasn't quite as one-sided as Ketzshanass implied," Jackie said. "If there was a degkhidesh colony on Proxima-b. . . ."

"It's the nearest red dwarf to the Solar system. Was Earth being watched?"

"We know the Kesh were watching it, the Belize wreckage proves that. If the degkhidesh were watching the Kesh. . . ."

"Or maybe they felt a bit possessive about red dwarf stars, and got annoyed if yellow star inhabitants intruded," Rico said. "Turf wars can be nasty."

Carson didn't see any way they were going to resolve anything this evening; there were too many unknowns. This would shift his priorities from investigating pyramids and possible pyramids, to going back to the Zeta Reticuli system and attempting to recontact the Kesh. They were the ones who held answers. He just hoped they'd be willing to share them.

There was another question that had been nagging at him since seeing the images of the wrecked ships. "By the way," he asked, "what was, or will be, the Velkaryan reaction to having a half-dozen of their ships destroyed on the ground? And, do they know it was aliens, or will they assume the Space Force did it?"

Ducayne's expression turned as grim as Carson had ever seen it. "That," he said, "is the big question. So far, we don't know. If there were survivors of that attack, they'll know it wasn't Space Force. The tactics and weaponry were wrong. We also know that the Velkaryans are aware that there are other spacefaring aliens out there. Vaughan may not know what attacked his *Carcharodon* back at Zeta Reticuli, but he knows it wasn't the Space Force. He'll figure out it was aliens, if not which aliens.

"As for Velkaryan reaction, not good. I expect they might leak some version of it, using that to stir up anti-alien sentiment."

"But it had nothing to do with aliens on any of the terraformed worlds where we have settlements," Boutelle protested.

"They'll gloss over such details," Ducayne said. "They'll also redouble their efforts to build up an armed space fleet, and now they have more justification for it. I'm sure our official position will be that that's the Space Force's role, and Velkaryan's arming makes the chance of interstellar conflict that much greater. It does, but I'm just not sure if that war will be a Velkaryan war for independence from the UDT, or between them and the degkhidesh, or whoever it was that shot up their base. If it's the latter, we'll get sucked into it; the aliens probably won't make fine distinctions between one group of humans and another."

Ducayne forced a smile. "But," he said with false cheerfulness, "maybe it wasn't the degkhidesh. Maybe the Velkaryans have some kind of internal squabble, or maybe it was space pirates."

"I doubt it," Jackie said. "Either way, somebody seems to have better particle beam weapons than I'm aware of."

Ducayne shrugged. "Technology marches on. Hell, maybe it's the Chinese, we haven't heard much from them recently."

"But they're part of the UDT," Boutelle said.

"Yes, and it hasn't stopped them from running their own independent operations in the past. No more than it has the United States, for that matter. It's all technically legal so long as nobody violates the UDT Charter."

"Surely shooting up a Velkaryan base violates the Charter."

Ducayne nodded. "Yes. Without some justification, I suppose it would. Pity." He looked around the table. Nobody else seemed to have anything to add.

"All right," he said, "I think that's enough for tonight. Rico, Burnside, be back here in the morning for some strategizing. Boutelle, thank you for your reports, you're free for the next few days. I may have something else for you then."

He turned to Roberts. "How's the *Sophie*?"

"She's had three and four people living aboard for a month. She needs a clean-out and her systems need flushing, the usual. The antimatter reserve could use a top-up, and there a couple of minor trouble tickets I need to see to. We had a radiation surge from hitting something in warp. There was no serious damage, but an in-depth diagnostic is recommended. Except for the antimatter, I can get it all taken care of in a week, unless the diagnostic turns up something unexpected."

"Pull it into the hangar and I'll have my guys take care of all that, if that's okay with you."

"Perfect, I could use a break. As long as you don't mind me hanging around to supervise."

"I wouldn't dream of trying to stop you," Ducayne said.

"Good, that's settled then," she said.

Carson felt a twinge of disappointment. With the ship being worked on in the aging hangar atop the hidden Homeland Security base, Jackie might be sleeping aboard, but that's all it would be. He had hoped that the last night before she'd left for Delta Pavonis might be turning into something more.

"All right," Ducayne said. "Carson, thanks for dropping by on short notice. We'll get together in a couple of days to discuss the extended mission we talked about a few weeks ago. Thanks again." He rose from his chair. "You all have a good evening and get some rest. I think things are going to start going a little crazy soon."

As the others filed out of the briefing room, Carson hung back with Jackie Roberts.

"I missed you," he said. "It sounds like you've got some stories to tell."

"Maybe a little more interesting than hanging around campus teaching classes, but you know me. Space travel is supposed to be boring."

He reached up and flicked a wisp of mostly-black hair away from her face. "Uh huh. With nothing but time on your hands you decided to color your hair."

She grinned at him. "Something like that."

He scanned her face. Her eyebrows were dark, which was new, as were her lashes. He couldn't remember if those had always been dark or she'd somehow dyed those, too. "Oh?"

She laced her arm through his and walked him down the corridor toward the elevator. "I'm not planning to put *Sophie* in the hangar tonight. She can wait. But I do need to make sure she's secure for the night. Walk me to my ship?"

"Of course," he said, a little confused about the abrupt change of subject, but he wasn't about to complain.

"Good," Jackie said, and smiled. "Maybe you'll find out if the carpet matches the drapes."

Epilogue

New Toronto

Vaughan had insisted on inspecting the damage personally. The hull of AC-37, callsign "Utahraptor," showed scars he had seen before, on his own *Carcharodon*. He had been attacked in the Zeta Reticuli system, by some kind of charged particle beam weapon. As far as he knew, the UDT didn't have anything of the kind. Perhaps a Homeworld Security secret? It was possible, although PB weapons research was generally considered to be a dead end. The charged particles tended to repel each other and diffuse too quickly to have much range.

The other possibility was more disturbing, but the *Utahraptor*'s crew swore that the Sapphire they'd been pursuing had never fired on them, or the other ships. They hadn't spotted any other non-Velkaryan ships, but then neither had the *Carcharodon* in the Reticuli system.

The damage to the heavy hydrogen facilities at Base 734 was a setback, but they could be repaired. As could most of those ships on the ground that had been damaged, either by explosion debris or the mysterious particle beams. Apparently, the latter had hit only a few, but he'd know more when his investigation team returned.

There was no question that there were, or had been, high-tech, spacefaring aliens out there. The Velkaryans had artifacts to prove it. If they were still around . . . well, would they know or care about different factions among humans? Maybe the Velkaryans could find a way to use those aliens to their advantage.

∞

More to come. . . .

The stories will continue. Carson and Roberts, together with Carson's timoan colleague Marten, will head back to Zeta Reticuli and beyond to recontact the Kesh and search for Spacefarer relics.

Meanwhile, the Velkaryans grow increasingly belligerent. Homeworld Security, and in particular Ducayne's agents Rico and Burnside, face the task of forestalling the inevitable until the UDT Space Force is up to the challenge.

Glossary

Chara: G type star 27.5 light-years from Earth, also called Beta Canorum Venaticum.

Kakuloa: Alpha Centauri B II - terraformed planet orbiting the second largest star (B) in the Alpha Centauri system.

Kapteyn's Star: a red dwarf star about 12 light-years from Earth. It is known to have at least two planets, each larger than Earth, and orbiting in or near the habitable zone.

Kesh (or kesh): Aliens encountered by Carson, Roberts and Marten at Zeta Reticuli, possessing advanced technology. They neither confirmed nor denied that Zeta Reticuli was their home system, but it is currently (so far as Carson knows) uninhabited.

omni: Short for omniphone - compares to today's smartphones as smartphones compare to walky-talkies. (Look for "Nokia Morph" on YouTube for a nearly-there concept video.)

omniphone: See omni.

parsec: A distance of approximately 3.26 light-years.

pykrete: a very strong composite material made of water ice and sawdust, invented during WW II.

Sapphire: A class of small interstellar ship (S-class), capable of sleeping about six if they're close friends, with a range of just over 20 light-years on full tanks.

Sawyers World: Alpha Centauri A II - second planet orbiting the largest star (A) in the Alpha Centauri system, the first extrasolar planet settled by humans. (See the Alpha Centauri series.)

Tanith: 82 Eridani IV - fourth (hypothetical) planet orbiting the star 82 Eridani. In real life, this star is known to have at least three planets, all larger than Earth.

Taprobane: Epsilon Indi III - Third planet orbiting Epsilon Indi, home world of timoans.

thruster: High-efficiency reaction drive, a kind of fusion-powered arc-jet.

timoan: (Analogous to "human") The sentient natives of Taprobane. Descended from the ancestral species of terrestrial mongoose and meerkats the way humans are descended from the ancestral species of monkeys or lemurs.

T-Space: from Terraformed (or Terraform) Space - Usual term for "known space," a spheroid of stars centered on Earth and about 20 parsecs in diameter. So-called because many of the sun-like stars within it were found to have planets that were not merely Earth-like, but deliberately terraformed.

Unholy War: A nuclear war which took place in the first half of the 21st century, involving primarily the smaller nuclear powers, purportedly for religious reasons.

Union de Terre: Union of Earth, successor to the United Nations, formed because of the events of and immediately after the Unholy War.

Velkaryans: Church of Divine Stellar Providence. A core belief is that God created the terraformed planets for humans, and, not as loudly stated, specifically for them.

Verdigris: Delta Pavonis III - third planet orbiting the star Delta Pavonis, so named for its greenish hue and the heavy jungle covering the habitable areas.

warp bubble: The thin shell of highly-curved space surrounding a ship in FTL flight. Based on Van Den Broek's lower-energy configuration of an Alcubierre warp metric.

Zeta Reticuli: A pair of G type stars separated by about 0.1 light-year at a distance of 39.2 light-years from Earth. (Technically, Zeta 1 and Zeta 2 Reticuli)

Acknowledgments

First, thanks to my readers, whose enthusiasm for the series keeps me going. As originally envisioned, the events following *The Eridani Convergence* were to be covered by a single book, titled *The Pavonis Insurgence*, but not *this* one. It was soon obvious that that book would be twice as long as originally planned, and far more complicated, so I split the events from the point of view of Carson, Roberts, and Rico into *The Centauri Surprise* , (adding detail in the process), and events from Burnside's point of view into this one (again, adding more details), and merging both plot threads together in Part III of *Pavonis*. All of which meant this book took a *far* longer to finish than I expected it would, and so I apologize to those of you who have been waiting patiently (for the most part) for it. I think you'll find it worth the wait.

Burnside's parachuting scene in Chapter 1 is partly based on my own few parachute jumps, a long time ago. My thanks to Joe Chow, my instructor and jump master, who never got me caught in any trees. The reentry pack is based on a 1960s concept called MOOSE, for Man Out Of Space Easiest (later renamed Manned Orbital Operations Safety Equipment). No flight units were ever made.

Thanks also to Robert, Jill, and the other Robert, for their feedback on the manuscript. Any remaining errors are mine, not theirs.

-- Alastair Mayer, Colorado, 2020

The stories will continue.

Meanwhile, the T-Space story starts with *The Alpha Centauri Trilogy*, available as a single omnibus ebook volume, comprising *First Landing*, *Sawyer's World*, and *The Return*.

Coming in late 2021, "Raven's Rift," the story of Carson and Roberts first meeting, will appear in the Space Western anthology *Gunfight at Europa Station*, edited by David Boop and published by Baen Books.

Get free stories
Sign up for my newsletter at www.alastairmayer.net

Subscribers get occasional free stories, announcements and special offers. Email addresses are only used as above and never shared.

See my blog at www.alastairmayer.org, which also links to the T-Space Wiki.

About the Author

Alastair Mayer was born in London, England, and moved to Canada with his family as a young boy. He describes his interest in space flight and science fiction as genetic: his father, Douglas W.F. Mayer, had been an early member of the British Interplanetary Society as well as a science fiction fan (who in fact published some of Arthur C. Clarke's first tales in *Amateur Science Stories*).

Alastair became involved in both the L5 Society (now the National Space Society) and computers, publishing articles in *Byte*, *Final Frontier*, and other magazines, as well as becoming an accomplished scuba diver and a private pilot. In 1989 he moved to Colorado, where he still lives, and where, after working in the computer and satellite networking businesses, he now writes full time.

His short stories have been published in several anthologies and his work has appeared often enough in *Analog Science Fiction* magazine to gain him entry to the "Analog MAFIA" (Members Appear Frequently In *Analog*). Many of his works can be found in e-book format on Amazon, Barnes & Noble, Smashwords, and other e-book vendor sites.

The Pavonis Insurgence is the fifth in his Carson & Roberts series, one of several set in the T-Space universe, which also includes the *Alpha Centauri Trilogy* and the in-progress *Kakuloa* series.

Visit his web site at www.alastairmayer.org, *which also links to the T-Space Wiki.*

Other books by Alastair Mayer

Mabash Books trade paper editions are available from Amazon or order through your favorite bookseller. Some volumes are also available in hardcover.

The T-Space™ series comprises:

The Alpha Centauri Trilogy: ISBN
- *Alpha Centauri: First Landing*   978-153-913229-5
- *Alpha Centauri: Sawyer's World* 978-154-691328-3
- *Alpha Centauri: The Return*   978-197-403548-9

The Kakuloa Series: ISBN
- *Kakuloa: A Rising Tide*   978-1-948188-074
- *Kakuloa: The Downhill Slide* 978-1-948188-227*
- *Kakuloa: Crash and Burn*   978-1-948188-241*
- *Kakuloa: The Tide Turns*   978-1-948188-265*

The Carson & Roberts Series: ISBN
- *The Chara Talisman*   978-1-948188-098
- *The Reticuli Deception*   978-1-948188-111
- *The Eridani Convergence* 978-1-948188-159
- *The Centauri Surprise*   978-1-948188-180
- *The Pavonis Insurgence*   978-1-948188-203

* forthcoming

Ebook editions are also available.